W9-ACF-509

SIEGE OF SILENCE

By the same author

MAN ON FIRE
THE MAHDI
SNAP SHOT
BLOOD TIES

SIEGE OF SILENCE

A. J. QUINNELL

HODDER AND STOUGHTON
LONDON SYDNEY AUCKLAND TORONTO

For Roger:
   The Patriarch

British Library Cataloguing in Publication Data
Quinnell, A. J.
   Siege of silence.
   I. Title
823′.914[F]   PR6067.U56

ISBN 0 340 38600 2

Copyright © 1986 by Sandal A. G. First printed 1986. All rights reserved. No part of this publication may be reproduced or transmitted in any form or by any means, electronic or mechanical, including photocopy, recording, or any information storage and retrieval system, without permission in writing from the publisher. Printed in Great Britain for Hodder and Stoughton Limited, Mill Road, Dunton Green, Sevenoaks, Kent by Biddles Ltd., Guildford and King's Lynn. Typeset by Hewer Text Composition Services, Edinburgh.

Hodder and Stoughton Editorial Office: 47 Bedford Square, London WC1B 3DP.

AUTHOR'S NOTE

I am not an American
North or South

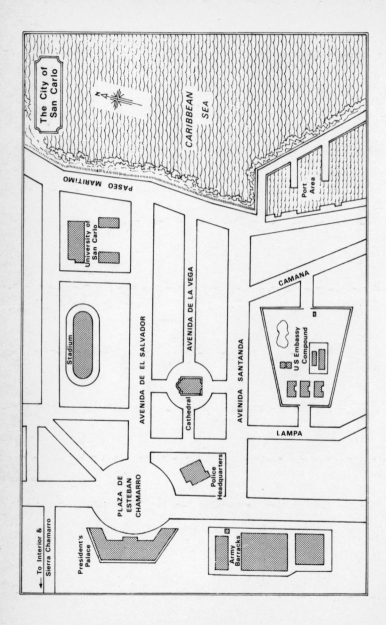

PROLOGUE

PEABODY
San Carlo

As I enter the room the hostility is tangible. It radiates, and my skin prickles with the sensation. I find it agreeable.

The room, lit by two oversized chandeliers, is full of people and odours, uniforms and medals, long dresses and diamonds, sober suits and polished shoes, tobacco, perfume, sweat, and the ever-present ambience of lust and jealousy. All the hallmarks of a diplomatic reception; and now the added aura of hatred.

The Venezuelan Ambassador approaches, his plump body cut diagonally by a red sash, his hand outstretched, a smile stuck on his face like peeling tape.

"Excellency, so good of you to come – an honour."

His handshake is damp. I utter the ritual words.

"Thank you, Excellency. Congratulations on this auspicious day. My apologies for being late; work, you understand."

His head nods enthusiastically. My tardiness is welcome.

"No matter. Your Embassy is very well represented."

I find this hardly surprising. Unlike most Foreign Service Officers my staff, given the prospect of free, copious champagne, would tramp barefoot across a mile of broken glass. I catch a peripheral glimpse of Dean Bowman and wife grouped with Arnold Tessler, Martin Kerr and the Argentine Military Attaché. In one hand Bowman is holding a glass of champagne and a thin smoking cigar. In the other a plate laden with open smoked salmon sandwiches. No doubt he will do his usual trick of smoking, drinking, eating and talking more or less at the same time.

A waiter approaches with glasses on a silver tray. I take one.

"We waited," the Ambassador says ingratiatingly. "Would you mind?"

"Of course."

I step forward and a silence works its way through the room. I am the focal point of resentful looks. Some are curious. If they expect a speech, they're wrong. I raise my glass and glance at the Ambassador. He has stretched himself to full height and puffed out his chest. He looks ridiculous. I nod towards him. "Your Excellency." I nod towards a cadaverous figure in the corner. "Mr Foreign Minister; ladies and gentlemen. On this the occasion of the National Day of Venezuela I would like to offer a toast to President Lusinchi." I raise the glass high, murmur "President Lusinchi," and take a sip amid the chorus of response. God, I hate champagne. I smell rather than see the Colombian Ambassador approach. He is marked by the twin curses of stupidity and halitosis. Quickly I move away towards the french windows. A path opens for me as though I carry the plague bacillus.

Out on the broad portico the air is sweet with the aroma of jasmine and bougainvilia. Plants never have halitosis. Not true. What about those stinking fruit they eat in Malaysia? Durian. Supposed to give potency. Well anyway, they stink but don't talk.

I envy the Venezuelan only his garden. Flagstoned paths weave through beds of plants and flowers and tall palms etched into a pattern by subtle floodlights on the high wall. A shadow materialises into the form of a guard sauntering along a path, sub-machine-gun slung over one shoulder. It typifies the situation in San Carlo – violence in paradise – as though the luxuriant beauty of the country is a greenhouse accelerating the growth of hatred.

Behind me I hear the murmur of conversation, the clinking of glasses and the braying laugh of the British Ambassador, a man invariably amused by his own jokes.

"I'm told you prefer Scotch, Excellency."

I turn to find the Venezuelan Ambassador behind me. He holds out a glass and I exchange it for the champagne

"Do I disturb you?"

"No, I stepped out to escape the hubbub."

He smiles conspiratorially. "You mean the attentions of our Colombian colleague. He can be exquisitely boring . . . as can those receptions." A theatrical sigh. "But then we have both been diplomats long enough to bear them . . . to close our ears and merely nod at regular intervals . . . and smile when required."

He waits for an answer but I'm in no mood for small talk. I shrug, hoping he will go away. I'm disappointed.

"I wanted a word with you in private, Excellency. I heard a disturbing rumour this evening."

"Oh?"

"Yes; apparently you are considering sending home all dependents and non-essential personnel."

Irritation washes over me. Damn them! And damn their loose, useless mouths! He is looking concerned and my irritation grows, knowing that my face reflects it. He says apologetically:

"You know how it is, Excellency. We are all in a fish bowl. It is always so."

He is right. Always so. A confidential chancery meeting in mid afternoon and by early evening the word is out to every Embassy in the city and doubtless right through the Government. It's the blabbering wives, of course. They always tell their wives and it's the same as writing it in the sky.

I speak to him coldly and formally. "Understand, Excellency, I have been Ambassador here for just one week. Naturally I have had meetings with my senior officials, including those from Military Aid and Security. I have examined all aspects of the situation and have to take all options under consideration. At this time I have taken no firm decision as to repatriation. It is, therefore, as you say . . . merely a rumour."

"I understand. May I speak to you not as a diplomat . . . that is to say in a straightforward way?"

"Sure."

There is more braying laughter from the room behind. He takes my arm.

"Shall we walk in the garden?"

He gently propels me down the steps on to a path. I hate people touching me. Not so gently I extricate my arm and we walk side by side between the shadowy trees.

"You are very experienced and knowledgeable, Senor Peabody. Even your Spanish is of a quality to bring me soothing relief in a country where my language is tortured beyond belief. Permit me to say that it is rare for an American."

"I thought you were not going to talk as a diplomat."

He is unruffled. In the semi-darkness his teeth show in a smile.

"I will, but the compliment was sincere. Now to the matter. In spite of your experience and length of service I believe I'm right in saying that this is your first posting as Chief of Mission."

"Correct."

"I, on the other hand, have been an Ambassador for over twenty years, although I now find myself in a backwater like San Carlo." He glances at me, perhaps looking for sympathy. Not finding any he continues. "As the doyen of the diplomatic corps here I feel I have the unwritten privilege to offer advice to new Ambassadors . . . especially in matters concerning the diplomatic community."

I insert a warning note into my voice. "And you're going to offer me unsolicited advice?"

"Not really, Senor Peabody. I'm going to point out certain consequences that may arise if you do issue a repatriation order."

Curtly I say, "I told you it's only under consideration."

"Exactly, and what I have to say may have a bearing. Such an order can have three possible consequences: first, to start a snowball effect among other Embassies, particularly as it is your Government which is propping up this regime with its aid . . ." He stops abruptly. "Ah! Is that it? Are you just flying a kite? To convince some of your Congressmen that the situation here is so dangerous that they must vote for the new aid package."

Jesus! The devious little pimp. He is watching me

expectantly. I know what's worrying him. If I give the order and the Italians follow suit, the wife of their First Secretary will be sent back to Rome, so ending her affair with this porcine idiot. I may have been here only a week but we're all in the same fish bowl. I know what's going on.

"Certainly not, Senor. Whatever decision I take will be based solely on the factor of personal safety."

Clearly disappointed he resumes walking and talking.

"The second effect would be to weaken morale among the locals . . . the Government and the Civil Guard . . . the business community. It would generate an even more disastrous outflow of capital. Third, such an announcement could only give encouragement to the Chamarristas."

We turn a corner on the path and are confronted by a patrolling guard, spectral in a paramilitary uniform. He stands to one side at semi-attention as we pass.

"Point is," he continues, "none of the other Chiefs of Mission have seriously considered such a move. They feel that Vargas has things under control . . . with American help of course."

I gesture over my shoulder with a thumb.

"Armed guards, day and night. It's hardly a normal situation. Besides you forget that we Americans are the prime targets. I'm aware of the consequences if I decide on repatriation. You point out that this is my first posting as Ambassador . . . but I was an officer in the Havana Embassy in January '59."

"Really? But surely there are differences?"

"Sure, and there are disturbing similarities, as there are with Nicaragua."

The path turns again towards the lights of the residence and the faint sound of music.

"Of course, Senor, and naturally with the great American aid and large covert presence here you must have more and deeper information than the rest of us."

There is condescension in his voice. The man really is a fool. He can't see beyond the garden walls and his own comfort and pleasures. I've had enough.

"That's exactly right, Mr Ambassador . . . and I'll make

my decision based on that information. At that time I'll inform you prior to the others. That's a common courtesy. There will be no announcement . . . just a quiet and gradual withdrawal of absolutely non-essential personnel."

We are facing each other on the path. I am about a head taller. Having lost the point, his face, sweating slightly, carries a sullen look. He opens his mouth to argue but I've had enough. I lean forward to cut him off.

"Now, Excellency, although I've only been here one week and I'm not the 'doyen', allow me to offer you some advice. Your Economic Attaché, Senor Borg, is the main supplier to the diplomatic community here of marijuana and cocaine. Again common courtesy makes it necessary for me to believe that you are unaware of this. His activity is a stain on the reputation of yourself, your Embassy and your country. I suggest you do something about it. My thanks for a pleasant evening . . . good night."

I walk up the path leaving him mute behind me. I feel good. I haven't done much to improve US-Venezuelan relations but that's the job of our Ambassador in Caracas. Let him earn his damned pittance.

JORGE
Havana

I should not care about time. I'm a Latin like my father and all my forefathers. It must be the Scottish blood of my mother that makes me impatient.

I check my watch again; just five minutes short of two hours. The woman is watching me. She smiles sympathetically then goes back to her work. She is reading through a stack of foreign newspapers and occasionally marking an item with a thick black pencil. She is a linguist, fluent in most European languages. During the night the marked passages will be translated and Fidel will read them with his breakfast. She is not attractive. Her face is dominated by a large forehead and nose. Her neck is short and her shoulders box-like. But she is very intelligent. I wonder if she would trade her intelligence for beauty. But naturally. Stupid people never recognise their stupidity. Beautiful people enjoy their attraction every waking moment. But the ultimate is to be beautiful and intelligent. We are so very few. I glance across the room where Gomez from Agriculture also waits. He is patiently reading a magazine.

Again I check my watch; exactly two hours. Abruptly I reach the decision and stand up. The woman raises her head in query.

"Tell him I'll be in my office – I have much work to do."

As I reach the door she says in puzzlement and consternation, "But . . . ?"

Outside I brush past the security guards and enter the open lift. They look at me blankly as the doors slide shut.

On the ground floor I am almost at the entrance when the phone on the security desk rings. I pause while the guard picks it up. Watch as he listens and see his eyes swivel towards me. Still holding the phone he points upwards with a finger.

"He'll see you now, Senor Calderon."

Going back up I consider my actions. Have I gone too far? Will he explode? People are filing out of the inner office: Moncada, Perez, Valdez and several functionaries. They seem preoccupied but they all greet me respectfully. Inside the woman is standing by the desk. She points at the open door. There is sympathy in her eyes. I go through and immediately know that I have truly gone too far. Fidel is sitting behind his huge desk. Cigar smoke and tension fill the room. His face, his whole demeanour, throws out impatience and anger. Immediately he says, "Calderon! I order you to stand by and you walk out. Impertinence! You show me no respect!"

I know the man and I know the only course.

"No, comrade. You show me no respect."

He straightens in his chair. Both fists come hard on to the desk. There is going to be an explosion. I have seen it with others; seen them demolished. The risk I am taking excites me; it is always so. At this moment of extreme danger I remember my final legal exams at the university. It is a memory in a millisecond. The night before the crucial paper, an old school friend had returned to Havana from Angola where he had fought for their revolution. In the morning he was to travel north to see his family. We went out for a drink which turned into a drunken party. I turned up for the exam without sleep and still partially drunk. For two and a half hours I stared at the questions without comprehension. By the time my head had cleared and I could think there was only half an hour left. With no time to answer the questions I wrote, instead, a letter to the chief examiner. I explained my condition and why. Then I argued the case that a suitable greeting for a homecoming friend and patriot who had repeatedly risked his life for his country far outweighed the selfish consideration of my getting a law degree. It was a brilliant letter and they gave me my degree.

Now I have to be equally brilliant to snuff out the fuse spluttering into Fidel's brain. Calmly I say, "On July 26th,

16

1969 when I was thirteen years old I watched you for the first time make a speech commemorating the attack on the Moncada barracks. You spoke for four hours. During those hours I became a revolutionary. Your theme was the continuity of revolution. I can remember almost every word. I will quote you some of them: 'We must learn from the mistakes of others, from every socialist revolution of the past; the French, the Russians, the Chinese, all of them. The greatest mistake is to allow the worship of bureaucracy, the idolising of the official and the functionary. The people are the revolution. They are the masters.' "

I have slowed the fuse. Underlying his anger is a hint of intrigue. Still feeling the excitement of fear I continue.

"In another speech, four years later to the day, you said: 'Every hour, every minute, every second is vital! To waste even a second is to dishonour the cause.' "

He is looking at me as at a toad in his bath water. I can only go deeper.

"My office is ten minutes from here. As you know I am busy on the Cubelas case. I was summoned here two hours ago and since then have wasted seven thousand, two hundred seconds." I gesture at the piles of paper on his desk. "In the ten minutes it would have taken to summon me you could have done six hundred seconds of work." I indicate the door behind me. "Gomez has been waiting out there for over an hour. He also is very busy working for the revolution."

Fidel takes a long pull at his cigar then blows the thick smoke at me. His voice has the timbre of rolling thunder.

"Did I really say those words?"

"I can't remember; but if not you should have."

He makes a sound like an old steam-engine pulling out of a station and I relax. He is laughing.

He points his cigar at a chair and I sit down. For a long time he studies me with distaste. He looks at my clothes and long hair, then at my face. I stare back. He will soon be sixty but apart from a greying and a fuzziness on his beard he hardly looks it. Only the eyes are tired but they are always so except when he is orating. I know what gives him power over others. I know exactly for I have the same power. He is first a

17

dreamer, second an activist and third a taker of risks. For him the risk is everything. To combine the dream, the action and the risk is to create the stuff of life and power. The magnet to draw others; men and women – especially women. Others call it personality; I call it the "essence". It is given to few.

Finally he sighs, mashes out his cigar and says, "Jorge, the last thing you resemble is a revolutionary. You look like the kind of specimen Lenin had in mind when he said: 'Burn the leeches and vermin'. "

Before I can answer he presses a button on his desk console and says, "Maria, tell comrade Gomez to return to his office. I'll call him when I need him." He sighs again. "Tell him I regret keeping him waiting."

He stands up, moves around the desk and starts pacing behind me. He will continue pacing until the interview is over. I turn my chair.

"We had word this morning from San Carlo via Managua . . . you read the file I sent?"

"Of course."

"What do you think?"

"Bermudez is crazy."

He laughs. "Maybe, but very imaginative. He's your age, you know. Even younger than I when we threw out Batista." He muses on that, then says, "If they succeed in all phases we have the chance to interrogate Peabody . . . you read that file too?"

"Of course."

He stops pacing and faces me, chin tucked into his beard. There is excitement in his eyes. Cautiously I say, "But for a few days only . . . maybe less."

A shake of his head. "You don't understand the Americans. You've had little contact. You are clever and shrewd in human nature – cunning; but I tell you they will not react quickly. I have much experience. We may have weeks, even months."

He moves back to his desk and lights another cigar. Puffing contentedly he resumes pacing and talking. "From our Intelligence we know three things. The operation against us is code-named 'Cobra'." He snorts in derision.

"After so many operations and code-names they lose imagination. We know that two of our top people are involved . . . so far passively. They are most likely ministers. Also two or three others in the army and the militia. We know that Jason Peabody advised on the operation before being posted to San Carlo. That is fortunate . . . the only luck we had."

I ask, "Do you suspect any particular minister or official?"

He walks to the window and looks out. Late afternoon sunlight filters through the cigar smoke as it writhes above him. The smoke appears to come from the top of his head. He turns and answers me obliquely. "Jorge, I have survived for over a quarter of a century. At least twelve tries at assassination and half as many coup attempts." His teeth show through his beard in a mocking smile. "Were I not so modest I would think myself immortal." He paces again. "It's become a question of demography. Over half our population was born after we threw out Batista. All they know of the old days are stories which grow dimmer. They grow impatient with struggle not knowing that a revolution takes generations. That's why it is very dangerous now. The traitors perceive that they might have a following . . . and that is possible. They must be crushed. We must find out who they are." He jabs his cigar at me. "I trust Raul . . . but that is the trust of blood. I trust you, Jorge Calderon . . . that is the trust of necessity. Only you and Raul know of my intentions. The word is that the Chamarristas will move at any moment. As soon as they are in control we will send in people – just as we did to Nicaragua. Doctors, teachers, engineers and so on. You will go in with the first plane. I want you to leave for Managua tonight."

"What about the Cubelas case? It is important."

He shakes his head. "Next to this it pales to nothing. You are the best interrogator we have. You broke Frias and Guijano and above all Pazos." He shakes his head again. "I would never have believed that. You are arrogant so it cannot make it worse that I call you brilliant. I need that brilliance now. We need one name. That will be enough. From him we will get the others. Now go and see Raul. He will arrange details and a communications set-up."

I get up from the chair saying, "I'll be sitting in Managua doing nothing. That Bermudez is crazy."

Very thoughtfully Fidel answers, "So was I. With eighty compatriots I made a revolution. Bermudez has many more than that."

I reach the door and say, "I hope you're right."

He is watching me; his head slightly on one side. I sense before the question comes that it will be important.

"Who is the girl?"

I feel no confusion. I answer immediately.

"Inez Cavallo – as I'm sure you know."

"What does she do?"

"Looks after me and nothing else . . . you know that too."

He nods. "I never took advice about women so I don't like to give it. But she is dangerous, that one. She is amoral, complex. Totally selfish . . . and beautiful. She is dangerous, Jorge."

"I know."

We look at each other for a long time. It's as though Inez is in the room. He makes a characteristic gesture with the fingers of his left hand, dismissing the subject.

"I'm planning to take her with me," I say. "I get bored doing nothing."

Have I gone too far? I feel the tingle again. Another long silence, then again the dismissive flick of the fingers.

"Just get me one name."

In the outer office the woman is marking an article. I lean over her shoulder. The newspaper is the *Washington Post*, the article is headlined: "San Carlo National Guard Starts Decisive Sweep Against Chamarrista Insurgents."

PEABODY
San Carlo

It's luxurious, but it's a prison. From my study window I look across the roof of the staff apartments to the high wall. Floodlights illuminate the wires running across its top and the television cameras at each corner. In the security room the duty officer will be manning the consoles and electronic equipment. Or will he? Maybe he's asleep or gone off for a game of poker. I make a mental note to spot-check; but not tonight. Yes, it's a prison. We are fifty-two souls locked into our compound. Even the glass in front of me is bullet-proof. The window can't be opened. How marvellous it would be to leave this artificial air and stroll down the tree-lined Paseo Maritimo and hear and smell the dark Caribbean surging up the beach. Impossible without a dozen bodyguards and a truck full of National guardsmen trundling along behind, plus the anguished face of Fleming from Security – the chief gaoler. I miss long walks. This is what I am now. The most important man in the country, including the President; and I'm a specimen in a zoo. The irony of power. The position makes me a target of any crazed commie – or any other crazy.

I'll do the job fast. With the new aid package and the new trainees and my clout they will be swept away. Then to his surprise that fat slug of a President will have to face elections, and with enough money and influence, a decent right wing Government – or a decent right wing General will run the country on decent lines. And decent men will be able to walk down Paseo Maritimo day or night.

Through the thick glass window I hear the faint, single chime of the cathedral clock. It reminds me of my fatigue, just as the throbbing of my big left toe reminds me of the gout. I walk painfully through the bedroom to the bathroom and take down the bottle of Zyloric tablets.

At last the maid has remembered to put the flask of chilled mineral water on the bedside table, together with a glass. Ten days I've been here and wasted a vast amount of time teaching the residence staff the fundamentals of hygiene and comfort. Calper must have lived like a pig. But it's to be expected. He was very lax in his policies, in his personal and general discipline and in his reports. I inherited a pigsty.

Christ, the glass is not clean! I go back into the bathroom, rinse it, pour water and take two pills. Then I brush my teeth. It's a pleasurable duty. I use a "water pik" and enjoy the tingling sensation of the tiny spray against my gums. Churchill used one. I read it in his memoirs.

The maid has also remembered to turn down the bed and lay out clean pyjamas. She was astonished when I told her, "clean pyjamas every night – and clean sheets". God knows how Calper used to live. The whole residence stank of cigar smoke until I had all the air-conditioning filters changed and banned smoking.

I dress my dumb valet with tomorrow's clothes. It is made from polished mahogany. I brought it with me from Washington – a mother's gift forty years ago. The only one I can remember.

In bed, I pick up a tract on the Sandinist revolution by Henri Weber. I have trained myself, no matter how tired, to read for half an hour before sleep. In that time I can read twenty pages. In rough terms it means thirty books a year. Just for that half hour!

Tonight it depresses me to read about such a bad cause so ably argued. It is a relief when the half hour has passed. I switch off the light and rearrange the pillows. They are feather pillows – I brought them from Washington. It's something learned from much travel. Most pillows nowadays are filled with some synthetic foam and you may as well lay your head on a trampoline. I read somewhere that the Queen of England travels with her own pillows but I was doing it long before her.

I rarely have difficulty sleeping and I am sinking into

22

unconsciousness when the bedside phone rings. It is Gage, Chief of Station. His voice is nervous. I guess it's because he's had to take a difficult decision in phoning me at this hour. He mumbles apologetically saying that the CIA deputy Chief of Station has an unsubstantiated report that a large column of Chamarristas has passed through the village of Paras, twenty miles north-east of the city, during last night. Gage is sorry to wake me but to his knowledge they have never operated this close to the capital before.

I ask the obvious question.

"Haven't you discussed this with Fleming?"

A painful pause, then:

"No, sir. He went to a party at the Brazilian Embassy. I rang there but he left an hour ago – they don't know to where."

Again I feel sharp resentment towards Calper. His laxity has rubbed off on to all the staff. There are strict procedures: a 1.00 a.m. curfew and hourly whereabout reports between sunset and that time. You'd think they were staffing the Embassy in Luxembourg. Gage's tentative voice again, "I checked with the National Guard Headquarters, sir. They dismissed the report as nonsense. They have a garrison in that village . . . but I thought I'd better call you, sir . . . your standard instructions . . ."

"Gage, you did right. Stay in touch with the CIA and the National Guard. Call me if anything develops and meanwhile let Fleming know that he's to report to my office at 8.00 a.m. . . . sharp!"

I cradle the phone, rearrange the pillows and try to sleep. It evades me; not due to the report but because of irritation. The Embassy is a sloppy mess and it's going to take weeks to straighten it out. There's going to have to be changes of personnel, starting with Fleming and Bowman, the deputy Chief of Mission. Gage is all right. He's only been here as long as me, flying in on the same plane. It took guts to phone so late on a flimsy report – and incidentally to ditch his boss.

Over the next few minutes I mentally rearrange the entire senior officer structure and my anger wanes. I'll definitely

keep Colonel Sumner, the Military Attaché. His briefing this
morning was clear and concise and he's a crisp, well-turned
out officer. My mind dwells on the man and his briefing and
abruptly, like a tiny electric shock, I remember something. I
sit up and call Gage on the phone and instruct him to wake
Colonel Sumner and ask him to meet me in the tank in fifteen
minutes. If Fleming returns in the meantime he is to be sent
straight there.

Sumner makes it in twelve minutes. He looks sleepy but I
note with approval that he's dressed in a well-pressed suit
and tie.

I'm standing at the large wall map. I've stuck a red pin on
the dot of Paras.

"Sorry to get you up, Colonel. I've ordered coffee." I tap
my finger on the map. "There's an unconfirmed report that
Chamarristas have passed through this village heading for
the city."

With the heels of his hands he rubs his eyes and nods.

"Gage told me. Also that the National Guard discount it.
That village is well garrisoned and it lies at the foot of a steep
valley. There's no way a large column of rebels could move
through there undetected."

"Terrorists, not rebels, Sumner," I remind him irritably.
"And what if they were detected?"

Now he is both sleepy and puzzled.

"But . . ."

There is a tap on the door and it opens to reveal a young
Mestizo with a tray holding two steaming mugs of coffee. He
puts it on the table and withdraws. I gesture towards it and
Sumner drinks gratefully, then says carefully, "You're
suggesting that the garrison may have collaborated?"

"Is it a possibility? Would they be from Lacay's brigade?"

Wide awake now, Sumner nods. He is looking at the map.
I say, "This morning at your briefing you talked about
Generals Cruz and Lacay. Recently Cruz has been in more
favour with Vargas than Lacay. You stated that the latter
was bitter over Vargas's decision to post all the Fort Bragg
trainees to Cruz's brigade. Also in a confidential report last

month the agency suggested that if we ever contemplated supporting a military coup against Vargas, then Lacay would prove more amenable."

Sumner is looking very sceptical. He drinks more coffee and says, "Mr Ambassador, let's slow down a bit. First there's an unsubstantiated report about reb . . . terrorist movements. Now we're talking collaboration by the National Guard. That's way out. Those guys know that if the Chamarristas ever take power they've had it. They're dead. It's like hitching a ride across a river on an alligator's back. Half way over you get eaten."

"Okay. But what about that report?"

He shrugs. "We get an awful lot of worthless stuff coming through. Even disinformation. I've been here two years, sir, and sifted through any amount of crap."

He is very confident and his allusion to his length of service is meant to contrast with my brief tenure. Let's wake somebody else.

"Well, the report came from our own assets here." I point to the phone. "Get Tessler over here and find out exactly where it came from."

He picks up the phone with enthusiasm, obviously pleased to spread the suffering.

It takes Tessler twenty minutes to appear. He is rumpled and in a foul mood. I don't care. He might be the Chief of Station and he might have an important father. I'm the Ambassador. I don't bother ordering coffee for him; merely instruct him to check out the report.

He is on the phone for a surly ten minutes. Then hangs up, sighs dramatically and says, "We have informers in most villages. They're very low grade stuff. They get a little monthly stipend and a small bonus when they come up with something. This guy hasn't had a bonus for over a year so he's trying it on. Our regional guy passes through there and gets what's known as a 'scam' report. By regulations he has to file it. Anyway consider it worthless. If the Chamarristas are trying to move close to the city, they sure as hell wouldn't use that route – and they wouldn't be in a large column.

They'd infiltrate in groups of three or four . . . normal procedure."

He can hardly keep the disdain from his voice. He's young and cocksure and barely makes the effort to be respectful. I glance at Sumner. He is studiously gazing at the wall map. I can read both their minds. I've been here ten days and I'm panicking. I've already sunk to total unpopularity by proposing the repatriation of dependents. Now I'm getting people up in the middle of the night because I've got the jitters. I'm considering a tactical withdrawal when Tessler decides to give me a little lecture.

"Look, sir, it's a classic guerrilla situation. The Chamarristas number at most six thousand men. They can hit and run and that's all. Four days ago they occupied San Pedro in Higo province. General Cruz takes the entire Marazon brigade, stiffened by the Fort Bragg trainees and chases them out. Now they're running for the mountains with Cruz right behind. Meanwhile Lacay's got eight thousand men in and around the city. Not counting the Presidential guards – another thousand . . . elite troops."

Casually he takes out a packet of cigarettes and lights one. He is insolent. He knows the new regulations. He watches me, enjoying his insolence. I am about to tell them both coldly to go to bed when the phone rings. Sumner picks it up, listens for a minute, then says, "Call immediately if anything else happens."

He hangs up, turns to face the wall map and says, "Two bridges on the Tekax River and one on the Chetumal have been blown up."

Offhandedly Tessler says, "It happens all the time."

Sumner holds up his hand for silence. Tessler takes a pull at his cigarette and blows out the smoke in a noisy hiss. We are all studying the map. At first, very slowly, very thoughtfully, Sumner begins to talk, but his voice soon becomes brisker as his military mind asserts itself.

"Three strategic bridges . . . well guarded . . . three major assaults with heavy Chamarrista casualties . . . rainy season . . . rivers swollen . . . impassible to vehicles. Marazon brigade – half the National Guard; sweeping the south west and cut off

26

until bridgeheads are retaken and bridges rebuilt. At least five days to a week. Limited air transport facility."

He turns back to the table, picks up the phone and while he dials says to me, "That call came from Major Anderson who heads up our military advisors. I gotta check something."

I'm irritated that he reminds me who Anderson is. I take it out on Tessler.

"Kindly put that butt out."

Without taking his rapt attention from Sumner he grinds it into an ashtray. Tomorrow I'll give orders to clear the whole damn building of ashtrays.

Sumner says urgently, "Paul, what's Vargas doing?" He swings to look at the map. "Shit! I could've guessed. Listen, can you talk him out of it . . . ? Because it could be a set-up . . . No I'm not. Look at the damned map. Assume that the occupation of San Pedro was a feint to draw the Marazon brigade. The Chamarristas withdraw slowly maintaining contact; pulling Cruz towards the mountains. Then they blow the bridges. Cruz and his brigade are effectively cut off from the capital. Vargas orders Lacay to retake the bridge-heads. Lacay sends half his force, far too many for the job . . . what . . . ? Okay, it's conjecture but there was a low level report about Chamarristas passing through Paras last night . . . yeah, from friends . . . you didn't . . . well chew them out but meanwhile persuade Vargas to pull those units back to San Carlo. Let Cruz look after himself . . . No way, Paul. Don't screw Lacay up, it could be coincidence, just tell Vargas it's bad tactics. Get back to me."

He hangs up and Tessler says incredulously, "Jesus, Ross! You're ready for the cuckoo factory! You think Lacay has turned?!"

Sumner sighs. "No, but let's take the worst case scenario. He's not in great favour right now. He's got a conscience somewhere. It's rumoured that he even complained to Vargas about the Mestizo massacres in Higo last year. Vargas put all the new trainees in Cruz's brigade. For the last few months he's kept Lacay close to hand . . . maybe . . . just maybe, Bermudez got to him."

27

I'm about to say something but Tessler laughs in derision. "Ross, Lacay is as corrupt as all of them. Shit, he's on our payroll. We know everything about him from the size of his underwear to the vaginal dimensions of his new mistress. There's no way he could've been in contact with Bermudez or anyone else without our knowing . . ."

The man is disgusting. I cut him off.

"Tessler, button it!"

He looks shocked as though he'd forgotten I'm in the room. I ask Sumner: "Colonel, following your worst case scenario, what would be the next step?"

He points at the map. "Lacay has already thinned out the city's defences by sending an over-large force to the south-west to retake the bridgeheads. He would have sent those units and commanders who have the least loyalty to him. Then he sends loyal units to the airport and other strategic sites. He puts his best – and most loyal – officers and units into position to engage the Presidential Guard when the rebels . . . terrorists, attack."

Tessler is shaking his head in disbelief. To me the next step is obvious. I am about to state it when Sumner does it for me. It is annoying.

"We must monitor all troop movements in and around the city."

I agree testily.

As Sumner reaches for the phone, it rings. By the law of relativity its clamour sounds louder and shriller than before. He picks it up.

"Paul, yeah . . ." He listens for a minute during which his body hunches lower in the seat. Then, "Hang on, he's here."

He cups a hand over the phone, runs his tongue over his upper lip and says nervously, "Mr Ambassador, we have a crisis situation. Units of Lacay's brigade are moving towards the airport, the Presidential palace, radio station and police barracks. There is gunfire a few miles north-west of the capital at Tandala where Vargas has a 'hacienda' guarded by units of the Presidential Guard."

*

At this moment I can only think of the foul, rank, detestable incompetence of those around me and who preceded me. Nausea overwhelms me and I struggle not to vomit. Tessler, his face ashen, is unconsciously putting a cigarette between his lips.

"You will not smoke!"

Into the petrified silence drops the distant, coughing rumble of gunfire. The nausea passes. Calmly I say to Sumner,

"Colonel, start pushing all the buttons."

I have never been in such a situation before. In Havana in 1959, events built up slowly and concluded logically. Now there is no logic and I discover immediately how plans, honed to perfection over the years, can go abruptly wrong. Since Teheran and Beirut some of our best minds and a hell of a lot of money have been devoted to Embassy security. Typically they have neglected the common denominator of human idiocy.

It starts with the discovery that the DCM, the Chief Security Officer, the Economic Counsellor, together with their wives and several other middle rank staffers, are all out of the compound. Sumner, no longer nervous but very decisive and military, tells me that they are at a big party at an industrialist's beach house ten miles up the coast. This, in total contravention of standing instructions.

I rebuke myself. I have already imposed discipline and order at the residence and had planned to start with the rest of the Embassy in the morning. It should have been the other way round. I allowed my personal needs and comfort to take precedence. I feel the rare discomfort of having to admit to a weakness. No matter that I've only been here a few days; but I thought that the least I could expect from these supposedly mature and experienced people was self-discipline.

Well, it's done. Now the palliative of action. Within minutes procedures are being followed. The crisis team is assembled and working. In the absence of Fleming, Gage and Marine Gunnery Sergeant Cowder take charge of the compound security. I draft the first cable to State. There is

29

satisfaction in knowing that it will get a lot of people out of warm Washington beds, and that very shortly a similar crisis meeting will be taking place in the Situation Room at the White House. I had been there only ten days before listening to the President expound his policy on Central America. It had been a little woolly except for the main theme: at all costs communism must not, cannot, will not prevail in our own backyard. He had expressed his pleasure that my nomination had finally been confirmed by the bleeding heart liberals in Congress. He would sleep better knowing that I was down there "kicking ass". Will they wake him up? I doubt it. They'll wait for follow-up information.

There are now eight of us in the tank and information is flowing in. Chamarrista units have already linked up with elements of Lacay's brigade and are assaulting the Presidential palace and the police barracks. It must have been well thought out and co-ordinated. They already have the radio station, and taped messages by Bermudez are going out over the air proclaiming the revolution and urging an end to all resistance. A phone call comes in from Dean Bowman who has managed to get through from the beach party. He tries to bluster, saying that to leave early would have upset the host – a man influential with President Vargas. Now they have no choice but to stay put. I content myself with informing him that his career is over, and hang up. Then Major Anderson comes through on a radio net and tells me that two of his MAG team have already been killed and he's ordered the rest back into the MAG compound. We consider whether they should make a dash for the Embassy itself and decide against it. Apparently there are road-blocks in most streets and anything moving is shot at. My concern now is Embassy security. Thank God I made that my first priority on arrival and reviewed all procedures.

We have a squad of fifteen Marines commanded by Cowder the "Gunny". We have sandbagged machine-gun emplacements on the roofs of the chancery, a staff apartment block and the residence. They cover the three wide abutting streets. The compound walls are three feet thick and reinforced with steel. They are topped with wire which is now electrified. In addition to the Marines, we have a team of twelve third-country bodyguards and security guards. Eight of them are displaced Nicaraguans and the rest Panamanians. They will fight.

The main gate to the compound is solid steel and there is a machine-gun emplacement built into the top of the wall at its left. There is a guardhouse inside the gate manned by our Marines, and another outside manned by a platoon of San Carlo National Guards. I am informed that they are still in place.

Inside the compound we number forty-two, of whom twenty-seven are Americans including eight women. Momentarily I wish that I had given the repatriation order yesterday. I am worried about the women. Since "Beirut", Congress has been very generous in allocating funds for Embassy security in the so called "danger locations", but the use of this money has been tardy and work has only just begun on a "security bunker" next to the residence. Again I blame Calper. The money was allocated months ago but he had bumbled along constantly changing the plans and specifications. The tank, though, is secure. Next to it is the "burn room". After the fiasco of Teheran when it was found that to destroy all sensitive documents would have taken over twenty-four hours, there have been drastic improvements. I'd been assured by Fleming that our own "burn time" is under thirty minutes. The incinerators are ready. The tank and the "burn room" are in what is called the "safe haven" area, surrounded by steel walls and doors; the air cleared by special ventilators. Apart from the crisis team the rest of the Embassy staff and dependents are gathered in the cafeteria. I order mattresses and blankets to be sent there.

Are we in immediate danger? I think not. Although the phone system has now broken down we are getting continuous reports by radio. The British Embassy which is close to the police barracks reports that resistance there is dwindling. Major Anderson radios that fighting around the Presidential palace is fierce, with many casualties but the Chamarristas appear to have the upper hand. He expects

31

the siege to be over by dawn, and other pockets of resistance in the city to die out a few hours later.

I review the possibilities. General Cruz and his brigade can't play any part in the fighting for several days. By that time, the city will be secure and he would have no chance against the combined forces of Lacay's brigade and the Chamarristas.

It is certain that by dawn the city will be in their hands. Together they are too strong to be dislodged by General Cruz – unless he has the active support of American troops. So now I have two paramount problems: what advice to give Washington as to active American involvement? And what to do in the event of violence against the Embassy compound?

The second problem is more immediate. I discuss it with Sumner, Gage and "Gunny" Cowder. Much will depend on the division of early power between General Lacay and Bermudez – leader of the Chamarristas. Sumner believes that in the early stages at least, Lacay will be in the ascendancy. Only with his support can Bermudez be confident of holding off Cruz and the Marazon brigade. Later the position could change. We agree that it is unlikely any co-ordinated attack will be made on the compound. The Chamarristas are the most extreme of all the Central and South American terrorists but once they see the prospect of power they will not wish to alienate the gringos totally. Like the Nicaraguans they will go through the motions of seeking détente. The only danger is posed by undisciplined units who, in the heat of the moment, and fuelled by years of Marxist propaganda, may act stupidly.

Both Gage and Cowder see no difficulty in holding off such units for several days. Particularly as they will only have light weapons. Sumner considers any threat to the Embassy as unlikely. Bermudez will be wary of direct American intervention and will risk nothing to precipitate it.

I incline to agree. We will only be in danger if the President does send in American troops. That would take several days. First to get them in place and second to orchestrate the diplomatic offensive. Obviously it would be preferable to be "invited" in, but who would issue the invitation? It's doubtful that Vargas and his crowd will survive the night. There has been no word from the palace for over two hours. Anyway I decide to check our defences and make the rounds with Gage and Cowder. I am comforted. Our Marines are alert and confident. The "third country" security contingent is nervous but they try not to show it. Gage assures me they will fight if necessary.

I look in on the canteen and am reminded of pictures of the wartime blitz in London. Mattresses and blankets are laid out at one end of the room. Wives and secretaries are checking through the food supplies. One of them, Julie Walsh, wife of our PAO, brings coffee and looks at me with anxious eyes. I recall the same eyes watching me at the Venezuelan Ambassador's reception. Then they were filled with hostility. With the sound of gunfire in our ears I feel vindication. I gather them around and say a few words.

"You know that the city has been overrun by terrorists with the collaboration of certain units of the National Guard. You know that I was considering sending many of you Stateside and I regret that I didn't. However I perceive no immediate danger. Our lives will be disrupted for a time until the situation clarifies. Meanwhile I want you to remain calm and do all you can to help."

There are murmurs of assent and one woman asks, "Is there any news of the group at the party?"

I recognise her as the wife of the Political Councillor.

"Not for the past two hours, Mrs Levy. Why were you not there?"

She looks close to tears, then straightens herself and says: "Because I didn't know about it. The bastard told me he was working late on something delicate – I'll bet he was!"

I hate to hear women swear. I shrug and say lightly to Mrs Walsh, "I know the Foreign Service regs. I can't order you wives to do anything but I'd be real glad if you'd kind of take charge here. Apportion people to help the kitchen staff and to keep the place clean and so on."

She is a small, bird-like woman and she nods her head vigorously. "Sure thing, Mr Ambassador."

I leave and walk across the compound to the residence.

Out of the air-conditioning it's moist and hot. There's only the occasional sound of gunfire. I am sweating slightly and resolve to take a quick shower and change my shirt. There is a faint paling of the eastern sky. It will be dawn over Cuba. Bitterly I visualise the celebrations over there.

Half an hour later, back in the tank, we all listen to the radio. Bermudez, live now, proclaims the revolution victorious. He has a high pitched, educated voice but speaks in moderate tones. I have seen photographs of him. Small and thin with a black moustache and thick-lensed glasses. Only twenty-eight years but looking older. I can detect both exhilaration and exhaustion in his voice. He announces the death of the dictator Vargas and his brother, and the arrest of dozens of henchmen. They are to be tried by People's Courts. He orders the immediate surrender, on pain of death, of all other Vargas functionaries. He praises General Lacay and all "loyal" elements of the National Guard who forthwith are joined as comrades and brothers with the Chamarristas in an "Army of National Liberation" which will crush all reactionary elements! Jesus! I've heard all this before. He's just dusted off Castro's old manuals. I loathe the myopic little punk.

He praises and thanks Cuba and Nicaragua. Curiously, he makes no mention of the United States. No messages of hate. Maybe he will be conciliatory. Then Lacay comes on urging all officers and men of the Marazon brigade to lay down their arms and save further bloodshed. Some chance.

A long "immediate" comes in from State, obviously drafted by an idiot. Maybe even the Secretary himself who thinks that every situation can be assessed in the light of "practical and permissible parameters". For sure the President appointed him only to brighten, by comparison, his own intellect. There are scores of questions demanding immediate answers. Most of them are insane, such as: "Give Sit. Rep. morale and sentiments local population." What am I supposed to do? Take a clipboard and wander around the city asking everybody how they're feeling? I send back a six word flash. "Wise on it. Hold your water."

34

I do the rounds again. There is a strange gaiety in the compound. Early fears have been transposed into the excitement of anticipation. Dawn has arrived and with it a sense of participation. People will look back and say, "I was there." For career officers it will be a leaf in the book of experience. For others, the piquancy of shared panic. I go back to the tank where coffee and sandwiches are being passed around by a wifely delegation from the canteen. The mood is jocular. Mrs Walsh is playing den mother with a vengeance. Her husband is subdued. He's drafting a reply to State's message.

Abruptly the mood changes. Look-outs have reported the approach of a convoy of five trucks heading towards the compound down Avenida Santanda.

They pull up at the main gate. We are given a running commentary by transceiver from the "Gunny" up on the roof of the inner guardhouse. The trucks are full of National guardsmen. A Colonel climbs down from the cab of the front truck. There are television monitors in the tank. Sumner recognises the Colonel. An aide to General Lacay. "A sensible guy," Sumner describes him. He approaches the gate and speaks into the intercom requesting to be allowed into the compound. The soldiers remain in the trucks. Sumner looks at me for an order. I nod and he instructs the Marine guard to open the small door let into the gate. Together with Gage we walk out to meet him.

It is barely dawn, but the Colonel wears very dark sunglasses. Behind them he looks unhappy. His complexion is very dark denoting Mestizo blood which is rare in senior officers of the Guard. He greets Sumner then turns to me and says, "Excellency, I am sent by the Revolutionary Council to assure you of the safety of the American presence in San Carlo."

I reply stiffly, "Already two of our MAG personnel have been murdered."

He shrugs mournfully.

"Excellency, I regret to tell you that two more of your compatriots have been killed: Mr Watson and Mr Packaro . . . they were lynched by workers at the Coca-Cola bottlers."

35

I am not surprised. Both were southern Texans who had the local "Coke" concession. Two very right wing guys constantly battling the local union which resulted in several disappearances and deaths. Their ideology was sound but their methods wrong. I cannot summon up sadness but I am very concerned about other Americans in the city.

"Inform General Lacay that I hold him personally responsible for this outrage."

The Colonel nods vigorously. "Of course, Excellency. That is why I am here – sent personally by General Lacay. The situation at the moment is . . . well, fluid. There is some indiscipline among the Chamarristas. They are vengeful. General Lacay needs time to impose order. Meanwhile all Americans are being collected by our own units and taken to your MAG compound. They will be safe there. It is guarded by a large contingent of disciplined National guards. Also we collected some of your own staff who were at a party up the coast. They are also safe at the MAG compound."

"Why were they not brought here?"

He is carrying an ebony swagger-stick which he taps constantly against the top of his polished boot. He looks nervously around the compound and says, "The route was dangerous . . . and General Lacay is worried about security here . . ."

Sumner interjects. "Why? We are well defended. It would take a major assault to breach the walls."

The Colonel now looks extremely mournful. Directly to Sumner he says, "You know how it is. Until the Chamarristas are integrated, everything is dangerous. There are now more than five thousand of them in the city. Many are getting drunk."

Sumner waves a dismissive hand. "But they only have light weapons."

The Colonel taps his boot in agitation. "No. They took the Presidential Guard Armoury. They have mortars, field guns and anti-tank rockets."

Sumner's face turns sombre. He is about to say something when I cut in. I don't like being a bystander to this conversation.

36

"Cannot Lacay disarm them?"

"Not yet, Excellency. There must be much discussion first with Bermudez and the other Chamarrista leaders."

I can't believe this fool.

"Are you telling me that Lacay collaborated with these terrorists without having a fixed agreement? Doesn't he know what will happen now?"

He holds up his swagger-stick as though to ward off my contempt. "Excellency, General Lacay knows exactly what he does. He and Bermudez are close as brothers. Together they have rid San Carlo of the curse of Vargas. Now all our people will prosper." He makes a sweeping gesture with the swagger-stick. "But for a few days there is danger to all Americans. You are, not unnaturally, hated by the Chamarristas. They blame you for the Vargas dynasty. Many of them are hotheaded and difficult to control, even by their leaders. The General is concerned. He has sent me with a hundred of our Guard to protect the Embassy – until arrangements can be made for repatriation."

"Very kind," I comment sarcastically. "You can deploy them around the outside of the walls."

He shakes his head. "Excuse me, Excellency. They must be inside the compound. Only then can we be sure the Chamarristas will not molest you. They will never risk firing on the National Guard. With the Marazon brigade loose they need us desperately."

Sumner is shaking his head emphatically. "No way, Colonel. They stay outside."

At that moment there is a distant thump. Sumner's head jerks in its direction, then he looks up at the roof of the guardhouse. The "Gunny's" head and shoulders are visible over a sandbagged emplacement. He has binoculars to his eyes.

Sumner is about to call when there is the crump of a loud explosion. I feel a slight pressure in my ears.

"Mortar!" the "Gunny" shouts down. "'Bout three hundred yards away over Santanda. Came from somewhere near the stadium."

I say to Gage, "Get moving to the 'safe haven' – fast. Tell them to start the burn – immediately – and all the women are to go into the vault."

He runs off towards the chancery.

The Colonel is very agitated. "Excellency! We must enter the compound. I urge you to lower your flag. It incenses them. We must replace it with ours."

The idea is repugnant and I dismiss it with an angry wave of my hand. There is another distant thump and we all turn. A few seconds later, another explosion, louder and closer. Laconically, the "Gunny" calls down, "Hundred yards. They're ranging in. You guys better take cover."

We move quickly into the guardhouse, past a marine who looks calm but ridiculously young.

The Colonel has a grip on my arm now. I smell garlic as he says urgently, "Think of the others. The women. Those fanatics have over a dozen mortars . . . and rockets that will blow through your gates. Senor, if we run up our flag they will stop firing . . . and Senor, if I order my men to defend the compound from outside I doubt they will do it. Sorry, Senor, I think they will not sacrifice their lives for Americans."

Sumner is cursing softly about the security bunker not being ready. Big help. There's another explosion from the opposite direction. Grimly, Sumner states, "We're bracketed. They have the range and can lob them right in."

I try to keep my face calm while inside frustration rages. The Colonel is still gripping my arm. I shrug him off violently then force myself to think. It is true that if Bermudez needs Lacay against Cruz he cannot risk killing his troops, no matter how much he hates Americans. Furious at myself for having to do it, I decide to compromise. Sumner is watching me urgently. Strangely, the Colonel has lost his agitation. He is slowly tapping his boot again with the stick. I wish I could penetrate those glasses and see into his eyes.

Formally, I say, "Very well, Colonel. Your men may enter the compound. I will lower the Stars and Stripes but permit no flag to be raised in its place. I suggest you send an officer to tell those imbeciles to stop firing, or face the consequences from my Government . . . Sumner, see to the disposition of his men!"

They file quickly out of the guardhouse. I remain, wanting to be alone for a moment, probing my decision. I hear orders shouted and then the rumble of the huge gates and the revving of engines. I walk to the door beside the marine and watch as the trucks move into the compound. Through the open gates I see a khaki staff car with only a driver at the wheel. Two of our security guards start pulling the gates shut. The Colonel is talking to Sumner, and the "Gunny". They look surprised as he turns and walks out briskly through the narrowing gap towards the car. Puzzled, I watch the guardsmen pour out of the trucks. They are all armed with sub-machine-guns. There have been no more explosions.

Suddenly, like the end of a losing chess game, the moves click in my head. The guardsmen are scattering in disciplined groups. Guns held high and ready.

There were only three mortar rounds. The Colonel relaxed after the third. He knew there would be no more. They were a mere persuasion to his argument. The "Gunny" and Sumner are looking around them in bewilderment. Beside me the young marine whispers, "Sir, it stinks! They're carrying PPD sub-machine-guns – Russian. The National Guard is supplied with our M3s."

I turn and look into young anxious eyes. He too is holding a sub-machine-gun. For a moment, rational, clear and precise, I want to take it and blow my brains out – my useless, stale, incompetent brains that have been tricked by a half educated, half-breed. I feel neither panic nor anger, but a deep, searing humiliation.

I watch the act played out.

Sumner and the "Gunny" already face a circle of guns. Sumner is watching me in consternation. I look up and see guardsmen already on the roofs of the residence and chancery covering our machine-gun emplacements.

Suddenly there is a noise at the gates. Half a dozen of our security guards are frantically pushing them open. An order is shouted in Spanish and my ears vibrate to the sound of bullets clanging off steel. The guards are tossed about screaming. The marine pulls me down beside him in a crouch. He raises his gun but I grab at it. "No! Wait."

Sumner and the "Gunny" have thrown themselves to the ground. They are still circled by guns. There is silence. I look back at the gates. Six bodies, corpses twisted on the concrete. They are fascinating. In all my long life I have never seen a corpse. Someone is shouting. I wrench my gaze away. It's the "Gunny" lying on his side, one hand on the butt of his holstered pistol, his face a mixture of fear and something else ...yes, determination. He is looking at me. He shouts again. "Sir! Do we fight?"

In an instant I scream back. "No!"

I have not even thought. No process of logic; no considerations enter my head. The chess game is lost; why smash up the pieces?

A man approaches the guardhouse. On his shoulders are the bars of a lieutenant. He is very tall and wide with a boxer's face. He seems familiar to me. His black hair is brush-cut – very rare for a Central American. He carries a sub-machine-gun loosely in his left hand. He is grinning widely.

"Excellency," he taints the title with insolence. "Tell your marines and any others to lay down their weapons or they will die."

My frustration is gone. I only feel icy rage.

"Are you in charge of these killers?"

He nods equably.

"Then I protest in the name of my Government and all humanity and . . ."

"Shut your mouth, pig!"

The marine beside me stiffens and starts to rise. I put a hand on his shoulder pressing him down. To the man in front I say, "You will suffer. My Government will see to that!"

"Fuck your Fascist Government!" His grin is gone. He raises the gun and points it at me. As I look at the tiny black hole he says, "Give the order, pig, or I fire. How I would love to shoot you, honourable Excellency!"

He will not shoot. I know it. I think I know it. Alive, I am a hostage. Dead, I am retribution for this scum and all the rest. But he will shoot others. I look at Sumner. He is sitting on the concrete, his arms around his knees watching me forlornly. I nod at him.

"Colonel, go with the 'Gunny' and tell them to lay down their weapons."

He and the "Gunny" scramble to their feet and, still surrounded, move off towards the chancery. Next to me the young marine lays down his gun carefully and straightens up. There are tears on his cheeks. I am praying that the incinerators have done the job; that all the documents are ashes. I have to keep the imbecile in front of me talking.

"Who are you?"

He grins again. His face is pitted with pockmarks. He bows elaborately. "Carlos Fombona."

I recognise the name. During the past week and in pre-arrival briefings I have seen it often in reports. He is a lieutenant to Bermudez. Known for cruelty.

"I know of you and your filthy reputation."

His smile widens as he enjoys the recognition. He lowers his gun to the ground. Still grinning, he unzips his combat blouse and shrugs it off. Underneath he wears a white tee-shirt emblazoned across the front with a red, jagged bolt of lightning. Underneath is a portrait of Lenin. He unzips his camouflage trousers and steps out of them, revealing a pair of faded jeans. He shouts an order and I look around as other "guardsmen" in the compound discard their uniforms. They all wear tee-shirts covered with Marxist slogans.

Fombona picks up his gun and walks forward. He prods the young marine in the chest with it and tells him to go over by the trucks. The marine looks at me and I nod. As he passes me I pat him on the shoulder.

Fombona is very close to me. I smell cologne on him. Even terrorists wear the damned stuff. He kicks the marine's gun back into the guardhouse, then prods me in the chest with his own gun. There is pleasure in his eyes as he says, "I have nothing to do with Bermudez or any of them." That cruel

41

grin again. "Me and my friends here are acting alone . . . We are . . ." a dramatic pause . . . "militant students!"

He leans forward, his face inches away. I feel a fleck of spit on my face as he hisses, "Militant students of the revolution."

I laugh derisively. "Sure. Forget the charade. Within hours you and your crowd will be thrown out. Are you really so stupid? You think my Government will stand by after this outrage? You think we've learned nothing? You're crazy!"

He shrugs. "I think not. We also have learned."

He turns and shouts an order and some of the "students" jump into a truck. They reappear carrying several packages. One of them comes over to us and gives Fombona what resembles a heavy, canvas flak jacket. A thin black wire trails from it to a small plastic box. Fombona hefts it in his hands with satisfaction. "Put this on."

I shake my head and see the cruelty in his eyes.

"Put it on, pig, or I'll call some of my men to force you."

There is no doubt he will, so I turn and he slips it through my arms and up over my shoulders. It is heavy and smells musty.

There are several canvas straps hanging on each side of the front. Carefully he ties them, pulling the jacket tight around me.

"Don't worry, Excellency, soon you will get used to it. You will be wearing it night and day."

He moves back, trailing the black cord, and hands the small box to the "student". The wire is about five yards long. Fombona points at the jacket and says, "That garment is packed with three kilos of plastic explosive. The wire is connected to a detonator. You will wear it all the time. Awake, asleep – even when you take a shit. Every American pig in this compound will be wearing one." He points at the student. "Pedro will be always by your side. At the first sign of a Fascist rescue attempt Pedro will turn that button and they will not find one square centimetre of you or any other American around here."

The man is crazy! We are twenty-seven. If they blow us up, twenty-seven "students" go with them. Acidly and with pleasure I point this out. His face is very serious. He nods solemnly. "Pedro is prepared to die for the revolution. So are the twenty-six others. They volunteered. Hundreds volunteered. What is twenty-seven when thousands have died already?"

I look at Pedro. Young, thin . . . almost emaciated. He holds the little box in his hand as though it is sacred. His eyes are glowing. I believe it. He will die. The jacket feels like lead. I can imagine watching those glowing eyes as he turns the button, imagine the flash of extinction.

Fombona is studying my face. He reads the belief in it and nods in satisfaction.

"And now, Excellency, we have to make sure that the chief pig in his White House pigsty understands that too. The photographers will be here soon. By tomorrow you will be famous. Your photograph and your lovely new jacket and umbilical cord and your faithful attendant will be in the newspapers all over the world."

I want to puke all over him. If he grins I will. He does not. Thoughtfully he says, "You will be the most famous pig in the world."

DAY ONE TO NIGHT TWENTY

JORGE
San Carlo
Day 1

I decide to use the guardhouse. It comprises an outer office and an inner room with four bunks and an adjoining toilet and shower room. The office has already been ransacked and papers are strewn around the floor. I give orders for it to be cleaned up and then I send for him. I arrange two chairs on either side of the desk. While I wait my mind ranges back over the past two days. I am still vividly excited by what I have witnessed. Throughout history nothing can stir the blood or the brain more than the violent overthrow of a dictator. It was like being dropped into the centre of the wildest carnival; at the airport, frenetic joy and exuberance as we filed down from the plane. Hands clutching at us, and our faces wet from a hundred kisses. It was a passion communicated and later, at the hotel, I coupled with Inez in a frenzy. She jerked into orgasm within seconds, and then again and again. She would have rutted all night but I left her screaming frustrated abuse at the closing door.

A jeep was waiting together with an armed escort. As we drove through the crowded streets people ran out and showered us with flowers and tried to touch us. The revolutionaries had flowers in the barrels of their guns. From almost every window hung red flags or pieces of cloth. Women and girls wore red flowers in their hair. We turned a corner and there was a pot-bellied man being dragged out of a door towards a waiting truck. Terror radiated from his wet face.

"Probably from the 'Model Platoon'," my escort said. "Vargas's pet death squad."

"What will happen to him?"

He patted his sub-machine-gun eloquently. "A quick trial by a People's Court and then up against a wall. We'll shoot a few hundred of them – just like you did in '59."

It's ironic. In 1959 I was three years old. Anyway, later Fidel regretted those killings, but at the time they were justified; the people demanded them. We drove past the Presidential palace. It was badly damaged; the white Christmas-cake façade pockmarked with black holes. I observed to the escort, "A tart's face covered with acne."

He liked the expression and laughed and repeated it several times. Then he told me that he had been in the assault force. Over one hundred Chamarristas had died. They had hanged Vargas and his brother from the chandeliers in his office. Chandeliers imported from Venice and costing thousands of dollars! It was only two nights ago. They were probably still hanging there. Would I like to look?

"At what? The bodies or the chandeliers?"

He laughed delightedly and repeated it to the driver. I was the comedian from Cuba.

But I was impatient and urged them on. Bermudez had set up headquarters in a squat building close to the palace. It was surrounded by heavily armed Chamarristas. I noticed the anti-aircraft guns on the roof.

I was shown immediately into his office. There were a dozen people with him and there followed a very emotional few minutes. He embraced me in a bear hug and although he was only a slight man I felt my bones would be crushed. He then kissed me fervently on both cheeks. I doubt that even Inez ever put such passion into the business. He was followed by all the others, including a stout young woman whom I recognised from photographs as Maria Carranza, right hand woman to Bermudez. She had a round, plain face and also round, large breasts. I passed reluctantly from her to a hug from a man who was almost a caricature of Che Guevara. It gave me a start. Had there been a resurrection? But then I remembered him. Another top lieutenant of Bermudez who had once trained in Cuba. He even spoke like Che.

Finally Bermudez made a short, highly charged speech: in

the name of the Chamarristas and all the people of San Carlo and all the freedom-loving peoples of the world, he wished to thank Fidel and the Cuban people for their comradely help and support for the revolution. In the face of such steel-like solidarity all Fascists, capitalists and imperialists quake with fear. In our hemisphere Fidel and the great Cuban revolution are a beacon of hope casting light into darkness; faith into despair; fear into dictatorship. If Juan Chamarrista's memory had been the father of this revolution then Fidel was the uncle. Every Cuban was a brother . . . a blood-brother. As soon as the country is pacified he will go to Cuba himself and tell this to Fidel and all the Cuban people.

The usual stuff, but as I glanced around the room I noticed they were gazing at him raptly. He has it. There is no doubt. He has the "essence". This almost waif-like little rebel is a singer and can turn his audience into an echo chamber. I'm impervious to it, but he held the others in his hand. They believed it because he made them believe it. I could even see that his eyes were moist behind the thick lenses.

I made a few similar noises but I was impatient and he saw it. With the exception of Maria, he ushered the others out and we got down to business.

He had just received some international newspapers via Managua. He spread them on the table with a conjurer's gesture. On the front pages they all had photographs of the hostages together with their "suicide" escorts and "militant student" guards. There were descriptions of the Embassy takeover and a detailed list of the students' demands. There was also a beautifully worded disclaimer by the Chamarrista Revolutionary Council. They had been powerless to affect proceedings. They were doing all they could to make the "students" see reason, but their first concern was the safety of the hostages. If an attempt was made to storm the compound by anyone at all, then the hostages would be blown up instantly. Meanwhile during negotiations, and in a humanitarian gesture, medicines and fresh food would be supplied to the compound daily.

I looked up to see Bermudez watching me with an

49

expectant smile and said, "I told Fidel you were crazy. I'm telling you the same. All right you got them. But the mood in the US is different now. They won't sit on their arses for months squealing in outrage and doing nothing."

The smile left his face. "I don't care. Whatever we do they will interfere. They cannot let San Carlo be the next domino. What does a cat do when cornered by a huge dog? It goes for its eyes! Claws its eyes! That's what I have done. The only way . . . to attack!"

He surely does have the "essence". Maria had run a hand down his sleeve in a gesture of admiration. Maybe he's right. I really don't care.

He said, "A closed truck will go in every morning and evening with supplies. You will go and come with it. Fombona has been told to give you total co-operation. If you have any difficulties you come direct to me."

I nodded. "I'll start tomorrow. Today I wish to interview anyone who worked in the compound. Servants – whatever. Especially if they had personal contact with the Ambassador."

I was staring down at the photos. At the tall spare aristocratic figure of Jason Peabody. On his face was an expression mixing extreme contempt with utter disdain. Now, at the sound of the door, I turn and look up into the same face and the same expression.

PEABODY
San Carlo
Day 1

There's a hippy in the room. I look around. No one else. He slouches in a chair behind the desk, one leg up on an arm rest, swinging. He is wearing faded, frayed jeans and a black tee-shirt. His hair, reddish-blonde and curling slightly, falls almost to his shoulders. There is a newspaper on the desk in front of him and a stack of files with black covers. The clod Fombona pushes me from behind and I stumble slightly into the room. I feel a jerk on the wire and then the little suicide punk is beside me. The hippy studies me, then says to Fombona, "Take that jacket off him and get rid of the kid."

Fombona moves past me with his sub-machine-gun. I have never seen him without it. He is shaking his head emphatically.

"No. He wears it every second . . . and the others."

The hippy sighs, swings his leg to the floor, stands up and stretches languorously; then he moves around the desk. He's wearing cowboy boots! I'm tired, I've hardly slept in three nights. Is all this a fantasy?

I watch the boots approaching. They are highly polished with an elaborate design stitched into the uppers. They are in front of me and I lift my head. With the boots he is almost as tall as me. His eyes are blue. It is a young face . . . no, old . . . young and old. He starts to untie the thongs holding on the jacket. I glance at Fombona. He is watching in astonishment. He snarls, "Leave him alone. You can talk to him. Nothing else!"

Oblivious to Fombona, the hippy continues unlacing the thongs. Fombona's face tightens in rage. I watch as he raises the sub-machine-gun and cocks it with great deliberation.

51

The ratchet sound hangs in my ears. The muzzle is pointed at the hippy's back.

He smiles and then astonishes me. In perfect, British accented English he says conversationally, "Spare the rod and spoil the child. The trouble with all students, 'militant' or otherwise, is the occupational lack of discipline."

It must be a fantasy! I glance at the punk. His eyes, huge in fright, are switching between the hippy and Fombona's gun. The detonator box is clutched in his sweaty right hand. The hippy reaches forward with both hands. His face is close to mine. Irrationally, I note that he is not wearing cologne. I feel the weight of the jacket being lifted from my shoulders. I put my arms back and it slides down. The hippy hands it to the punk, pats him on the shoulder and, speaking again in Spanish, says softly, "Here, chico. Live for another day, another sunset, another girl."

He turns the boy and pushes him gently out of the door, then without even glancing at Fombona or his gun, he walks briskly back to the desk, his boots clomping comically on the concrete floor.

Fombona's rage has intensified. He is quivering. He swings the muzzle to cover the hippy and moves forward two paces. The hippy appears to be reading the newspaper. When he looks up it is directly at me. He points a finger at the chair opposite.

"Excellency, kindly sit down. We have much to discuss and our time may be limited."

There is silence – almost a silence. I can hear Fombona's breath made heavy by fury. I can literally feel it building to an apex. At any second he will fire. I am certain. I look into the hippy's eyes, trying to detect any sign of fear. There is absolutely none. They gaze back with languid unconcern. Abruptly, I know that this man's life is in my hands. I walk forward slowly but positively, past the gun barrel. I have the sensation of moving over ice. I sit down. The chair squeaks – shrieks in my ears. The hippy smiles and says over my shoulder,

"Comrade, on that uncomfortable journey in the supply truck I noticed some bags of your wonderful San Carlo

52

coffee. Please arrange to have two mugs sent over here . . .
very strong. And again in an hour."

He does not know the man. He has gone too far. Yesterday
I watched Fombona beat one of his own men half to death
because of a minor infraction. He enjoyed it. Now I can
imagine his finger tightening on the trigger. I have an ache in
my back. I wish to move even slightly but I stay rigid. There
is total silence. Apparently Fombona has even stopped
breathing.

Seconds pass, or minutes. My nerves jangle at the scrape
of a boot, then again at rapid footsteps and the slam of a
door. I want to let out my breath in a great gasp of relief but I
don't. I let it out very slowly and quietly through my nostrils.
I will not show the relief. I cross my right leg over my left and
adjust the crease of my pants. The hippy notes the action,
smiles and says, "I learned never to argue with such people.
Debate gives them a false sense of importance."

I am pleased. I have managed to control the trembling in
my fingers. Casually, I say, "Had I not moved when I did, he
would have shot you."

"That's very probable."

I don't know how to answer that. I feel again the fantasy
surrounding me. He was close to death and knows it. I
believe he may even be savouring it. The whole emotion is
alien to me.

The silence grows while we study each other and then he
says, "My name is Jorge Calderon."

He says it as though I must know it. Even as a man might
say: "My name is Winston Churchill or George Washington
or Albert Einstein or Sigmund Freud or Karl Marx or . . ."
With a terrible mental explosion I realise that I *do* know it.

Has my face registered the shock? I pray not. I simply look at
him. He waits. I wait. I raise an eyebrow, glad of that facial
facility. He shrugs, leans forward and says, "I'm from the . . ."

I've won a tiny but deeply satisfying victory. I cut him off.
"The Cuban Directorate of Intelligence. Jorge Calderon . . .
rising star . . . one of the whizz kids."

He smiles and leans back. I am still astonished. As an

53

expert on pre and post Castro Cuba I am very familiar with the top echelon of their Government. I vividly recall a meeting a few weeks ago. Jameson, the CIA's top man on Cuba, talked at length about Jorge Calderon. Under thirty – he looks much older – obviously a dissipated life – one of the new generation of leaders brought in by Castro to regenerate his damned revolution. You'd think the idiot would have learned something from Mao and his Red Guards. But I know that the man in front of me is both brilliant and dangerous. An intellectual revolutionary; the worst kind. His father was Spanish, a wealthy painter. His mother a Scotswoman. The father left Cuba shortly after the revolution. Mother and child stayed on. Calderon trained as a lawyer and went straight into Intelligence, becoming a brilliant analyst and interrogator. Described by Jameson as cynical and unconventional . . . and a Marxist with all the fervour of a convert. He sure as hell doesn't look it. He might have shambled off the campus at UCLA. What is he doing here?

He pushes the newspaper across. It's the *Herald Tribune* dated the previous day. I look down at my own face. I'm gratified by the expression. I quickly read through the article. I can't help it. The words come out. "They're crazy!"

"I agree."

I look up. His face is serious.

"But your presence means that your ever-meddling Government is behind it."

"Wrong. My presence here has nothing to do with the Chamarrista revolution, or with your Embassy."

"Then?"

He waves a hand dismissively. "We'll get to that." He points at the newspaper. "What do you think your people will do?"

He's impertinent. He really expects me to give a professional opinion so he can run off to Bermudez and pass it on. I say, "They have several options, all of which will be bad news for your friends here."

He shrugs non-committally and pulls the paper back towards him, reads for a moment, then says, "Two and a half billion dollars is not unreasonable. After all, your budget deficit this year will be a hundred times that."

"It's blackmail."

"True." He smiles slightly and runs a hand through his hair. It's a mannerism I've already seen repeated a few times. "But only in the method of asking . . . or if you like, demanding. There's a basis to it. Morally your Government owes them money."

"Bullshit."

He prods at the article. "Three US corporations, Andana, General Metals and Universal Foods, over the past fifty years, have raped this country, with the active aid of successive US Governments, just as they have raped others in the region. If Universal Foods had paid a fair price for their half million acres of prime land, and if Andana and General Metals had paid normal royalties for their ores, then at least three billion dollars would have accrued to the State of San Carlo. Bermudez is being generous . . . He's offering half a billion discount. After all, most of those ores are now exhausted . . . and bananas aren't what they were."

Is it only three nights ago that I was reading Henri Weber trotting out the same inanities? Coldly, I say, "I don't need a lesson in the history of Central America. Anyway Bermudez won't get a cent from my Government."

"He doesn't expect to."

"What?"

He grins. "At least not directly, and he doesn't expect two and a half billion. He'll settle for a billion."

In spite of myself I'm intrigued. Without doubt this man has recently been conferring with Bermudez.

"So?"

"So Bermudez is a realist – and a Marxist. If he even holds on to the country he's facing a disaster. It's bankrupt. Its main assets, the iron and bauxite ores, are almost finished. It's overpopulated with one of the lowest per capitas in the world. Where will he get money? The World Bank? It's controlled by your Government. So are most of the other international aid agencies. He has the example of Cuba and

55

Nicaragua in front of him. Because of their ideologies they got and get nothing."

He's supposed to be brilliant but he talks rubbish. I'm unable to keep the derision from my voice.

"If he survives, he's blown whatever chance he had of getting aid. The western world doesn't give money to kidnappers."

He laughs good naturedly. "Unless they're Fascists. But you see, Peabody, Bermudez does expect to get aid – at least a billion dollars."

"From where – Russia? He's dreaming."

"No, from the World Bank. The European Community. Japan and so on."

"He's crazy. So are you."

"I'm not. He might be. But he has a plan. Of course the 'militant' students are a charade. Everyone knows that, but sometimes charades are necessary. The students demand two and a half billion dollars in reparation for the past economic rape of their country by the USA. Bermudez knows that it will never be paid. Meanwhile, stalemate. The students have graphically demonstrated what will happen to you and the other Americans in the compound if any rescue is attempted. By the way, one of your aircraft carriers, the 'Nimitz' is already sitting on the horizon. But it's a question of fire power being impotent."

He gives me comfort with this news. I say, "Maybe my President doesn't see it that way."

He runs a hand through his hair again. "I hope for your sake he does. Anyway assume a stalemate. North Americans don't like stalemates. They'll pressure for action. Your President's in a spot." He smiles. "It's a beautiful coincidence. One of your so-called staffers is Arnold Tessler. We know he's CIA. His father is the president of none other than the Andana Corporation. He's also one of the powers behind your President. His millions went towards getting him elected." He points at the photographs, at the row of hostages and smiles sardonically. "Now, daddy Tessler is going to see his little boy all trussed up in explosives and a lunatic fanatic next to him just dying to press the button.

He's going to urge his friend the President to be a mite cautious and the President is going to have to listen. I don't think the marines are about to land any second."

He is watching me, waiting for a reaction. There is truth in what he says but I won't give him the satisfaction of confirming it. I remain silent and he shrugs and continues. "So after a while, Bermudez, through third parties, will offer a solution. He'll let it be known that the students will release the hostages if an international aid package of one billion dollars is put together, say over five years. Oh, the suggestion could come from anywhere, even the Red Cross. Obviously, due to pride and politics, the USA cannot be seen to contribute even a single cent; but of course these things can be arranged. It will contribute all or most of it."

Again he is waiting for me to comment. I am tempted, but determined not to give one clue as to what I think. I don't have to. He tells me exactly.

"You know your President. You know he won't go along with that. He'll try threats first and then third party pressures and then, in a matter of weeks rather than months, he'll order a rescue attempt and a simultaneous invasion."

He's got it exactly right. The President will agonise and try to see everything in moral fables and his china-doll wife will stroke his arm, look admiringly into his eyes and say, "Honey, whatever you do, you'll know it's right. The country will know it's right. Honey, God will know it's right!" And with a heavy heart he'll give the order and go off for a good night's sleep. So what is this long-haired commie doing here if he knows all the answers? I ask him.

"What's all the talk about? I thought you had nothing to do with it."

"I don't. I'm just indulging myself in curiosity. I wish Bermudez well, but he made a mistake taking you people hostages. But the mistake benefits Cuba."

He pushes the newspaper away and puts a black file in front of him. He is about to open it when there is a knock at the door. He shouts, "Enter!" and even as the door opens I smell the rich aroma of coffee. I recognise the young man who carries the tray. He is a Mestizo employed in the kitchen on menial tasks. Apparently the students are too idle to cook for themselves and have kept some of the local staff on – or more likely trapped in. He is nervous and avoids looking at me. After he leaves, Calderon pours the coffee, making a little ceremony out of it. Without asking me he puts three lumps of sugar in my mug and a little milk.

"That's how you like it I understand."

"How do you know?"

He sips at his coffee.

"I've been finding out a lot about your personal habits."

"Why?"

"Because I'm going to be spending a lot of time with you."

"Why?"

He taps the file and smiles very pleasantly. "Excellency, you're going to tell me about 'Operation Cobra'."

JORGE
San Carlo
Day 1

It's going to take time. I hate this man; what he is; what he
represents. An elegant, foppish scalpel cutting into the flesh
of millions. Sucking the blood of whole nations and peoples,
in the false name of democracy. I loathe him with his crisp
suit, perfectly knotted tie and groomed hair. He's been
attached to that kid for three days but he looks as though he's
just walked out of a barber's shop. It's oven-hot in here and
he sits in his three-piece suit without a glimmer of sweat. I
detest him; but he will be difficult. He was probably terrified
during the business with Fombona but he concealed it. He
recognised my name and its implications but his face showed
nothing except the supercilious raising of an eyebrow. He
won that one. Now when I mention "Operation Cobra" he
merely looks politely puzzled. He's very good. Were I to play
him poker with a thousand dollars at stake I would win, but
it might take a week. I have to be careful and very cautious;
remember my own words to Cruz when he messed up with
Cubelas. "Interrogation is seduction and, like seduction, is
an art form." The subject must be prepared and conditioned
with great patience. The brain must be disorientated, the
senses confused, the emotions chasing through a maze. Only
then can the real interrogation start. I recall the Russian
instructor Kubalov, was it only six years ago? All that
rubbish with drugs. The subject gets turned into a babbling
monkey and all you get is monkey chatter. It's an insult to
the art, like slipping knock-out drops into a girl's drink and
then fucking her inert body. No satisfaction; no art. Interrogation is a long fencing match. Probing for an opening.
Recognising it when it comes. The sudden lunge and the

subject transfixed and flapping like a pinned butterfly. Above all, the art consists of the osmosis of transference. Of sucking in the thought process of the subject; his mental strengths and weaknesses; his fears and desires and conceits. You must know him better than your mother or child or lover. Your knowledge is his weakness. Finally, having exposed the weakness, you must be the strength to which it is drawn. When the subject finally talks he should weep with relief; and you know you have the truth.

From this Peabody I need one name. In a conspiracy one name leads to all the others. He knows all the names but he will be difficult. In the file in front of me is a single positive weapon. It is the weapon to break him but it must be used at precisely the right moment. Too early, and the wound will not be severe enough. Too late and it could be fatal. He must be made ready for the wound as a patient is prepared for an operation.

While these thoughts have been moving through my mind I have been watching his face. The expression of slight, unconcerned puzzlement is still there. The face is like his clothes – all in order. Smooth cheeks, neat eyebrows, brown eyes with identical crease lines at each outer corner. A perfectly straight long nose that certainly has never been broken. Thin lips, parted now, showing very white, even teeth. A wide, cleft jaw. His dark hair is short, flecked with grey and carefully combed straight back. He is sixty-three but looks ten years younger. He would be attractive to women. His normal expression is haughty and condescending but the face reflects his confidence, strength and intellect. He has the arrogance of intellect and the dignity of the position it has given him in life. I must undermine the dignity, and the arrogance will collapse with it.

Like every art form, interrogation requires inspiration. Suddenly, unexpectedly, I have it. I see a path opening up that will lead to a point where I can use my single weapon. I feel the warm flooding of my senses which comes at the moment of inspiration. For a moment I indulge myself in the enjoyment of my intellect, then I consider the time element. I do not have the luxury of an open ended time-scale. But with this man it would be fatal to rush. Mentally I give myself twenty days. I would like more and maybe I will get it. Maybe I will get less but I will pace myself, and Peabody, for twenty days.

I open the file in front of me and say, "We are both intelligent men. I know a lot about you and assume you know about me. I have an advantage. I've been studying your file for many days now."

He shrugs with feigned disinterest, reaches for his cup and takes a delicate sip. I harden my voice. " 'Operation Cobra' is yet another attempt by your Government to destabilise mine. Operations mounted against us by the CIA now number in the twenties. They have all failed and so will this." I tap the file emphatically. "You were the State Department's top expert on Cuba. This CIA operation is the most significant act of aggression against Cuba since the 'Bay of Pigs'. You were certainly consulted about it in great detail."

In a bored voice he says, "I'm a Foreign Service Officer. I have nothing to do with the CIA."

I turn two pages of the file and read, "On 28th November subject had lunch at the Metropolitan Club with Kirk Jameson."

I look up. His face is impassive. I harden my tone further. "Fact one: Jameson heads up the Cuban section of the CIA. Fact two: for the seven months prior to this posting you have acted as an advisor to that section on Cuban affairs particularly in relation to Government structure and person-alities." I turn more pages. "In the past three months you attended at least a dozen meetings at Langley. In fact you seem to have spent more time there than in your own offices at State." Did I see something in his eyes? A subliminal flicker? I press forward. "Peabody, we never underestimate the CIA, though from their past performance we have good reason to. But you people underestimate us. I don't mind telling you that eighty per cent of our budget is devoted to our USA Department. In addition, the KGB give us a vast amount of information that relates to Cuba. I know exactly what your role has been over the past months and your connection with the CIA and 'Operation Cobra'. You are intelligent. There is no point denying it!"

Good. He is angry. He stands and leans over the desk, thin lips compressed. He points a finger at my face and in a clipped voice says, "Deny? Why should I deny or confirm anything to you? By international law this compound is sovereign territory of the United States of America. You have no more right to be here than those terrorist scum. You are as guilty as them of an invasion of US territory – a fact that will outrage my Government when it learns of it . . . and will further sour relations with your jumped up little island!"

I laugh loudly, watching his face get angrier. For a moment I think he might strike me. I hope he does. But no. In seconds his face is impassive again. He sits down and looks past me at a spot on the wall above my head. A pity.

"Peabody, relations between our countries are as bad as they could be. So the US will be outraged; so what? Your Government is outraged with us all the time. Anyway no one has seen me come in here and naturally my Government will deny any knowledge of it. Now let's get back to 'Operation Cobra'."

Scornfully he says, "Calderon, if you think you have the impertinence to try to interrogate me, you are totally wrong. The only thing I have to say to you as a Cuban official, is to protest at your presence here."

He fixes his gaze again over my head. His mouth is set in a straight line as though sealed by clear tape. Good. The interrogation has started well. He is addressing me by name. He has taken the first rung up the ladder. He thinks he will go no further. Now is the time to start him up the next few rungs. The time to put into effect my earlier inspiration. I stand up and walk to the door of the other room and open it. There are two high windows with bars on them. It was obviously built to act as a detention room if necessary. I turn; he is watching me intently.

I say, "You will not have to wear that explosive jacket again. You will be separated from the others and will live in here." I indicate the empty room. Did I see a flash of relief in his eyes? If so it was not about the jacket. The other hostages are being held in two big rooms in the chancery; men in one, women in the other. Peabody is a private man. The thought of being alone pleases him. He will shortly be less pleased.

"Peabody, I'm going to come back in a couple of days. In the meantime I'm going now to give orders to Fombona. The bunks will be cleared out of the room and a straw palliasse put on the floor. The doors to the toilet and shower will be sealed. A bucket will be provided for you to piss and shit in. There will be another bucket with water to drink from and wash yourself... but no soap. You will get one meal a day... not what you're used to. Thin soup, rice, beans, plantain, cabbage and so on. Occasionally some stewed meat or fish." His face is no longer impassive but incredulous. I continue, "You are to take off your clothes and leave them on the desk. You may keep your underpants on. Anyway it's too hot for all those clothes. I suggest you do that as soon as I leave. Fombona will have orders to take them off forcibly if you are still wearing them when he arrives. That would be undignified. He would enjoy it."

He is standing now; shocked and furious. His mouth opens and closes, then he asks icily, "You expect me to live like that? Me!?"

"Yes, Peabody. Thanks to people like you who put people like Vargas into power and keep them there, millions and millions of campesinos in this country and others in Latin America live exactly like that. They sleep on dirt floors, shit in buckets, drink only water and eat the sort of food you'll be eating. Campesinos who worked like slaves on Vargas's estates; picked thousands of tons of coffee and could not afford to drink a single cup of the stuff... Think about that. When I come back we'll talk about 'Operation Cobra' and the traitors in my country."

He shouts the word.

"Never!"

I cross the room to the outer door, open it, turn back and say, "You will tell me about them. Be sure of it. One way or another."

He takes a step back, coming up against the desk. His

voice rising in disbelief, he asks, "You would torture me . . . ?
An American Ambassador?"

I shake my head. "No, Peabody. I never use torture. It's
usually counterproductive. Also no drugs. Drink your water
and eat your food without fear."

He thrusts an arm towards the inner room, his face mobile
with indignation.

"Forcing me to live like that is a form of torture . . . mental
torture!"

I laugh.

"Peabody, even being in love is mental torture . . . you
know *that* . . ."

PEABODY
San Carlo
Day 3

My rage has subsided. It has taken a full day and night. It subsided only slowly and marginally, but enough for rational thought to surface. During the same time, the hatred has distilled into a single burning, vibrating spot inside my core. Perversely, it brings a form of serenity. At last, after all the years, my amorphous enemy has solidified into the form of one man. It is twenty-five years since I felt such hatred. Then it was hatred with a passion. Blind and consuming and ultimately sterile. Now it is refined and logical and targeted. It burns in my brain and the rage cannot compete and so subsides. Rage is meaningless. Hatred is wonderfully logical. I read him easily. I am not a half-educated reactionary, or an agent dimwitted enough to get caught. I am trapped by circumstances beyond my control, but I can control my own mind and he will not tamper with it. He expects to take away my dignity. He is a devil in his perception, for it is a solitary weakness. In all men of taste and breeding and high position, dignity is a lynchpin. It's why a bankrupt financier throws himself from a twentieth-storey window. With the loss of his millions he also loses his dignity. It's why Hemingway blew his brains out. For him dignity was physical strength. When senility stole that away, his life was over. It's why rage consumed me. Not discomfort but the loss of dignity. Standing in my shorts, thin and almost naked, while that animal Fombona sneered and laughed. It's true, I have always been conscious – over conscious, of my thin legs. Ever since childhood.

It's true I have not made friends easily. Scarcely at all. I don't know exactly why. It was always so. Solitary people often take solace in style and order. He saw that already. Of course he will have questioned the residence staff; know that there is pleasure in a perfect cup of coffee or a correctly pressed shirt. So he tries to pry me away from my dignity. He knows the revulsion I feel having to crap into a bucket and eat slops with my fingers and lick up fetid water from a bucket. But he miscalculated. A man will suffer much if sustained by hatred.

He does not know, cannot know how intensely I hate him and the man and the system that sent him. He will not find me pleading for comfort. I pray this will end; but he will never know it.

I have just eaten what they call food. The little tin bucket lay on the floor for hours. When Fombona had water brought and saw it untouched he told me there would be no more until that was finished. He enjoys my humiliation. He probably spat in the food. Logic forced me to eat it and I did so almost retching throughout. I need physical strength. I ate it thinking about Calderon. Seeing his cynical eyes and arrogant mouth. The hatred helped me force it down and keep it there. Later I felt a twisting in my bowels. The food or the filthy water will surely give me diarrhoea . . . then more indignity at the bucket. He has thought about all of this.

What did he mean, "Being in love is mental torture . . . you know *that* . . . ?" Is it in that file . . . ? All those years ago? I doubt it. I have never spoken about it. Even now it is painful to think about it.

I am sitting on the straw palliasse with my legs drawn up under my chin. My big toe is swollen from gout, and throbbing. It's going to be a bad attack. When I asked Fombona for my pills he laughed scornfully. I fervently wish the gout on him with all its pain and immobility. Perhaps Calderon will give them to me. Will he come today or tomorrow? What will his next move be? I think about 'Operation Cobra'. Of course I know all about it. I was in on the debriefing of the defector Llovio, and saw the possibilities immediately. I virtually planned the whole thing with Jameson. Calderon is right. It's the most significant move against the Castro regime since the Bay of

66

Pigs. In October, Castro will surely go to Moscow for the big anniversary celebration and the bastard will find out what it's like to be on the wrong end of a *coup d'état*. Find out how he likes his own medicine. The thought gives me immense pleasure. Imagine sending that damned hippy here to try and make me talk. To humiliate me like this. They will pay for that. Calderon will suffer. After "Cobra", I'll make sure he suffers.

I'll be able to return to Cuba again. I can never think of that island without a mental picture of her coming to my mind. Strangely in recent years the picture has changed in subtle ways. Certain of her features have become more distinct, particularly her lips and eyes. Sometimes lately, in dreams, that is all I see – lips and eyes. I wonder at the significance. I hate people who constantly interpret dreams – who love talking about them as though they are anything more than disjointed ramblings of the subconscious. But why do I sometimes only see her eyes and mouth? As though all her other features are not blacked out, but burned away by a bright light. It was the eyes that used to watch me; always strangely mournful; and the lips that used to touch me, always soft, even in passion. My memory moves back across two decades. The pain, never diminishing, spreads through me yet again. For me, the gift of memory is nothing but a curse.

JORGE
San Carlo
Day 3

She stands naked by the window and I change my mind again. It was not a mistake to bring her. We have passed through the ritual. First we made love; as always, long drawn out; as always with her pounding her heels against my buttocks and screaming my name as she soars into orgasm. As always lying still for ten minutes and then watching as, lying on her back, she masturbates herself quickly to a second orgasm. I had been greatly offended the first time, my manhood impugned. But she had laughed and told me what a pleasure it was, lying next to a lover, remembering the past moments. She called it the "instant replay orgasm" and the next time made me try it, watching avidly. She understands such things. For me it was not quick but it was erotic in the extreme and afterwards, for the first time, I was truly sated.

Is it that which draws me to her? Only the physical? I partly wish it were, for then I would be able to control it, and her. But the other part, the darker part, knows that the difficulty of control attracts and fascinates and draws me to the edge.

She turns and walks to the bathroom. Her walk is a strut, almost boyish, but the body is outrageously female; its curves a miasma distorting the eye. I told her that once and she asked me what the word meant and laughed when I told her: "A vapour rising from a marsh, corrupting the air or the mind." But her face appears innocent in its dark beauty. Set on a long neck, she always holds her head proudly high. As a child I saw an old film with the American film star Ava Gardner. I must have remembered her face well because when I first met Inez the similarity was vivid, even down to the sensually cleft chin.

After a minute she comes out of the bathroom carrying a mirror like a tray. She sits down on the bed and lays the mirror between us. On it is a small bottle, a straw and a razor blade. She unscrews the bottle and tips some white powder on to the tray: cocaine.

"Where did you get it?"

"Here in the hotel. It's American owned. Lots of foreigners stayed here. The staff sold them everything from heroin to twelve-year-old girls. I got this from the room-service waiter."

Using the razor blade she is carefully sifting the powder and pushing it into two thin lines. I ask,

"How much?"

"Nothing."

"Nothing?!"

Her lips curve into a conspiratorial smile.

"Nothing, Jorge. I told him that later, when you are not here, he can come up and for ten minutes do anything to me he likes."

"Anything?"

"Anything . . . for just ten minutes. He became very excited."

I swallow. She is watching me, the smile wider now. I know that my face is expressionless. Would she do it? Probably. I cannot analyse my emotions. They are a mixture of impotence and fury. For an instant I want to smash my fist into her angelic face. She wants it also, for then whatever shred of control I have over her is gone. She invites the attack. She has done it before. Once at a party she threw a glass into the face of a drunken girl who had touched me in a suggestive way. Again in my apartment when an old girlfriend rang to ask a favour. I had spoken with affection in my voice. Inez smashed every glass and cup and plate in the place while I listened to Bob Marley at full volume. She wants to draw me into her own madhouse of jealousy and violence. The moment she does, I am lost.

She offers me the straw which I refuse with a shake of my

head. She shrugs with indifference and leans over the tray. Her breasts hang down, caressing their reflections in the mirror. Her left nipple is inverted into the breast. It only appears when aroused. She calls it her little penis. She quickly vacuums the two white lines into her left nostril. Even in Havana this one found drugs. She could find employment at any airport sniffing them out in smugglers' luggage; more expert than any hound.

I met her three months ago during an interrogation. Her husband of two years was a subversive. We had turned him and a month afterwards he was found hanging by his neck from electric cord from his kitchen ceiling. I suspected foul play and Inez was the first I interrogated. She was brought to my office wearing a multi-coloured gypsy skirt and a white frilled blouse. She was barefoot. My first question was whether she knew of any reason why he might have killed himself? Her answer was direct and devastating.

"Certainly. I left him for his friend. He couldn't exist without me. He was boring."

His friend turned out to be also boring but he did not kill himself when she moved in with me a few weeks later.

She stretches out on her back at the foot of the bed across my legs. While she waits for the coke to kick I get a vivid mental impression of our situation. She is a dangerous animal in a circus cage . . . a lion or a leopard . . . no, a tiger. I am the trainer, the showman who dares to enter the cage without even a whip or a chair. I have seen it on old films. The audience marvels that with only his personality he controls the beast. That control is balanced on the edge of the sharpest mental blade. One sign of weakness – more – even the slightest odour of fear and the balance is tilted and the showman is slashed. Why does the showman do it? It is surely akin to a sexual experience. The same thing that drives a man single-handed up a rock face; or to jump out of a plane with only a piece of cloth to bring him down.

She is rubbing herself against my legs. Soon she will move; licking her way up my body.

The bedside phone rings. It is an aide to Bermudez.

Excitedly he tells me, with much invective, that the Americans have just announced a total sea and air blockade against San Carlo which will come into force at dawn. Any ship crossing a three mile coastal limit will be sunk; any aircraft approaching to within ten miles of San Carlo airspace will be shot down by fighters from the "Nimitz". There is a plane leaving for Managua in an hour. Do I want seats? I decline and hang up. As I expected, the Americans have reacted swiftly and forcefully. They have the example of Nicaragua behind them. They will not allow a military build-up in San Carlo. I look at my watch; 7.30 p.m. The supply truck leaves for the compound in half an hour. I had meant to leave Peabody languishing for another day, but now I may not have my twenty days. I pull my feet out from under Inez and scramble out of bed and start dressing.

Petulantly she asks, "Where are you going?"

"The compound. I'll have to stay there till morning."

"What about me?"

I gesture at the television. "There'll be some video films on. Order a meal from room service." I had forgotten about the waiter.

She is sitting up on the bed looking hostile. She gives her "I don't give a shit" shrug and says, "Maybe I'll go out somewhere to eat."

"No. The streets are still dangerous. Eat in the hotel or in the room . . . or go to the airport. There's a plane to Managua in an hour. If you want I'll fix you a seat on it. There won't be any more for some time."

She is silent. Is she considering it? Do I want her to go?

I finish dressing and pick up the canvas bag holding my files. At the door I turn to look at her. She is kneeling now, looking at her face in the mirror.

I open the door and she says, "Leave me some money."

"Why? You can sign for anything."

She looks up at me. We are in the cage. Her eyes tell me that a test is coming. Very quietly she says, "I may decide to pay the waiter in cash . . . not kind."

She is probing for a weakness. Casually I reply, "Money is short . . . so is ten minutes."

I close the door behind me. Five paces down the corridor I hear a splintering crash as something hits the door; presumably the mirror. The animal has clawed and missed – and is still in the cage.

SLOCUM
Washington
Day 3

I, Silas Slocum, have been in this man's goddamned army
for twenty-eight years and nothing like this ever happened to
me. I'm at Anacosta. It's raining and there's a fat, black
limousine waiting at the foot of the helicopter steps with a
smart airforce captain standing alongside getting wet. As
I reach the bottom he salutes crisply and opens a rear door.
I'm puzzled as all hell, but I'm beginning to feel like one very
important cat. Some difference from a few hours ago. I duck
into the limo, the door clunks shut and we glide away.
There's a guy sitting next to me . . . a civvy in a dark suit. He
holds out a hand and drawls, "Good to see you again,
Colonel."

It's quite dark and I can't make out his face; then we pass
under the arc lights at the security gate and I get clobbered
by yet another shock. I'm looking at Mike Komlosy,
National Security Councillor to the President. But what's he
talking about? He's never seen my face before. The limo lifts
up on the flyover crossing the river.

"Mr Komlosy, I know who you are. I've seen you on TV
and in the papers. But I never met you."

"Sure you did. April 25th, 1980. Late at night in a bar in
Raleigh, North Carolina."

He is watching my face; amused at my puzzlement. With a
chuckle he says, "It was the night after the hostage rescue
failure in Iran. You were drunk. You talked a lot. I listened. I
was a bit drunk myself."

I remember hazily. I'd gotten drunk out of frustration.
Sure there was a guy sitting at the bar next to me, and sure
I'd sounded off. But that guy had a beard.

"You had a beard?"

"Yes. I was in Raleigh doing advance work for the election. You'd come out of Fort Bragg hell bent on getting drunk."

"I did just that."

"Sure, and you talked for about two hours. Talked in a rage. Colonel, a lot of it made sense to me. It stuck in my mind. So did your name. Last year when I became NSC I checked you out. You were still a Major and I couldn't figure out why; thought it might be the other thing. When I read your record I understood. For a career army officer you kinda speak your mind."

"Yeah. Always did. Figured I'd end my days as a Major – or a DD."

"DD?"

"Dishonourable discharge. I still might."

He nods in agreement but there's a bitty smile on his face.

"Did you have to hit him?"

"I did . . . an' would again."

He shrugs as we turn into Independence Avenue and says, "Anyway last year I pulled some strings and had you made Colonel."

"Thanks, pal. That explains it – one of the less unhappy surprises of my life. Why?"

Komlosy is looking out of the window. A girl is hurrying down the windy sidewalk. One arm aloft holding an umbrella, the other vainly clutching her skirt. Great legs. We pass and he turns back and says, "I'd like to think that I anticipated this day, but I didn't. I just thought your ideas might get a better hearing if delivered from a higher rank. Also maybe I got a kick out of using my new influence. It's kinda fun at first. Anyway, I immediately forgot all about you . . . until around midnight last night."

"How so?"

"San Carlo."

Ding dong! The bells ring.

"You're gonna get 'em out?"

He sighs. "It's a major option. But there are problems that would freeze a polar bear's balls."

74

"Sure, there's gotta be. Those boys are cute. They got it sewn up tight." I'm feeling real excitement. For six days and nights sitting in my quarters waiting for the axe to fall, I'd followed the news about San Carlo; imagined our great military machine swinging into action. Just before I left Fort Bragg I'd heard the news of the executive order proclaiming the total blockade. It was a good move. The right move. Trying to keep excitement from my voice, I ask, "You want me to be in on that?"

He shakes his head. "No, Colonel. Since Teheran, special units have been set up. You know about that of course."

"Sure. The Joint Special Operations Agency. So what am I doing here?"

He reaches into his pocket for a packet of cigarettes and offers me one. I shake my head. He lights up and blows smoke at the back of the driver's head. It swirls up against the glass partition. He sighs as if disappointed.

"Colonel, last night the Chairman of the Joint Chiefs of Staff briefed the President and the NSC on a possible plan to rescue the hostages. As I listened, I kept thinking about you and your drunken words all those years ago. I'm a lawyer by training, and not really competent to comment on the plan. I'm telling you that but no one else. The plan seemed ingenious, but a little complicated."

I can't help it. I laugh. "I'll bet. If the JSOA planned it, then the Normandy landings were a beach picnic by comparison. But what am I here for?"

Komlosy blows more smoke, then impatiently mashes the cigarette out.

"Colonel, I'm close to the President right now. Who knows for how long? After the briefing he asked his military aides what they thought. They were all enthusiastic."

"Sure they were! They're not about to criticise the Chairman of the Joint Chiefs."

"Exactly. Well I persuaded the President that we should have another opinion . . . a maverick opinion."

"Aha . . . Enter Slocum."

"Exactly. And in your present position you've got nothing to lose by offending General Grant."

The idea warms me.

"Do I get to meet the President?"

"I doubt it. The briefing was taped and recorded. You'll watch it. Think about it and then make your comments to me."

I'm disappointed and maybe it shows in my voice.

"Then I go back to Fort Bragg and the chopping block."

"We'll see."

We are turning into the White House. I'm excited. Me, ol' Slocum, at the White House.

The gate is heavily guarded by what look like ordinary cops, but I guess they're Secret Service men. One of them peers through the window at Komlosy, nods respectfully and waves the driver on. We move slowly to an entrance that's covered by a canopy like a door to a fancy restaurant. Inside there's another Secret Service guy sitting at a desk. He throws a semi-military salute and says crisply, "Good evening, sir."

Komlosy nods vaguely and walks on. I follow, surprised by the lack of formality. He stops at a door on the right side of the corridor. It's got a cypher-lock on it. Komlosy twists the dial one way, then the other. There's a click and he pushes it open. I follow into what looks like the general office of a small corporation. A couple of secretaries at typewriters, a guy talking on a phone with another cradled against his shoulder. They look at me without interest. We pass through another door – another office, this one equipped with word processors and a girl working a Xerox machine. Komlosy says to her, "Hi, Gail. Ask Rogers to come into the Sit. Room."

Then we go through another door and are inside. I'm disappointed. This is the nerve centre of the White House; the whole damned country! It's small, cramped and wood-panelled. With a couple of dozen people it would be crowded. There's a polished wooden table with a dozen chairs around it. One wall is covered by large television screens. There are several telephone consoles and map tripods scattered around. On another wall is a map of the world. It looks scruffy. The air is slightly perfumed.

I tell Komlosy, "It smells like a barber's shop."

He smiles. "Yeah, I think the admin. guy is gay."

There's a knock on the door and a small man comes in. He wears thick frameless glasses and a rumpled suit. The knot of his tie is pulled down. He looks tired and mighty intelligent. Komlosy waves a hand at him.

"Ken Rogers. One of my staffers. He'll work the equipment. Ken, this is Colonel Slocum."

We shake hands. His is damp and soft. He winces slightly as I squeeze it.

Komlosy looks at his watch and says, "The briefing lasts about forty minutes, after that I'll see you in my office."

He goes out. Rogers indicates a chair at the head of the table. There's a pad of lined yellow paper and some ballpoints in a silver mug. Also a flask and a glass. I sit down as he walks to the television console and pushes a button.

General Mathew Grant appears on a screen. Behind him, to the left, is a diagram "Embassy Compound". To his right a large-scale map of San Carlo. He is one handsome cat. Square face; greying, tailored hair; great teeth; thrusting jaw. His uniform is moulded; his voice a blend of honey and cut glass. For ten minutes I'm mesmerised by it. Then, as the individual words penetrate, my toes begin to curl. Rogers is sitting on my left gazing at the screen as though he's listening to the Sermon on the Mount. After thirty minutes I have a pain in my guts. After forty minutes I've a pain in the brain. The briefing ends and I ask Rogers to get me six aspirins and leave me alone for twenty minutes.

He brings the aspirins. I pour water and swallow them. He watches in fascination, then says primly, "Six is too many."

"How many would you take?"

"Three max."

"How much do you weigh?"

"One fifty-five."

"Drugs are prescribed by body weight. I'm close to three hundred so go away."

He leaves and I gaze down at the yellow pad. I haven't taken a single note. I look up at the blank screens and imagine the President and his advisors sitting at this table listening to what I've just heard. The pain is going. I stand up and start to pace. I try to wipe from my brain everything that I've just heard and seen. I glance at the map on the wall. San Carlo is so small they had to print the name out into the Caribbean.

It comes to me. Not in a logical, orderly way. It just appears in my head and washes away the last of the pain. But who's going to buy it? Sure as hell not Grant and his generals. Maybe Komlosy, but he's ignorant of the military. The President must know that. He's got to listen to his generals . . . unless . . .

Rogers opens the door and silently taps his watch. I follow him through into Komlosy's office. He is slouched back in his chair, feet up on a vast desk, a telephone in one hand and a cigarette in the other. He waves at a chair and says into the phone,

"Yeah, sure, Hal, but don't forget the goddam Tessler factor . . . Sure it's never off his mind . . . 'kay, but keep it up front . . ."

The door closes behind me. Komlosy swings his feet to the floor, cradles the phone and grinds his cigarette out into a stub-filled ashtray.

"Coffee?"

"No thanks."

"What do you think?"

"It's a crock of shit!"

He runs a hand through his hair. He looks close to exhaustion.

"Why?"

"That's immaterial."

His head snaps up.

"What!?"

"You heard me. Now I guess since the Embassy takeover you've had little sleep. You're a smart guy with a logical mind. Why waste time listening to words that have no way of affecting the outcome? Get some sleep instead. It'll be more productive."

He's looking very pissed off. Behind his casual exterior

he's a guy who enjoys authority. I could get slung out but there's no other way. With great deliberation he lights another cigarette. The smoke curls out of his mouth and then one curt word: "Explain."

"Sure. That plan has less than a thirty per cent chance of success. I can give you a dozen detailed reasons why. If you understand them and believe them and are able to make the President understand them, he may order a revision of the plan. Then the generals and their whizz kids go back to the computers and fuck around with the details – different plan, same result."

Very coldly, and with a tinge of sarcasm he says, "And in the few minutes since you watched that briefing, you've formed a totally radical plan."

"You got it."

"Don't be flippant, Colonel."

I stand up. "Mr Komlosy, sir. You know what's waiting for me back at Fort Bragg. If I sweet talk you, maybe you'll pull another string. But sweet talk gets stuck in my throat. You may as well get it straight. You brought me here to massage your ego. You watched that briefing last night with the President and all the brass. On the surface it's damned impressive . . . to a civilian. Afterwards there had to be a discussion. As far as the military aspects were concerned, you couldn't have had much to say. A guy like you – close to the President – that must have rankled. You'd have been on the side-lines . . . NSC or not. You gotta get back into the ball game. So before the next discussion you whisk me up here by jet and chopper to look it over. Then you debrief me on it and pick up a load of pointers. That might do you some good with the President but what's the bottom line? You want to get those hostages out alive or in body bags?"

He blows smoke at me.

"That's a disgusting question."

"You're a politician."

"And that means I don't care?"

"If you care . . . get me in to see the President."

I expect scorn, or even laughter. I get a contemplative look.

"And then?"

"And then I tell him what's wrong with his armed forces." I hold up a hand. "Okay, I know. He's the CIC. He's put the 'P' back into patriotism, he's built up the forces like no other President in thirty years. He thinks his Generals and Admirals emit pure sunshine from their asses. If he keeps thinking that there's a seventy per cent chance those hostages are going to die. You personally can't tell him that. Admit it!"

I am angry and I guess it shows. I don't care. I think of all the years. All the goddam stupidity. All the waste. Komlosy is looking up at me. He's tapping the finger nails of his right hand on the polished desk. He asks, "And you can tell him?"

"Damn right. I'm a soldier. He's my Commander-in-Chief. It's my duty to tell him. You brought my ass here – he's only yards away. What have you got to lose . . . ? Your influence . . . ? You said I talked sense that night in Raleigh. That's why my ass is here, so let me talk to my President!"

He's looking past me now. He's considering it. Really considering it. Slowly, not to interrupt his thoughts, I sit down again. In spite of his exhaustion this man gives off all the vibes of power. He's only just passed fifty, but looks younger; kind of boyish with lank blond hair and a face active in its movement. Guys like this must be born with more energy than most. Real achievers. They've just got to be top dogs in school and college. Then in whatever career they choose. We've got Generals like this guy. They get there by pure effort. No difference whether it's the army or a corporation or politics. But at least this one listens and sometimes even thinks.

I guess there's only a one in ten chance, but it was worth a shot.

He lights yet another cigarette and asks, "Colonel, that plan is wrong for all the reasons you talked about in Raleigh?"

"And more."

He sighs. "And you don't simply want to tell me about them."

"Waste of time unless you just want to score points."

Another sigh. But he's nodding his head slowly.

"Okay, Colonel, I'll give it a try. He may want to call General Grant first."

"If he does it's a non-starter."

He stands up and stretches. "Yeah, I know it. Wait here. Don't get your hopes up."

When he reaches the door I say, "I'd sure appreciate some coffee now."

He nods and goes out. I get up and start to prowl around. It's a plush office with real leather chairs in one corner grouped around a glass coffee table. There are pictures on the wall. They look so goddam awful they must be expensive. There are also lots of framed and signed photographs. Komlosy with visiting Heads of State; Komlosy with Cabinet members; even Komlosy with the Pope I'm impressed. This is one top cat. There are two doors set in a wall. I open one of them. It lets into a small room which contains a cupboard and an army cot. Even the blankets are army issue. I open the other door; a tiled bathroom. I go in and splash cold water on my face. The towels are snow-white and fluffy and decorated with the Presidential seal. Back in the office I look at a leather-framed photograph on his desk. A smiling, pretty woman flanked by a young boy and a younger pretty girl. This cat's got it all wrapped up. He even hit home runs on his children.

The door opens and a young woman comes in carrying a tray. She gives me one of those smiles they paint on Barbie dolls. She puts the tray on to the glass table and I walk over and sit down. She leans over, picks up the jug and pours. Her blouse opens a little. The jug bears the Presidential seal; she has great tits.

"Cream? Sugar?"

"No thanks, just as black as me, lady."

She laughs nervously and I smile up at her.

"I guess there's a lot of overtime going on here."

"Sure is, Colonel. Poor Mr Komlosy has hardly gotten home since the San Carlo crisis."

"I saw the cot." I gesture at the photograph. "Must be tough on the wife."

She shrugs. "Mostly they understand."

No doubt about it. The emphasis was on "mostly".

"I guess everyone puts a lot of time in. You all have your own cots?"

She shakes her head and backs off towards the door. She's blushing a bit. No doubt at all. Ol' Komlosy's pickin' up the perks that go with power.

"Call me if there's anything else."

"Sure thing."

The coffee's good. I drain the cup and pour another, then put my mind working. If the chance comes, I'm gonna have to be ready.

Twenty minutes later Rogers is at the door crooking a finger. The chance has come.

He walks with an important spring-heeled step, his head bouncing up and down. I am barely aware of the route or surroundings. Up some steps and along a couple of corridors.

We come to a large wooden door. There's a Secret Service type outside. He opens it. Rogers murmurs "Good luck," turns and bounces away. I go in to find Komlosy standing alone in a small room. His voice sounds harshly loud in the hushed atmosphere.

"Colonel, we're going in to see the President now. Tonight is a rare chance for him to have dinner alone with the First Lady, so try to keep it brief."

I nod and he turns to a door and opens it. We go through. It's true. It is oval. Large but kind of intimate.

I hardly notice it. I only have an impression of the spaciousness of the room and the man sitting at the desk in front of the tall window with a dark blue flag behind his shoulder. He is reading something. There is a pen in his right hand. Komlosy coughs and says, "Colonel Slocum, Mr President."

The President looks up. I snap out a crisp salute and see the brief impact of shock on his face. For a second I'm puzzled, worried, then I realise. Komlosy has not told him that I'm black. More than black; I'm goddam ebony. The Commander-in-Chief has just set eyes on the biggest, blackest soldier in his entire army – and was not expecting it. I wonder about Komlosy. Was it an oversight, or deliberate?

The President recovers quickly. A lowered glance at Komlosy and he rises and comes round the desk. His smile is genuine as he holds out his hand. His grip is firm. He puts his other hand on my shoulder and urges me towards a group of low chairs. We sit down. I'm excited but not nervous. The President is looking at the slab of fruit salad on my chest. He says, "Colonel Slocum, your many decorations tell me that you have long been a courageous defender of our country. But I wonder if it's appropriate that I receive a soldier who is shortly to be court-martialled."

He is smiling just a little. I'm not sure what to say. I hear my voice.

"We . . . yes, sir, Mr President . . ."

"After all, son, it's a serious offence striking a general officer."

His words confuse me. His tone is stern but I can't remember when anyone last called me "son". I think for a moment, then say, "Sir . . . Mr President. I've tried to be repentant but it doesn't work. Eight good men died . . . my men."

He nods solemnly. "It was a terrible tragedy, but you of all people know that these exercises are essential. We often have casualties."

"Yes, sir, but those were not necessary. Conditions were over the limit. In real combat, I'd have kicked those boys out of the aircraft and then jumped myself. He was just trying to prove how mentally tough he was. He was sitting on the ground in a nice safe command post. I just saw red. I regret it but I'm not repentant . . . Mr President, I'll take my chance at the court martial."

"Of course. Now Mike here tells me that you're worried about some aspects of the San Carlo rescue plan. Tell me about that."

I'm uncomfortable. The chair is low and softly sprung. My knees are just about up to my chin. I can't sit here for any time. I say, "Er . . . Mr President, do you mind if I stand up? I think better on my feet."

He waves a hand in agreement and I push myself up. It's no better. Now he has to crane his neck to look up at me. He smiles and stands and walks to his desk. "Go ahead. I'll sit here. Pace if you wish. Oh, and Colonel, you're having trouble whether to call me 'sir' or 'Mr President'. Make it 'sir' if it's easier."

"Thank you, sir."

Komlosy has pulled a chair up sitting off to my left. I decide that I may as well start as I mean to go on. I look the President in the eye and say, "Sir, Mr Komlosy asked me to keep this brief. You're shortly going to have dinner. Sir, either dinner gets cold or you only get to hear part of what I need to say."

I slide a glance at Komlosy. He's looking unhappy. The President glances at his watch, purses his lips and gives me a long, level stare. Finally he says, "Colonel Slocum, if I believe that what you're telling me is important, then my dinner can wait."

First hurdle over. I take a deep breath and state flatly, "Sir. It is my duty to tell my Commander-in-Chief that for the past thirty-five years the United States military establishment has been guilty of gross, professional incompetence."

Total silence, except for the faint wailing of a distant siren. The President is looking at Komlosy as though he were a cat that had dragged in a stinking, decomposed rat. He turns back to me and says harshly, "It is not your duty to malign the uniform and the medals you wear; and the thousands of fine men and women who have fought and died for freedom and their country over those years."

I shake my head. "No, sir. I honour them. I have been a soldier for twenty-eight years. The American soldier, airman and sailor is as fine as any in the world and better than most. I criticise the command. Its attitude, its structure and its thinking. In a nutshell your armed forces are incapable of being an efficient instrument of your global policies."

Another silence. His face reflects indigestion. In an ominous tone he says, "Explain yourself, Colonel."

"Sir, in the past thirty-five years, our country has not enjoyed a single military success."

He sighs. "What about Grenada?"

"Grenada was a mess. I was on it. But I'd like to come to that later. I'd like to start with Korea. The Inchon landings, 1950 – 'Operation Cobalt'."

"Oh! That was also a mess?"

"No, sir. It was brilliantly successful. It was our last success."

I start pacing in front of his desk. My steps make no sound on the thick beige carpet. I hold up one finger.

"Sir, it was followed by the advance to the Yalu River. MacArthur took no notice of all the evidence the Chinese would intervene. He didn't wait to consolidate, he pushed forward, over-extending his lines. The Chinese attacked and routed our forces and pushed us into the longest retreat in our history. Result: final stalemate, partition of Korea and our first overseas defeat."

He interjects, "Some wouldn't see it that way."

I swing around to face him.

"Sir, historians do and will. Our soldiers did. I knew many of them." I hold up a second finger. "'61. The Bay of Pigs. Okay, it was a CIA operation but our military was deeply involved in the planning. Another mess. Classical errors for an amphibious assault. No air cover. No dispersal of ammunition reserves, disgustingly bad Intelligence." A third finger. "Vietnam. With a massive superiority in all aspects of military power we lost because the generals at the Pentagon decided to rotate our boys in and out on six-month tours. Sir, I was there for six years and watched them coming and going. For the first three months they were learning. For the last three months they were taking the least risks possible. There was lack of cohesion and pride among fighting units. It's human nature. In the early days, the British were fighting a similar war in Borneo against the Indonesians. They sent their troops in and told them they would stay until they won. They did the job in under three years."

The President looks an enquiry at Komlosy who nods. I raise a fourth finger.

"'68. The 'Pueblo'. The navy sent an unescorted, barely armed Intelligence ship to the edge of North Korean waters. A volatile, hostile area. It was attacked. When it signalled for help the chain of command was inefficient. No help was available. The Commander failed to scuttle his ship as was his duty. It was taken . . . a mess."

He is watching me intently now. I am standing still, facing him. I raise a finger of my other hand. "'70. The Son Tay raid. A brilliantly planned mission to rescue American POWs from a prison in North Vietnam. When the Commandos got there . . . no Americans. They'd left months before . . . an Intelligence mess." I raise another finger and resume pacing. "'75. The 'Mayaguez'. American cargo boat and crew seized by Cambodians: a patched together rescue attempt. More bad Intelligence. Every branch of the services trying to get in on the act. We assaulted an island and then discovered that the crew had already been released . . . it would have been comic but we suffered forty-one dead."

I give up on the fingers. I'm running out of them. "'79. The Iranian hostage rescue attempt. Maybe the biggest mess ever. Colonel Beckwith and his men were among the finest soldiers on this earth. After five months of training, the operation never had a chance because of incompetent planning. So complex you'd have had to be a chess grand master to figure it out. Okay, long distances, big problems but . . . badly rehearsed; faulty command structure. No one in a position to compromise. No back-up. The computers said it was perfect. Did they feed in sandstorms? Pilot error? Civilians roaming about where they weren't supposed to be? Poor chopper maintenance? It just fell apart . . . a mess." I swing around. He's looking gloomily at his desk top. I glance at Komlosy, he's gazing at the far wall. Very quietly I say, "'83. Beirut." The President looks up. I feel a little sorry for him. "Beirut, sir. 241 marines killed mainly because of professional military negligence. Sir, in two days' time I'm gonna be court-martialled for hitting a General. He got a sore jaw. How many Generals were court-martialled for Beirut?"

He sighs and leans back in his chair. There is a long silence. I can feel the pain in my head again. Am I getting through? He looks at his watch, then at Komlosy. What's it going to be? With another sigh he reaches forward, picks up the phone and punches a button on the console.

"Julie, get me the First Lady." A pause. "Hi, honey. Now don't get mad, huh. I'm going to be a mite later than planned ... Yeah, honey, the San Carlo thing ... I know, honey. Wait a minute." He looks at me. "Colonel, how long you going to be?"

"'Bout half an hour, sir."

Into the phone he says, 'Half an hour, honey ... Sure. You did? That's just wonderful ... I sure am ... An' me, honey." He hangs up.

"Okay, Colonel. I'm gonna hear you out. Don't think I agree with everything you say. In these matters there are factors of chance, fate, call it what you like. But what was wrong with Grenada?"

"Well, sir. We won that one. We had no choice, I guess. We used a steam-roller to crush a walnut. And in the process the roller got knocked about a bit."

"How so?"

"We took unnecessary casualties. Again, all the services wanted in on the act. We should have done it with a thousand paras. We had so many troops running around they were in danger of colliding with each other. Ostensibly we went in to protect the lives of our medical students. It took us forty-eight hours to secure them. It should have taken two. Again, our Intelligence was God awful. The biggest damage we did was to a mental home. The only smart idea the Generals had was keep the media out. They saved themselves a scandal."

The President smiles slightly and stands up. He walks to a cabinet and opens it. Inside are glasses and bottles. Over his shoulder he says, "Colonel, I generally mix myself a martini this time of the evening. Mike enjoys one. How about you?"

"Yes, sir. Thank you."

I'd prefer a beer but how do you say that to a President? He mixes the drinks carefully. Komlosy walks over and collects his. The President hands me a glass and perches on the edge of his desk.

"Cheers." I take a sip. It's dry enough to numb my tongue.

"Great martini, sir."

He smiles. "Thanks, son. Now tell me . . . briefly . . . why those so-called messes happened."

I take another sip and marshall my thoughts.

"Sir, in one word . . . technology."

He is looking down at his glass, reflectively swirling his drink. I go on.

"We rely too much on it, sir. It's permeated and warped the thinking of our top command. They've neglected the simplest and most fundamental rule of war: battles are won by soldiers on the ground. We were beaten in Vietnam by an enemy comprised solely of infantry. In spite of our total air and sea domination. I'd guess that out of every ten million bullets we fired in Vietnam, only one hit a Vietcong. We were blinded to this by computers, sensors, avionics, electronics and all the other tricks in the bag. It's been that way since World War Two. They've forgotten. The first rule for a Commander is to get his men into contact with the enemy on the best possible terms. That's also the last rule. They're trying to fight without contact. That can't be done unless you go nuclear."

He nods. "Okay. Following that line what's wrong with the rescue plan?"

I drain my glass. "Sir, excuse the language. As I told Mr Komlosy, it's a crock of shit. . . ."

PEABODY
San Carlo
Day 3

I hear a slight clatter and open my eyes. The room is lit by a
single unshaded bulb hanging from the centre of the ceiling.
There are no shadows. No movement. But I heard a noise.
I hold my breath and listen. There's a slight snuffling.
Something catches my eye. It's hanging over the rim of the
food bucket by the door; black, thin and scaly. It twitches. I
taste copper in my mouth. I can hear my heart. Is it a snake?
Slowly, carefully, I push myself to my feet. The straw
palliasse makes a squeaking sound under my palms. The
black thing slithers into the bucket. I back up against the
wall, trying to think. Whatever's in that bucket is after
remnants of the food. I look around the room for a weapon.
There is only the slops bucket; half full and stinking. My eyes
jerk back to the food bucket. It topples slowly on to its side
and rolls a little. Something slides out. I press myself back
against the wall. I'm looking into two bright eyes behind
a pointed snout. It's a rat – black – about ten inches long.
It moves, disappearing behind the bucket. I try to think.
I can feel pain and realise I'm clenching my fists so tight
my nails are digging into my palms. The pain helps to ease
the panic. Keeping my eyes fixed on the bucket, I shout,
"Guard!"

It comes out barely louder than a squeak. The bucket
moves and the obscene black shape slips behind the bucket.
I push myself away into a corner and scream, "Guard!!
Guard!!"

I hear the sound of the outer door, then footsteps. It's
an eternity, then the lock turns and the door opens. The
guard is young; a round-faced teenager. He holds his

sub-machine-gun ready. He sees me crunched into the corner. I point at the bucket. The muzzle of his gun swings towards it.

"A rat!"

"A what?"

The rat moves. It's hurtling across the floor towards me. I throw myself to one side. I hit the floor feeling no pain. My hands are over my face. I twist and through my fingers see the rat concertina itself into a tiny hole in the corner where I was standing. It appears to get stuck and then like a lump of congealed black oil it oozes through trailing its tail.

I feel the pain now where my shoulder hit the concrete. The guard is laughing uproariously. With difficulty I climb to my feet. My hands are wet from the sweat on my face. Horror is replaced by rage. I scream at him, "Shut your mouth!"

He looks at my face and whatever he sees there stills his laughter. He covers me with the gun and moves back a step. Then with a sneer says, "Frightened by a little rat? Don't worry, Excellency, you are too skinny. You won't make him a good dinner."

I'm thinking of a retort as Fombona appears in the doorway. Still grinning the guard explains about the rat and pantomimes my hurling my body around the room. Fombona is vastly amused. With exaggerated courtesy, he offers me his sub-machine-gun.

"Here, pig. Take this to fight the great monster; or would you prefer a field gun?"

It's only a yard away. I'm tempted to hurl myself forward to try to grab it. He is watching me; daring me. Stiffly, I say, "I protest against this outrage. You will do something about the vermin in here. There are also cockroaches. Dozens of them." I point to a dirty brown pile in the corner, the corpses of cockroaches I've killed over the past two days. "There are pesticides and rat poison in the Embassy stores . . . which no doubt you've looted."

He shakes his head benignly.

"Forget it, pig. The orders are exact. Only the Cuban can agree to anything for your comfort or person."

"Then I demand to see him . . . immediately."

He shrugs. "He is not here."

"When is he coming?"

"Who knows? Who cares? He'll come when he wants."

"Then get word to him."

He gives me a scornful look. "Listen, pig, I'm not your messenger."

I control my anger and point at the food bucket.

"Get that disinfected."

He laughs and says to the guard, "He worries about catching a disease. What about the poor little rat catching something from him?"

They go out giggling like delinquents and the key scrapes in the lock.

I feel crushingly alone. So alone that I would even tolerate Fombona's company. I listen to hear if they stay in the office, but their footsteps recede and the outer door closes. I look quickly at the hole in the corner. Is there a snout there? Recessed eyes? No, it's hyper imagination. I check the rest of the room. There are two other holes, a bit smaller but they look ominous. I have to block them; but with what?

Another brief inventory. Apart from my shorts there is nothing, and they won't block all three holes. Besides they are the last shred to my dignity. I look down at the palliasse. Straw and sackcloth. It's all I have. There's a dull ache now in my shoulder as I squat down and start tearing the palliasse apart. I don't think about my future sleep; with those holes unblocked there will be no sleep. I tear three strips of sackcloth and roll them tightly round bundles of straw. I unpick the crude stitching and bind the bundles tight. I have made them too big. I cannot force them into the holes. It takes me half an hour to get the sizes right and the holes firmly plugged. I am sweating freely as I force the last one in, but I am pervaded by a sense of relief. I loathe rats.

I kick the remains of the palliasse back against a wall and sit down. I rub my shoulder and wonder how long it will take a rat to chew through a plug of straw and sackcloth. A day? A week? An hour?

When will Calderon come?

JORGE
San Carlo
Day 4

I climb out the back of the supply truck. Fombona saunters up with a young guard. They tell me about Peabody and the rat. Fombona, his eyes lit with malice, says, "He's terrified. Turn out that light and put a dozen oversize rats in with him – he'll babble in minutes."

This is an interesting development and I think about it carefully. It could be crucial to the next stage. Finally I give Fombona his orders. For a moment he's dumbfounded, then he spits on the ground and says in disgust, "You're wasting your time. Give me a few hours and he'll be singing."

"Do what you're told. You know your orders."

There is a hesitation. This one is another beast in a cage. The slightest flinch and he'll strike. I look steadily into his eyes. After a minute he drops his gaze and turns away with a curse.

I glance around the compound. Already the militants are losing their attentiveness. A group of them are sitting with their backs to the fence that surrounds the residence; their guns are at their feet as they smoke long cigars. The group at the gate are sitting in a circle playing cards. Fombona is getting over-confident. I'll inform Bermudez.

I walk slowly towards the guardhouse. A group of prisoners is led out from the chancery. Six women all attached to their suicide guards – girls who look to be in their late teens. With their short hair and scruffy clothes they are barely distinguishable from the male guards. Would they really blow themselves up? They look cheerful, talking loudly to each other as they walk in a slow circle. Their prisoners are morose and unkempt. One of them, a grey-haired woman, is looking at me with contempt. I turn away and walk to the guardhouse.

I don't unlock the cell door immediately. I put my files into a desk drawer and sit down and wait, analysing my strategy. After five minutes three guards arrive. They are carrying buckets and brooms and a shovel. They are grumbling good naturedly. I unlock the cell door and open it. A second later I'm covered in excrement and urine. Peabody is standing two metres in front of me; the bucket in his hand, a look of triumphant hatred on his face. For a slice of a second there is a searing white light in my brain and I want to kill him. I control myself, wipe my face on my sleeve and say casually, "I'm told there's a problem with rats here." I gesture at the guards. "They'll put rat poison in the holes, then plaster them up." I point at the bottom edge of the door. "There's a gap there. They'll put a board and make it flush with the ground. They'll disinfect the whole room and spray it with insecticide. Your food bucket will be disinfected." I notice the torn-up palliasse. "They'll bring you a new palliasse and whitewash the walls." His expression hasn't changed.

I say, "If it had been Fombona who opened that door you'd be dead now."

He throws the bucket across the room and sneers, "I'm not some common criminal. You forget who I am."

"I don't. Fombona would have. I'll be back."

I turn. The guards are trying very hard not to laugh. I give them all a look and they don't have to try any more. They are poker-faced while I give them their orders. I walk out and cross the compound to the residence. The female prisoners and guards are still circling. I'm the object of curious looks. My fury is fermenting. He threw shit over me! His own shit! No greater insult on earth. I suck in a breath. The odour fouls my nostrils; seeps into my brain. He threw shit on me! Wait. Control. I indulge myself. Fury is futile. I will turn the insult back on him. Revenge is more satisfying than rage – more permanent.

There is a guard at the entrance. He looks at me in

astonishment and steps back out of nasal range. Curtly I say, "Take me to the Ambassador's quarters."

I follow him through the door. The entrance hall is tidy. Bermudez has given orders that the buildings must be searched but not looted or damaged. I take little notice of the place. I'm desperate to rid myself of this filth.

The guard opens a door and stands back. I go through into a luxuriously furnished lounge.

"Where's the bathroom?"

He points at a door. "Through the bedroom, comrade."

"Follow me!"

I have to stop myself from running and retching. The bathroom is similar to the one at the hotel but bigger. All tiles and mirrors. I strip off my jeans and shirt and hold them out to the guard. He takes them between forefinger and thumb, distaste on his face.

"Have them washed and dried . . . and meantime find me something about the same size to wear."

He goes out quickly and I turn on the shower taps. After a few seconds, a miracle – the water is hot. They probably don't know how to turn off the boiler.

I make it so hot it's agony – and bliss as it washes me clean. His bottles and soaps are lined up neatly. I find shampoo and luxuriate in the lather. Three times I lather my whole body. Finally, I feel clean.

By the washbasin is a silver-backed monogrammed hair brush. I like its heavy feel as I pull it through my hair. The guards must have been mightily impressed by Bermudez's orders not to have looted even that. Wrapped in a towel, I go through to the bedroom. It's curiously neutral. A large bed, springy blue carpet, modern cream-coloured furniture, but almost devoid of any personal touch. Bedrooms usually reflect the character of their occupants, and this one does. Fastidiously tidy and impersonal. No family photographs, no personal knick-knacks. Just a place to sleep.

The guard returns. He's carrying a clean pair of jeans, but a very dirty tee-shirt. The jeans fit loosely. I toss the tee-shirt back at him and open several drawers before I find a pile of shirts. Plain white and plain blue. I choose a blue one.

Soft cotton with a button-down collar. It fits perfectly. I roll up the sleeves and look in the mirror. The combination of formal shirt and casual loose jeans looks great. I smooth down my wet hair. The lighter streaks are beginning to fade. It needs more lemon juice and sun. From the corner of my eye I catch the guard smiling.

"I'll be sleeping here tonight."

"But comrade, our leader has ordered . . ."

"It doesn't apply to me. When my clothes are dry put them in here."

He looks worried as I turn and walk out.

At the guardhouse, Peabody is sitting in front of the desk. He turns and his eyes settle on the shirt.

I say, "An immaculate fit. Compliments to your tailor."

He doesn't answer. His face is impassive. I look through into the cell. It's already clean and I see the fresh plaster in the corners. The guards are whitewashing the walls. I close the door and go behind the desk. He watches silently as I unlock the drawer and take out my files. I put them on the desk and without looking up say, "Peabody, you are an expert on the Latin mind and temperament. You know that what you did was, for a Latin, the worst insult possible short of sexually abusing his wife, mother or daughter. Understand this: if you ever try anything like that again, you will suffer more than your imagination can comprehend. Fombona is almost begging me to allow him a few uninterrupted hours with you. But he would be like a compassionate priest compared to what I would do."

I look up. The bastard has a small superior smile on his face.

"I thought you didn't use torture."

"I never have, but I remember what a Chinese once told me. 'Insult me once, shame on you. Insult me twice, shame on *me*.' I will accept no shame from you."

Airily, he waves a hand at the cell door. "Calderon, I know what you're trying to do."

"What?"

"The carrot and the stick. It won't work. You think you're

so damned smart but I can read you. I'm not some low level moron. I see right through you. You're transparent as glass."

"Yes?"

"For sure. First you come on hard to soften me up. Then you're pleasant. If I don't respond you get tough again. Then soft, then tough. It's standard technique by guys like you to confuse and disorientate. You don't give a damn if there's rats in there or if I get bitten half to death by bugs. Suddenly you're Mister Nice Guy, hoping for something in return."

"You're wrong."

"Oh yeah?"

I find myself telling him the truth.

"Peabody, years ago I was cutting sugar cane. All students help during the harvest. I was billeted with a peasant family. They all worked except for a very old, feeble man. He was over ninety. One night there was a party in a nearby village. All the family went except the old man and me. I was too exhausted – not used to the hard physical work. In the night I got up to take a pee – outside of course. The old man slept on a palliasse on the verandah. He must have died a few hours earlier. There were half a dozen rats on the corpse, feeding. I had to attack them with a stick before they gave up their meal. Since that night I've had a phobia about rats. I see that scene in nightmares. If someone locked me in a room with rats it would be torture for me. So I don't torture you like that." I gesture at the cell. "What I told them to do is no carrot. I don't use that technique."

I study his face. Does he believe me? I sense that it's important. He shows nothing; not a flicker.

"So what technique do you use?"

"There's no real technique. I try to persuade, to enlighten even."

He snorts cynically.

"And you're going to enlighten me?"

I open a file and select a page and start reading: " 'I spent thirty-three years and four months in active service as a member of our country's most agile military force – the

Marine Corps. During that period, I spent most of my time being a high-class muscle-man for big business, for Wall Street and for the bankers. In short, I was a racketeer for capitalism . . . Thus I helped make Mexico and especially Tampico safe for American oil interests in 1914. I helped make Haiti and Cuba a decent place for the National City Bank to collect revenues in . . . I helped purify Nicaragua for the international banking house of Brown Brothers in 1909 to 1912. I brought light to the Dominican Republic for American sugar interests in 1916. I helped make Honduras "right" for American fruit companies in 1903.' " I look up at him.

"Ambassador . . . Excellency. Do you know who wrote those words?"

"Sure. General Smedley D. Butler."

"And?"

"And what?"

"Don't you have a comment?"

He gives a bored shrug. "I guess he was unhappy with his pension."

I clamp down on my anger.

"You don't find it a damning indictment?"

"No. So there was capitalist exploitation . . . We're a capitalist country and it's been Government policy to support our businessmen internationally. Sometimes in the past there have been excesses. That's part of history. Over the decades, capitalism has become more enlightened." He leans forward. "During those same decades communism has degenerated into mental oppression."

I leaf through the file and quote quietly: " 'The day is not far distant when three Stars and Stripes at three equidistant points will make one territory. One at the North Pole, another at the Panama Canal and the third at the South Pole. The whole hemisphere will be ours in fact, as by virtue of our superiority of race it is already ours morally.' "

I look up and say, "Those words were stated by none other than a President of the United States of America."

He nods and his lips twitch into a smile.

"Yeah; Taft. And it sure hacked off the Canadians . . . but that was 1912. Things have changed."

I start to answer but he cuts me off.

"Listen, I've argued these questions a thousand times, starting before you were born. You want to judge a country by its historical crimes? Who decides how far you go back? Fifty years? A hundred? A thousand? You're going to blame a Spaniard today for the Conquistadores? You're going to blame me for the slave trade?" He points a finger. "Or you? What were your ancestors doing?"

Again I try to speak, but he's angry now, stabbing his finger at me.

"Listen. A few years back I overheard a couple of blacks arguing about the TV series, *Roots*. One of them was sounding off about the atrocity of slavery; the other said, 'Hell man, if they hadn't plucked my great grandpappy outa there I'd be sittin' in the jungle right now. I ain't got no complaints.'"

"And that justifies it? History condemns it!"

"No. History explains it. As a good communist you should know that."

This is said with a sneer. I find my anger rising.

"Communism is the antithesis of slavery."

"Oh yeah? Go preach that in the Gulags."

I'm going down a wrong road. This man, this leech, is impervious to logic. He's sixty-three years old and I'm not going to argue him out of something he's never been argued into. But he's clever. I have to go back and open him up from the beginning. He's talking again, confirming my thoughts.

"Calderon, you're crazy. You think you're going to sit there and convince me? Convert me to communism so I'll spout a couple of names that I don't know anyway? You're not crazy . . . you're stupid!"

With an inward sigh I replace one file with another. It's far too early to use my weapon but I must prepare him for it. I open the file and read out a name.

"Amparo Flores."

I look up and see the shaft strike into his eyes. The sneer is gone. I've scored. He struggles to react normally.

"What?"

"Amparo Flores. The reason you hate communism and particularly Cuban communism."

Now there is silence. I let it gestate; waiting for him to break it.

He doesn't. He sits mute. An almost naked statue. There is a difference in his face. Or was it there before? A haggardness. He has five days' growth of speckled grey beard. His hair is unkempt. His lean body is suddenly thin. His poker face is firmly in position but now I'm aware of something as yet intangible. With a single name we are no longer strangers. There is a link. For an irrational and disturbing moment I feel sorry for him. It passes, and although all the details are clear in my head, I look down at the file again. I intone: "Between May 1958 and March 1959, subject had a sexual liaison with Amparo, daughter of Juan and Nani Flores. They became betrothed during the first week of March. Amparo Flores arrested March 28th, 1959, for anti-revolutionary activities. Subject recalled to Washington May 4th, 1959. Amparo Flores died of cerebral thrombosis May 11th, 1959."

"That's a lie!"

The words are a scream. He's on his feet, hands on the desk, leaning over it. I feel a flicker of spit on my cheek.

The tirade goes on for several minutes; a litany of hatred and pain. It finishes with the stabbing finger and the words: "You murdered her! Cuban filth! You, you, you!" He swings away and, trembling, walks to a small window across the room and stands with his back to me.

I expected a reaction but this intensity surprises me. Softly I remark, "At that time I was just an infant."

His shoulders are still moving from the passion of his outburst. I hear his tight voice.

"You . . . them. No difference. They breed scum like you to replace scum like them."

Is it the time now? No, too early. He is not broken, not reliant. I affect a conciliatory tone and say, "It was a time of much passion . . . and vengeance . . . and excess. She was denounced as a spy . . ."

He turns. He looks his age now . . . and more. He walks back slowly and sits down. His voice is normal again.

"They killed her father because he was close to Batista. They killed her because she was close to me. She was nineteen years old."

I must draw closer now and ease off the subject.

"From the way you reacted to her name you must have loved her to the depth." I want a reaction but his face is set as he looks past me. "My family knew hers. I'm told she was a great beauty . . ."

No reaction. Time to move on.

"Peabody, Batista had an extensive secret police network. We inherited most of their files. Some of them are fascinating. They were culled from many sources. Maids, chauffeurs, brothels, bar owners, girlfriends. Did you know that one of your Ambassadors was keeping four mistresses?" He shrugs indifferently. I go on: "He kept them all satisfied. The officer who wrote the report was vastly impressed. Of course there was also a report on you. I'll indulge you and quote from it." I turn some pages in the file and then look up quickly and catch the glimmer of interest in his eyes. Of course, it's human nature. I read: "November 10th, 1958. Subject: Jason R. Peabody. Political Councillor, US Embassy. Further reports have come from informants (see appendix) that Peabody continues to make favourable comments during his social life on the Castro bandits. It is also known from other sources that he gives negative advice to Ambassador Smith who however takes little notice of this advice."

I close the file and look up. He says, "Batista was a fool and obviously so were his Intelligence people."

I shake my head. "No, Peabody. Some of them were good. They worked for Fidel even then. Also there were other sources. It's interesting psychologically. You arrived in Cuba in '56 a young, idealistic Foreign Service Officer already speaking fluent Spanish. I wouldn't say you were at all left wing – more like dead centre. You fall in love with a local beauty and plan to marry. Then comes the revolution. Your fiancée is arrested. At that time your Government was trying to reach a working agreement with Castro – trying to keep Cuba within its sphere of influence. Outraged at the arrest, you lost all objectivity and became a nuisance to your Embassy. You were recalled under vociferous protest. I guess at that time your career was just about over. Then the tragedy of your fiancée; the deterioration in US-Cuban relations; Fidel's historic embrace of Marxism and Cuba's friendship with Russia. Your career picks up again, but now with a difference. Your whole existence is a nemesis for Cuba, for Castro, and above all, for communism. Whatever idealism there was in you had imploded to nothing."

He is not looking bored, but neither totally fascinated. I decide to elevate the mood.

"Let's have some coffee."

His upper lip literally curls.

"More carrots."

I smile and shout the order to the guard.

PEABODY
San Carlo
Day 5

I understand in one startling moment. I'm raising the mug. The rich, deep smell of the coffee drifts into my nostrils. My mouth salivates. This is the sensation an addict gets at the end of deprivation. Five days only and my fingers shake and the mug rattles against my teeth. For a moment I wished I had never tasted coffee and so would never crave it.

He is watching. Those sleepy eyes that see everything. I feel my nakedness like a suppurating skin disease. I carefully take two sips and lower the mug. They have finished cleaning the cell and gone. He inspected it as if it were a queen's boudoir. I stayed sitting at the desk. When he returned I made another protest at my detention, the appalling conditions, and his very presence on United States territory. He listened attentively and then informed me airily that all the other hostages were in good health and not being mistreated. It's like spitting down a volcano. I ask him what's happening outside; the general situation. He spreads his hands.

"Nothing. Stalemate; no change. Your Government is issuing threatening statements and complaining to anyone who'll listen. Its puppets are dancing up and down on strings parroting protests."

He's lying of course. There must have been developments. Several times today I've heard jets fly overhead. They can only come from the "Nimitz". I'll bet the pressure's building up. He will tell me nothing, though. It's a deliberate strategy to keep me off balance. Even the punks who bring my food have orders not to say a word.

It's working. I am off balance. There have been times in

my life when all I wanted was solitude. I never understood that when enforced, it changed its character. After three days I'm getting a glimmer of the horrors of incarceration.

Also Amparo. I must be off balance. I lost my senses. It was hearing that name emerge from his lips. Hearing the lilt again of the Spanish inflection. It was obscene. And the rat. I believe him about his phobia. Why do I believe? This devil could invent anything. But I believe him. At this time, now I recognise the danger. This man in front of me, this boy, is more than cunning. More than intellectually brilliant. He has in him a strange power. A few hours ago had anyone told me that this boy could extract information from me I would have thought them insane. Now, thank God, the danger has infiltrated my mind. I must be always on guard mentally and emotionally.

I take more coffee, a gulp this time. He says musingly, "You devote your whole career, your whole life, to an anti-communist crusade, with great emphasis on Latin America and Cuba in particular. But your career does not take off. You become almost a recluse. Devoting yourself to study. You have no friends. You write anti-communist books which are widely acclaimed by your capitalist intelligentsia and your career spurts a little, then slows, then spurts, according to the ideological swings in your administrations. Finally you're made Ambassador to a Government that is ousted a week later. Tell me, Peabody, when did you last have a fuck?"

I'd been lulled by the cynical but accurate biography. I grasp for a retort. He has a half-smile on his face. I ask, "Why do you tint your hair? When did you last look in the mirror? Don't you carry one with you?"

He grins amiably. If I didn't know about him it would be engaging.

"I don't tint it, Peabody. I squeeze lemon juice on which streaks it as it dries in the sun."

"Why?"

"I don't know. I guess it's a kind of bleach in the juice."

"You know what I meant; why do you do it?"

"It suits me."

"You look damned ridiculous. Like a woman."

He shrugs, still smiling.

"You don't find me attractive?"

I feel a sudden chill. God, does this relate to the previous obscene question? Does he think the shock of Amparo and my self-imposed isolation turned me homosexual? Why am I even considering this? Why even allowing this dialogue?

Curtly I say, "I find you repulsive in every way. Now it's late. I'm going to sleep."

He looks at his watch and nods in surprise.

"Okay. But one more question: for the last three or four years, whenever you've been in Washington you've made frequent trips to Dulles Airport without flying out. On average about once a week. You get there about seven in the evening and leave an hour later. You've never been observed talking to anyone. Generally, you just sit in the arrivals hall. Sometimes you have a coffee or a drink. Then straight home. It puzzles our analysts. Why, Peabody?"

That's going to be the last shock today. I feel unsteady as I stand up. I walk towards the cell and manage to say, "Your questions are boring. I prefer my own company."

I go into the cell and turn at the door. He has an elbow on the desk, his palm cupping his chin. His eyes watching me are narrowed in thought.

Trying not to rush, I close the door and walk across to the far wall. The tart smell of whitewash is in my nostrils. Has he guessed? Even he could not guess. Can he look into my head? I hear the scrape of his chair. I pray he won't come in. Won't look at me again.

With relief I hear the key turn in the lock, then his voice.

"See you in a day, or two, or three."

I sink down on to the palliasse. My limbs are weak. How much does he know? How can he know? It's hot in the cell but as I clasp my knees they feel cold. I realise that I must have been a target of their surveillance for years. Of course I must have! For years I've been State's top analyst on Cuba; desk man for four years; political advisor to the CIA. The Russians would have channelled everything they got on me. Why do I worry? I'm clean. God knows I'm clean. No goddam skeletons in any cupboarrd. But they've been watchinng me foor years. I feel dirty. I look at my thin legs. I am dirty. How long can this hell last? Eating slops, washing out of a bucket. Crapping in a bucket. My spirits lift at the memory of Calderon standing at the door covered in shit and piss. But he was right. Fombona would probably have killed me. With a jolt I realise that at the time I hardly cared. That's what a single black rat can do to me. I must be rational. Today I've been through physical and emotional shocks which I haven't experienced for thirty years or more. I'm drained and exhausted, maybe even suffering the effects of shock. I have to get my mind on to something tangible.

About two weeks ago I'd been reading a book on the Karpov-Kasparov chess marathon. The thirty-fifth game had intrigued me. Kasparov fighting for survival; Karpov, an icy computer. I start to go through the moves, straining to remember. It's no good. Amparo played chess. Keen but over adventurous. Karpov fades from my imagination and Amparo is sitting there opposite me, her nose wrinkled in concentration. She lifts her head and I'm looking at the golden olive cameo of her face, framed in jet black silkiness. The picture has never faded, the face never withered. What would Calderon know or understand? I've never had a "fuck" since before I went to Cuba. What Amparo and I did, and had, could never be classified, or debased, with a four letter word. Why should I need anything after that but a memory?

Despite the heat, I shiver at another very recent memory. The shock as Calderon asked his question about Dulles Airport. The casualness of his voice belied by the probing stare. I felt an odd juvenile shame that anyone, let alone he, could ever crawl so close to my mind even to ask that question. All those years after the death of Amparo when, clearly, and for the first time in my life, I saw and recognised my enemy and exulted in the conviction of my purpose. It was so strong that I needed nobody, no emotion, no mental comfort, no affection, but a small recessed part of my brain refused to be cowed; stubbornly refused. Sometimes on rare occasions that refusal sent me out to Dulles Airport like a

105

prowler in the night. Afterwards, long afterwards, I would feel the guilt of my weakness. The guilt of a long-distance runner covering the course alone and sometimes stopping to draw breath. Sometimes cutting the surreptitious corner, unseen except by the gaze of his own conscience. I tried so hard but I could never banish that weakness. Now there are more doubts in my head. Should I ever have tried? Have I been running alone for nothing?

Five days in this cell. The word "cell" startles me with its succinct accuracy. It sounds like it feels and it rhymes with hell. Five solitary days and the loneliness sharpens my senses. I look at my feet. Grime growing between my toes . . . grime; the word so suits the substance . . . a fungus on my body. Does a man unable to wash measure time against the thickness of grime on his skin? No; a man would forget the squalor in time, forget this filthiness. That, for me, is another weakness. . . . How well Calderon knows it. I cannot forget. Each day the grime grows and humiliates me. Five days gone. How many more?

I try to get back to the thirty-fifth game but I've lost the sequence. I wonder if Calderon plays chess? Will he come in a day, or two, or three?

SLOCUM
Washington
Day 3

I savour the memory. There's not much else to do. My room is on the tenth floor but the view is confined to watching the side of a heavy rainstorm. In two days of sitting on my ass, I've seen enough TV re-runs and soap operas to want to go out and strangle every producer in the land.

The memory eases the boredom – the memory of the President's face. I'd finished telling him what was wrong with the rescue plan. I'd kept it brief; the cat was looking hungrier by the minute. I'd explained the over-complications. The plan involved five co-ordinated operations: a ground assault by infiltrated special forces; a simultaneous air strike to take out the city's electricity generator; a simultaneous air attack on the main army barracks, and finally the centre piece: a simultaneous helicopter-borne assault into the compound itself. Meanwhile aircraft and helicopter gunships would be "sanitising" the area around the compound to discourage any reinforcements getting close.

I had highlighted the one word "simultaneous". It's much loved in military jargon. What would happen if, because of miscalculation, error, or bad luck, just one of those operations failed to be simultaneous? Under the plan, the compound guards were reckoned to have no more than sixty seconds' warning before the assault force landed. But if one of five operations mis-timed or went wrong, they might have several minutes. I'd said that it was crazy to multiply the "fuck up" factor by four when it was big enough already, what with all the services competing to get in on the act.

Komlosy had coughed discreetly at the obscenity but the President was unruffled. Then came the moment. The President said: "The Joint Chiefs have emphasised that this is a major military operation."

I took a breath. "No, sir. With respect, World War Two was a major military operation. This is an itsy bitsy little one."

The memory is of his expression when I said that. I quickly went on, "It's an operation to secure a small compound right by the sea and only twelve miles from a major base of operations – the 'Nimitz'. To release twenty-seven people from a semi-trained bunch of youths and chopper them back to base."

"You make it sound a snip."

"It is."

He glanced at Komlosy and said sceptically, "What about the explosives strapped to our people?"

I answered firmly, "There aren't any."

"What?!"

"Sir, that's just a smoke-screen."

"How can you know?"

"I'm ninety-nine per cent sure. I've trained Central and South American forces for years – thousands of 'em. In Panama and at Fort Bragg. They're not religious fanatics. You might find one or two nuts in ten thousand to blow themselves up – but not twenty-seven. They don't believe eternal paradise automatically follows religious suicide. Besides those guys are not stupid. With twenty-seven people wired up, the chances of an accidental explosion are enormous. They know that one explosion would bring an immediate attack from the 'Nimitz'. Why risk it? Those jackets just contain padding."

"But you can't be positive."

"No sir, but anyway the plan, as it stands, gives them around sixty seconds to make up their minds and even if there are no explosives they could shoot our people. The way I'd do it they would only have ten seconds or less. It would be 4.00 a.m. Most of them would be asleep. There would be a few seconds of noise and confusion then we'd have our

108

people and the compound secured. Then the rest of our guys can come in like the cavalry."

Komlosy decided it was time to assert himself. He asked, "How would you get in, Colonel?"

Without taking my eyes off the President, I replied, "Silently. By Ultralights."

The President was puzzled.

"Ultralights?"

"Yes sir. Motorised hang gliders. We take off from the 'Nimitz' and climb to around eight thousand feet approaching the coast, cut the engines and glide right in."

The President was still puzzled. "But those things are made of cloth and metal tubes. I've seen 'em on TV. Hell, they're just bicycles with wings and sewing-machine engines!"

"Yes, sir." I knew I'd got to be real persuasive. "But to put it in perspective, parachutes are just made of cloth – and they figure high in many modern military operations. I've been experimenting with Ultralights for the last few months. They're simple but effective. Not much of 'em to go wrong."

He nodded thoughtfully. "How many men would you take?"

"Twenty, tops."

"But they have over a hundred in the compound."

"Sir, each of my guys is worth ten of theirs, or more. In that sense we'd outnumber them two to one. I could do the job with ten. The others are back-up."

A long silence, then the President muses, "It all sounds so damn simple . . . twenty guys."

"Sir, the opposite of simple is complicated. In military matters complicated should be a dirty word."

He glanced at his watch and said to Komlosy, "Mike, I'm gonna sleep on this. We'll discuss it at the NSC meeting tomorrow. Keep Colonel Slocum on hand . . . and incognito."

Komlosy said, "Yes, Mr President. What about the court martial?"

The President turned to me. He gave a small smile and said, "That will be postponed . . . on executive order."

"Thank you, sir . . . Mr President."

So I get sent up to this hotel room with a plan of the compound, a map of San Carlo and some large sheets of white cardboard. I work out my plan in twenty minutes and kick my heels for the next two days. Komlosy told me if I left the room or phoned out, he'd have me on a goddam treason charge. He's phoned once on each day. I guess to check I'm here. To my questions he just answered, "Wait."

That's one habit I never really mastered.

I know a girl here in Washington. Knew her real well. Great long legs and curves and a face to swivel heads. Transferred from Fort Bragg to work in the Pentagon as an analyst. A first class, uncomplicated lay. I seriously contemplate giving her a ring. She would sure help pass the time. Better not. If Komlosy found out it would blow all my chances.

I pick up the *Washington Post* and read the news for the third time. It's all front page stuff. UN resolutions; messages of solidarity; silence from Moscow. It's like one of those goddam TV re-runs. Only the location has changed. Teheran to San Carlo. I drop the paper. I'm trying to decide whether to ring down for a hamburger and fries now or postpone that treasured piece of action for another hour, when there's a sharp tap on the door. I open it to find Komlosy holding a brown paper bag.

"Hi."

He brushes past, casts a look round the room and then goes into the bathroom. He comes out with two glasses, puts them on the bedside table, sits on the bed, points a finger at the sole chair and, from the bag, produces a fifth of Johnnie Walker Black Label.

I sit down and watch as he pours two healthy slugs. He passes me a glass and raises his own.

"Cheers, Colonel. Here's to us."

"Cheers."

I drink and trying to be casual, ask, "We got it?"

He grimaces at the taste of the neat Scotch. "Not exactly. Not yet. The two plans are to go forward in tandem. At a later stage the President will take a decision on which one to use."

"Uh uh. What now?"

He pours himself another and offers the bottle. I shake my head. He drinks and says, "You go back to Fort Bragg tonight. Assemble your team and start training. You're to report to Brigadier Al Simmons. Okay?"

I feel a flush of relief.

"Right on! Ol' 'no shit' Simmons. We get on just fine."

He smiles. "So I understand. He'll keep the flak off you and also provide back-up engineering to build a mock-up of the compound. There's one problem. You can't use anyone from Delta Force."

"Hell! I know some good guys there."

He says firmly, "Forget it. They're out of bounds. All involved with the other plan. The decision as to which one to use might come late. You'd have no chance to retrain them in yours. Is it a problem?"

I think for a moment, then shake my head.

"No. I don't need many and I know where to find 'em."

"You got your basic plan ready?"

"Sure, stand up."

"What?"

"Stand up, sir."

He pushes himself off the bed and I lift the mattress, pull out a sheet of cardboard and lay it on the bed. It shows a plan of the compound and several crosses and arrows. He studies it.

"That's it?"

"That's it."

"Shit!"

"What's wrong?"

He shakes his head in awe.

"Six crosses? Six arrows?!"

"What do you want? A computer print-out? That's it, unless the Intelligence situation changes. What's happening on that?"

He pours more Scotch. "We could have got lucky, Colonel. We'll know in a day or two but maybe we got an agent on site."

"In the compound?"

He nods and I whistle in admiration.

"But we're not sure yet. I'll be coming to review your progress in a few days. I'll tell you more then. How soon can you be ready?"

I've been waiting for the question. "I'd like three weeks."

"Okay. Good. The other plan calls for five to six weeks minimum."

"I'll bet. You really think this is gonna be on?"

He looks up at the ceiling despairingly. "Who the hell knows? There are complications I don't even want to think about."

"Should I know about them?"

"No, Colonel. They're not military. But I can tell you it's a real bag of worms right now. Everyone's got their concerns. State, CIA, Defence. By the way, Grant's like a bear with a sore ass."

"Yeah?"

He grins happily and pours more Scotch.

"Slocum, the President's going to be pulled in all kinds of directions in the coming days. All kinds."

I ask anxiously, "You think the Generals will get to him?"

He takes a giant sip and says, "Maybe. But don't be misled by the President's laid-back manner. When he makes a decision he generally sticks to it. He can be tough as nails."

He drains his glass, looks at his watch and stands up. "I gotta get back to the madhouse. I don't have to tell you to keep that mouth of yours shut and stay out of trouble, but I just did. A car will pick you up at six and take you to Andrews. Transport to Bragg's been laid on." He hands me an embossed card. "Simmons has been given special authority. He should be able to handle anything that comes up. Any problems that he can't then phone that number. I'll see you in a few days."

"Okay, sir. There's just one more thing." I show him a report in the paper which tells how the "Nimitz" is sitting on the horizon as a dire reminder of America's awesome power. "Mr Komlosy, it's also a reminder to those guards to keep on their toes. That plus all the overflights. It's counter-productive. They should be kept to a minimum."

He thinks for a moment, then says, "I agree. I'll try to make the President see that."

I show him to the door and watch him stride down the corridor. At the elevator he turns and throws me a kind of salute. I grin and return it. That cat would just love to be a five star General.

Back in the room I check my watch. An hour to kill before the car picks me up. I walk to the window. The rain is easing up. Below me, down-town Washington looks wet and forlorn. I start going through names in my head. I'll need four squad leaders. The names pop up quickly. I'll talk to them before I select the rest of the team. I try to picture the situation right now in the compound. It's been a week since the takeover. If things follow the usual pattern, the guards will be getting sloppy now. Within three weeks they'll be bored out of their tiny skulls.

I wonder if I'm being too casual about this? Making a god of simplicity.

I try to imagine the feelings of the hostages. Twenty men, seven women. They'll be of two minds. One, just dying to get out of that place. The other, terrified of dying if we try a rescue.

I sure hope I'm right about those jackets being nothing but dummies.

JORGE
San Carlo
Day 6

I play the tape again. It has the same effect. I'm listening to a
different man. It throws me. Was I blind? Which man is
which? It's three days since I saw Peabody and I try to
match his personality to what I've just heard. It escapes me.
I check the time. The delivery truck will leave in an hour.
Inez is still sleeping despite the voices on the tape. She will
sleep through anything and for endless hours. It's fortunate;
it helps her pass the time. I stand up and cross to the bed.
She is lying with her head cradled on one arm. Asleep her
face is even more angelic than awake. She could have sat or
slept for Botticelli. I sit on the bed and brush hair away
from her forehead. I feel tenderness – or is it love? I've got a
great mind but can't tell the difference between love and
tenderness.

She stirs and opens one eye.

"Inez, I'm leaving soon."

"When will you be back?"

"Tonight."

The eye closes. I bend down and kiss it. She murmurs
unintelligibly.

Something bad happened. Last night I was jealous. It was
the first time in my life and the experience was terrifying.
At the dinner, Bermudez paid her much attention. She
seemed to react in her usual fashion, interested in him one
minute, apparently bored the next. But after dinner, as he
showed us around the floodlit gardens of Vargas's decadent
palace, it was different. She stayed always close to him,
occasionally touching his arm with the back of her hand. I
was jealous. At first confused by the emotion and then

alarmed. My hold on women – and sometimes men – stems partly from a natural ability to be above envy or jealousy, so it could never be used as a weapon against me. If I am jealous now maybe it means that affection and fascination have coalesced into love. The thought is catastrophic. If true, it must be possible to love someone whom you know is capable of causing you great suffering. I'm aware that this is naive but I never before experienced jealousy or its consequences.

Vargas even had a small private zoo in the grounds. Bermudez showed us round with a proprietary air. I began to wonder about that man. He's beginning to show disturbing symptoms. He's already moved into the palace with his inner circle and there have been subtle changes in his appearance and manner. His uniform is smarter, better pressed, his speech a little more arrogant. His people still look at him with the eyes of adoring spaniels, and maybe he's just flexing his charisma but like many before him he could be falling prey to the narcotic of power. He is also stubborn in the infallibility of his beliefs.

At dinner he had outlined some of his programmes. I reminded him of the many mistakes we had made in the early years of the revolution and how Fidel was always the first to admit it when we blundered. He had listened politely but not with great interest. He has also started the first executions. The People's Courts are sitting in constant sessions. He explained that the people demand them. Vengeance belongs to them. I reminded him that Fidel later regretted the relatively few executions that followed his victory. He replied equably that the situation was different. San Carlo is bordered by hostile regimes. We had the sea as a cushion. He must root out all radical elements.

He is surprisingly sublime about the USA. The "Nimitz" has pulled back over the horizon. Incursions into San Carlo airspace have decreased. I told him bluntly that he was indulging himself. Those moves were probably designed to lull him into a false sense of security. If the Americans were planning something, they wouldn't want the defences super-vigilant. I told him of the slackening of awareness in the compound. He was sanguine, merely saying that he would send word to Fombona. He is convinced that the Americans will soon negotiate. Already both the Red Cross and the Swedish Ambassador have put out feelers. I remarked that such moves were to be expected. I sensed his irritation at my words, but he was polite. He had to be. He needs us.

Back at the hotel, after we had made love, Inez lay on her back gazing at the ceiling. Then she said reflectively, "He has the power of death."

"What?"

"Bermudez. They bring him the decisions of the courts. He can veto them or sign them. He has signed more than a hundred. There will be hundreds more; maybe thousands."

She turned to look at me and I could see the awe in her eyes.

Studying her face now, a picture of purity and innocence, I know that she will find that power fascinating. In a disturbed mood, I stand up and pack the little cassette recorder into my bag and go out. The two bodyguards are both sitting on stools opposite. Both with their heads against the wall. Both asleep. They had been assigned to me two days ago. There is much talk in the city of American spies and agents. Should they know of my existence, Bermudez thinks they might try to kill me. Fidel would be angry. These two offer brilliant protection. Not at all gently I kick them both awake and walk down the corridor. They stumble after me apologising and, at the elevator, beg me not to tell Bermudez. I say nothing and at the truck tell them to wait for me at the same spot and not to leave. I am angry. If the Americans know what I'm trying to do they might well try to kill me.

There is another passenger sitting on sacks of beans: the young Mestizo boy who works in the kitchens. He nods at me nervously. As we pull away I ask, "They let you out?"

"Yes, sir . . . my mother . . . she is sick."

We bump along the road. He is small and slight. It's hard to judge his age but I think less than twenty. He has long, lank, black hair cut jaggedly. It falls down like petals. He looks like a dark chrysanthemum. He avoids looking at me.

116

"You don't like working there?"

His eyes flicker towards me and away.

"Why didn't you run away?"

He moistens his lips. "My family, sir."

"Ah. So you also are a hostage."

He nods tentatively and asks, "Will it be long, sir?"

"I don't know. I think not."

The truck comes to a halt and the doors open. He tries to pick up my bag but I shake my head.

In the guardhouse I leave my files in the bag but take out the cassette recorder and place it in the centre of the desk. Then I unlock the cell door, open it, and without looking inside go to my chair and sit down.

He appears at the doorway. His beard is visibly longer.

"Good morning, Excellency."

He is looking at the recorder.

"Calderon, I don't often swear, but if you switch that thing on all you'll hear from my lips are obscenities."

PEABODY
San Carlo
Day 6

He waves at the chair. "I don't want to record. I want you to listen to something."

As I walk painfully to the chair he says, "You have a very comfortable bed."

"You're staying in the residence? Does your impertinence have no limits?"

He smiles. "It was only one night."

"Then did you locate my pills? I'm having a bad attack of gout."

He shakes his head regretfully. "The guards must have taken them. Now Peabody, ex-President for life Fernando Vargas borrowed a trick from your President Nixon. He had his palace wired up and he taped everything. The revolutionaries found the tape library intact. They're working through it now. Believe me, there's some very interesting material. Yesterday they gave me this tape. We're going to listen to it and then talk about it."

He leans forward and presses a button. There's a pause and then from the small speaker comes the single harsh word, "Sebagos."

In an instant I'm taken back sixteen days. Can it truly be only a little more than two weeks? Since then I have passed through an eternity. It was my second day in San Carlo. I had requested a private audience with Vargas. As I hear my own voice the memory is vivid.

I was shown into a vast room by an aide-de-camp. He indicated a chair in front of an inlaid walnut desk and left. I studied the chair and sat down. It was genuine Louis Quatorze. It, and the others scattered around the room, must have cost enough money to feed an entire Mestizo village for five years, or equip a battalion of guardsmen with M16s.

I was kept waiting for five minutes, then he came in through a side door. I stood up and he said triumphantly, "Sebagos."

I was momentarily confused, then understood and looked down at my shoes.

"Yes, Mr President. I always wear them."

He had beamed. "So do I. When I'm out of uniform of course. Best shoes in the world. What size do you take?"

"Ten and a half. Triple Es."

"Good. My Embassy in Washington sends me regular shipments. I'll instruct them to include your size."

I started to say something about Foreign Service regulations but he waved that aside and approached with his hand out. After we shook hands he sat down behind his desk and I resumed my seat.

Vargas could have stepped out of a McNelly cartoon. Short body, short neck, short legs. Tight blue and gold bemedalled uniform. Gold rings on short fingers; pudgy face, small narrow eyes just discernible behind the obligatory dark glasses. He lacked only a wide moustache to complete the picture of a banana republic dictator. I recall wondering why most dictators are short. Two things in my life give me acute pain. The damned gout and the fact that all too often the first instruments of defence in Latin America against the communists are people like Vargas.

He said, "I enjoyed your book on contemporary Latin American literature."

I was jolted by the idea of Vargas reading any books at all, let alone mine.

"But I was surprised at your treatment of Marquez. Especially coming from the author of *Evils of Communism*. Was it only because he's a Nobel Laureate?"

"No. As I said in the book, the beauty of his language, if anything, obscures his philosophy."

He had shrugged as if beauty was banal. "He's a dangerous subversive. I must tell you I am very pleased with

119

your arrival. To be honest your predecessor did not fully understand our special position here and failed to communicate our feelings to your Government properly. I have heard good reports of you, and of course your disgust of communism is well known from your writings."

He stood up and started pacing in front of me. Light from the crystal chandeliers reflected like tiny arrowheads from high black boots. His voice slowed and became emphatically formal.

"It is essential that we receive the full military and civil aid package promised by your Government . . . by your President. The subversives grow stronger. They terrorise the people, disrupt the economy, spread the cancer of communism and pose, in the long run, as great a threat to your country as mine."

He paused, leaned forward and looked gravely into my eyes. "And Mr Peabody, they are being armed, supplied and indoctrinated by your greatest enemy, Russia, through their lackeys: Cuba, Nicaragua and others. Yet, even while your Congress talks and delays and listens to lies our life-blood is being sucked by the vampires of Marxism."

"Excellency, my Government is doing everything possible to get the aid package through. As you know, the balance, particularly in the Senate, makes things very difficult. The President himself is spending a lot of time with individual Senators. It's the human rights problem."

"Human rights!" He spat the words out like broken teeth. "The President himself has certified that there is improvement."

"True, but some Senators don't believe him. Others think that it's not enough."

"What do they know?" Angrily he resumed pacing. "They choose to believe traitors and leftists! Putas like Lopez!"

Without sympathy, I said, "He was your Ambassador in Washington, Excellency; and is your own brother-in-law."

He swallowed to control his anger. "He wanted to replace me. He plotted with others . . . Only when I recalled him did

120

he defect. A traitor. But they call him to your Congress and listen to him!"

"His testimony is damaging," I conceded. "But not so much as the continuous killings and disappearances."

"That's improved," he countered sharply.

"Only marginally. From 152 last month to 131 this month; and it's still got four days to run."

Vargas had shrugged dismissively. "It takes time. There is much passion in the country. My people hate the subversives. It is not always easy to control them."

"But Excellency, in twelve months there have been more than 1,500 killings and disappearances. Not one person has been convicted or even tried."

He spread his hands. "Courts need proof. It is hard to get."

"I'm sure it is, but Congress votes in two weeks and not even the President's personal intervention may save the aid package."

He passed a hand over his face. Rings glittered. "Only three days before you arrived, Bowman, your deputy, was here at a reception. He congratulated me on the progress we are making. Told me he was preparing a report for your signature emphasising that."

"That's correct. It's on my desk."

"You will send it?"

Slowly I shook my head. "I'll send my own. But not for ten days. And its contents will depend on three conditions."

"Conditions?" Amazement was creeping over his face.

"Yes, conditions." I had let my previously submissive attitude slip away. "For me to send a report and recommendation similar to Bowman's, genuine progress will have to be made – and within ten days, before it's too late. Otherwise I report negatively."

Vargas's mouth opened with astonishment. I could see gold fillings on his back teeth. Neither his brain nor his ego could believe that he heard the words. I went on, "The first condition; the killings and abductions stop. Don't tell me it's impossible. We know they are directed by your brother Colonel Jaime Vargas from an office in the north wing of this very building. I assume you approve the names of the victims. Second: the university is to re-open, the four detained lecturers are to be released and either they resume their duties or they are allowed to leave the country. Third: the officers commanding that company of the Marazon brigade which carried out the massacre of Mestizos in Higo province last April be immediately brought to trial."

Vargas stood there like a squat volcano. I wished I could see behind those glasses into his eyes. Abruptly he turned and walked to a high window. I could see the view over his shoulder. The expanse of the Plaza de Esteban Chamarro, and then the national football stadium and behind it the dull ochre walls of the university.

He turned and started talking. First the university. It was the womb of revolution, spawning the germs of destruction. He was eloquent in anger; precise in memory. The names rolled out: Roberto Bermudez, Carlos Fombona, the "puta" Maria Carranza and others. All of them had gone out of that place to the mountains – all of them communists with the obscene arrogance to name their movement after the founder of San Carlo: Esteban Chamarro – at this moment rotating in his tomb in the cathedral. The memory of the man who had washed in the blood of the Spanish was now painted in the red of Marx, his name libelled in propaganda for the illiterate.

Bermudez, from a poor family, had been given by the generosity of the Vargas family, a scholarship to the university. His thanks were to bite the hand, and sharpen the teeth of his contemporaries.

Fombona, son of a Colonel no less. A drug addict for sure. Hating his father. Hypnotised by Bermudez – becoming his right arm – even more vicious – educated at the university.

Carranza the witch. The puta! Her cunt a whirlpool sucking in the ignorant. Blinding them in sperm! All of them graduates of the university. The university endowed by the Vargas dynasty. Should he open it again like an old wound so as to bleed him to death?

My answer had been succinct. "You cannot fight communism with ignorance. The university must re-open."

We glared at each other. Then Vargas talked of the death squads. Argentina had stifled communists by using their own methods against them – terror. So had Uruguay and Chile. It worked. The only way to deal with them. They are all vermin.

I answered, "The killings must stop. For every death of a genuine communist you kill maybe five innocents. For every death of an innocent you create five communists. It's an equation of disaster."

He switched the subject. How could he prosecute officers for carrying out orders? The Mestizos of Higo had harboured the communists – sustained them. They were accomplices in murder and deserved the same fate.

Coldly, I reminded him. "Eighty-five children under ten. They didn't even waste bullets! Just smashed their heads with rocks. A child that young cannot have an ideology – cannot be a communist. It was murder – cold-blooded murder!"

Vargas gave up on explanations. His anger distilled into cold formality.

"Tomorrow my Washington Ambassador will convey to the State Department our displeasure at your appointment – our inability to work with you. They are not Congress – no primitive voting. It is certain you will be recalled." He smiled, cocooned in his ego.

I said, "Probably. It's also a certainty that on my return to Washington I'll be called to testify before the Senate Appropriations Committee. Excellency, here I'm a ticking bomb. There I explode."

"Your career would be finished."

"It's almost over anyway. I retire in a couple of years."

"You could retire a rich man – rich beyond your dreams."

I stood up. "I have enough money . . . and I seldom dream. Understand me clearly. I represent the country which sustains you. I abhor you and your principles, but I abhor communism more. I will be an instrument in your sustenance but only under the conditions I outlined."

Now as I look down at the little recorder I hear my parting words.

I had walked to the door and turned. He was standing very still on the red carpet, a dictator shimmering under the chandeliers.

"Vargas, the world of extremes is not flat. It curls around and melts into itself – you are at the joining point."

From the loudspeaker I hear the click of the door as I went out. The tape curls on until Calderon rouses himself, reaches out and pushes a button.

He slumps back in his seat. Silence. I raise my head and look at him. He gazes back. Today he's wearing a white shirt with a frilly ruff down the front, unbuttoned half way down the chest. He looks like he's about to produce a set of balls and do a juggling act. I tell him so scornfully. He just goes on gazing at me, then says, "Who would believe those were the words of Jason R. Peabody, Ambassador to San Carlo of the United States of America? A man whose political philosophy is slightly to the right of Ghengis Khan."

"What's so hard to believe?"

He stands up and stretches languorously. I'm conscious of my own cramped muscles. I haven't had exercise for more than a week; or had a taste of the outside air; but I'm not going to ask him any favours. He sits down again.

"Peabody, you are an enigma. You've got Ambassadors all over the world paying lip-service to human rights. You're the least likely candidate to really believe in it, but from the evidence of that tape you do."

"Why should that be difficult to believe?"

He smiles: "Maybe you don't understand yourself. Tell me. If Vargas had not been overthrown what do you think would have been the result of your little lecture?"

"Not much. He would have toned things down for a while."

"Exactly. After you left he called his brother in. It's also on tape. He told him to suspend the killings for a couple of weeks, re-open the university but cover the lecturers and find a couple of junior officers to serve as scapegoats for the Mestizo massacres."

I believe him. It's logical.

Fascinated, he says, "But you genuinely loathed him. Had he done nothing you would still have urged your Government to give him aid. Why?"

I point at the recorder. "You heard me. I abhor him. But I abhor communism more."

He is shaking his head in puzzlement. He points a finger at me.

"Peabody, we are going to talk about this. Now. Maybe for hours. Don't get negative with me. Don't indulge yourself by standing on your dignity. You are glad I'm here. You need to talk. After three days alone you were glad to see me. Don't deny it. I need a name and you are going to give it to me because you will want to."

"Calderon, as usual you indulge yourself on delusions."

He smiles. "No, Peabody. First understand this. The name you give me will lead me to the others. Don't grieve for them. They will not die. They will be re-educated."

I laugh, genuinely amused. "I'm sure. Like your name-sake Jorge Arrango."

He is immediately angry. "He was a *plantado*. Yielded nothing. Could see nothing of the progress under Fidel. Even his poetry was lousy."

I also find myself angry.

"So bad poetry can result in twenty years of imprisonment and maltreatment; physical and mental?"

He leans forward and says very earnestly,

"Peabody, you must listen to me. Every revolution has its victims. To find a cure for meningitis maybe half a million monkeys died. Progress demands sacrifices. Thousands were arrested after the revolution. Most of them responded to logic and persuasion. Most of them are now active in our society."

"And those who don't respond?"

"There are less than two hundred."

"And life is not great for them."

He shrugs indifferently and I say sarcastically, "You're telling me that if I give you a name, which anyway I don't have, that person will merely have his wrist slapped. Be given a strict talking to and persuaded by logic to give up all his naughty thoughts. Calderon, you insult both my intelligence and your own."

He thinks for a moment and then nods in agreement. "But they won't be maltreated. I'll be doing the interrogations myself. No matter. Now we are going to examine the roots of your ideology. But first, Peabody, why did you keep going to the airport?"

I feel immediate mental discomfort. A child caught in the act of misbehaviour. Quickly I say, "You better change the subject or it's the end of the conversation."

SLOCUM
Fort Bragg
Day 10

I'm at work. Sitting in a jeep on the edge of a disused airstrip. Komlosy is next to me. We are both looking up into the clear sky, at the circling Ultralights. At five thousand feet they are tiny specks, like a flock of wheeling vultures.

"There are more than twenty," Komlosy says.

"Twenty-four, sir. I got five back-up men in case of injury during training, or sickness. Watch now, they've cut the engines. They're coming down."

The flock breaks up and rearranges itself into four groups. They separate and begin a spiralling descent. A dozen giant white crosses have been painted about thirty metres apart on the concrete runway. There are two men standing to one side talking into hand-held radio sets. They are wearing jeans and wind-breakers and baseball caps.

"What are those guys doing?" Komlosy asks. "They're civilians?"

"Uh huh. They're giving me a helping hand, sir. I cleared it with Brigadier Simmons."

"Who are they?"

"The shorter one is Larry Newman. The tall one is his partner Bryan Allen. Two of the most innovative and adventurous guys in aviation."

Komlosy is sceptical. "They look damned young."

I laugh. "Sir, I guess Newman is in his late thirties. He first flew at age twelve. At twenty-one he was qualified on Lear jets. Since then he's flown F16s, F18s, 1011s, even Concorde. Besides that, he's a helicopter pilot, a top flight instructor, a sky-diver and a balloonist. Fact is, he was one of the three guys who flew that balloon over the Atlantic."

127

"Ah. I heard about him."

"Allen is around thirty. He's a world class pilot and cyclist. He won the prize for being the first person to fly across the English Channel using only human power."

Quietly Komlosy says, "I heard about him too. As you'd say, a couple of highly talented cats. What do you have to pay guys like that?"

"Sir, for a job like this you don't have to pay guys like that. They're probably the two best Ultralight instructors in the world. Some of my squad had flown them before, others hadn't. Believe me they're learning fast. Now watch."

The first two groups are coming in. There's about a ten knot head wind. They turn gracefully into it. The canard wings lift and they look to be hardly moving as they approach. Silently, one by one, they slide on to the concrete. Most are right on the crosses, some overshoot by a metre or two. One lands a little short: they come to a stop after about thirty metres. The pilots quickly step to the ground and pull their crafts clear and into line. A minute later the other two groups come in with similar performances.

With satisfaction I say, "Not bad. Not half bad."

The pilots are congregating around Newman and Allen. Komlosy says, "Shall we go over?"

"No, sir. They're being debriefed. Let's wait awhile."

He lights a cigarette. "Colonel, when we're alone you don't have to call me 'sir'."

"Thanks, Mr Komlosy."

"Mike."

"Okay. I'm Silas."

We sit in companionable silence for a few minutes, then he says, "They look easy to fly, but I guess it's tricky at night . . . and in combat conditions."

"It's more complicated, sure. You'll see it tonight at the mock-up."

The group of men breaks up. Two of them go back to their machines, start the engines, taxi clear and take off. Allen and Newman stroll across towards us. We get out and I make the introductions. Allen is shy and respectful in the presence of a top White House figure. Newman is ebullient and respectful.

Komlosy is grateful and respectful. There's a little mutual hero-worshipping going on.

He says expansively, "I want to thank you guys for what you're doing. It's a great job. Just great."

They mumble a few modest words. I say, "They're coming on real fine, the guys."

Newman grins. "Silas, you picked a bunch of naturals. Another week an' they'll be able to fly up a gnat's ass."

Allen points up at the two circling Ultras. "I sent Brand and Kerr up to do half an hour of touch and goes. After that I guess everyone should rest up for tonight."

"Okay, we'll see you at dinner. Larry, ask the squad leaders to come over here, please."

"Sure."

They turn away and walk back to the group. I ask: "Mike, can you give me an update on the Intelligence situation?"

"Sure. There's quite a bit, but I'd like to do that after I've seen the show tonight. Can tell you one thing though. I pressed your case about the 'Nimitz'. I guess you made quite an impression on the President. He didn't exactly give orders but he made a very powerful suggestion. The 'Nimitz' is over the horizon and overflights are limited to the essential. We have a second surveillance satellite in position so we're pretty well covered."

"Good. Listen, you'll meet all the men tonight but I want you to meet the squad leaders now."

We both turn to watch a giant C5 Transport lift off a distant runway. It looks like a warehouse rearing up on its ass. As it roars into the sky I ask, "By the way, did you tell the President I was black before I met him?"

He smiles. "No. Truth is, it didn't cross my mind until a few seconds before we went in. Then I thought 'what the hell anyway'."

"Did he bawl you out?"

"No, he wouldn't do that. He did comment that you were damned fearsome-looking, but that wasn't about colour. I mean you don't look exactly effeminate!"

The C5 is now a distant speck. We turn back and there are four men lined up at attention five metres away. I sneak a glance at Komlosy. He's gonna have to take lessons from the President on how to keep a poker face. He looks like he just set eyes on something from outer space. I savour the moment while he recovers, and then I say, "Mr Komlosy, sir. This is Lieutenant Sacasa; Captain Moncada; Sergeant Castaneda; Captain Gomez."

It isn't that they are all Latinos that stuns him. I may be fearsome-looking but the appearance of these guys would frighten a panzer division.

Sacasa is short and slight. He looks like a strong wind would give him trouble keeping his feet. But his face would freeze oil. It must have started out bad enough, but after God knows how many fist fights plus the close attention of some misdirected napalm he could've made a fortune in horror films. Moncada is also short, but is practically deformed by the shoulders and arms of a professional weightlifter. A wide scar starts beside his left eye and disappears under his chin. He has a low forehead and the kind of eyes that Picasso painted at one time or another. Castaneda is tall and slender. He has a pencil-thin black moustache and looks as if he is smiling cruelly. It's a sinister illusion caused by a shrapnel wound. Gomez has no apparent facial anomalies. In fact, he should be handsome but the mix of features has somehow resulted in a face that approaching strangers cross a street to avoid. I say, "Men, you know who Mr Komlosy is. Tonight he's going to be watching the exercise. I want a clockwork effort from you and all your men."

Four voices snap out in unison. "Yessir!"

Komlosy confines himself to a lame, "Keep up the great work, men. We're relying on you."

I dismiss them and we climb back into the jeep. As we head for my quarters, he mutters, "Christ, Colonel, where did you find them? Fort Levenworth?"

"Mike, they're all long time regular soldiers. Sacasa and Gomez are Chicanos. Moncada and Castaneda Cuban blood . . . they all speak Spanish."

"Ha! Got you. That's why you picked them."

"Only partly. They're tough and they're proven and they know how to lead."

"Is the rest of the squad like them?"

"More or less."

"All Latinos?"

"Hell no." I turn and give him a grin. "I've got a couple more blacks. A full-blooded Indian an' two Puerto Ricans."

He shakes his head. "Listen, is this gonna be an all-ethnic-minority assault force?"

I laugh. "No, Mike, about half of the squad are white. Not exactly your average WASP but ethnically they kinda balance it out."

"Well, those four sure look dangerous. Where did you find them?"

"Different special units. I've worked with them before and most of the others. Those units, when they screen volunteers, they don't want the fantasisers. They look for certain traits of character and tendencies."

"You mean homicidal?"

"Not exactly. They look for loners with imagination. You'd be surprised. Gomez, for example, is into classical music. Sibelius is his favourite. He'll talk about him for hours if you let him. Sacasa, he teaches in a local boys' club. They're not all what they seem."

We bump along in silence for a time, then he asks, "Silas, you don't mind me bunking in with you tonight. It's just that I'm real pissed off at hotels."

"No problem, Mike, I'll enjoy the company."

It's just after ten. We're standing on a platform high on a scaffolding tower. Behind us Newman and Allen are discussing the wind conditions. Komlosy is looking down at the mock-up.

"They built all this in four days?"

"In twenty-four hours. It's just plywood and canvas but all the measurements and distances are exact. Those Seebees are 'can do' guys. You ask them to part the Red Sea for a couple hours an' they'll sure give it a try. Now I'll fill you in." I point below. "Moncada's squad lands there behind the chancery. Castaneda's over there by the residence. Sacasa's there behind the apartments. Meanwhile Gomez's squad has approached a thousand feet higher. They circle down slowly. At the first shot they turn on their engines, dive down and circle over the compound dropping grenades and other goodies on all the roof-tops where the guards have emplacements. Their Ultras are equipped with small but powerful lights. Once those emplacements are taken out they land and secure a landing zone over there for the choppers."

"How long will the choppers take to arrive?"

"They'll lift off as we make our final approach. We figure four to five minutes. At the same time, fixed wing aircraft and helicopter gun ships will be closing out the whole area."

"So how long from landing to evacuation?"

"Eight to ten minutes."

He turns slowly, studying the whole compound carefully. "It's pretty dark, Colonel."

"Our boys have light-intensifying glasses, sir. They don't exactly show daylight, but they're damn good and a hell of an advantage."

"What weapons will they carry?"

"Knives. Ingram sub-machine-guns with suppressors and a variety of grenades: some the good old-fashioned kind; some new fancy ones. An' believe it or not in each squad one man will have a sawn-off, pump-action shot-gun. That's a weapon that for some situations can never be equalled." I glance at my watch and he asks, "They're about due?"

"Yes, sir, any time now. See how far away you can spot them."

For two minutes he strains his eyes into the darkness, first one direction, then another. Finally he remarks, "I guess they're late."

Very quietly I say, "No sir. They're here."

I point to a corner of the chancery building. Two black figures glide across the ground towards the entrance. I point again; black figures running towards the residence, others towards the apartments.

"How the hell . . . ?"

His words are cut off as two black shapes glide by twenty yards in front of our faces.

"How . . . ?"

The first shot. Then more. Above our heads, pencils of light appear, picking out the roof-tops. Then sharp explosions and flashes. Komlosy ducks down.

"Just thunder flashes, sir – simulating grenades."

After a few seconds the lights go out. I point as the last squad lands in front of the dark oval patch that simulates the Ambassador's swimming pool. There are explosions and bursts of fire all over the compound. Two minutes later, flares light up in a circle a hundred metres across. There's a clattering over our heads. A single chopper plunges out of the dark sky seeming on course for a crash. At the last moment it slows abruptly and settles to earth. From all points of the compass, twenty black-clad figures walk out slowly and form a circle around it. The chopper's rotor slows and stops. There is total silence, then twenty rigid arms hold up twenty sub-machine-guns and a chilling shout rolls and echoes up to us.

"Vampires!"

"Jesus!" Komlosy is gazing down mesmerised. I turn. Behind me Newman and Allen are grinning hugely. They know I stage-managed that little bit.

"What did that mean?" Komlosy asks in a whisper.

"That's what we call ourselves, sir. The 'Vampires'. Black vampires, flying at night, seeking blood . . . good for morale."

He shakes his head. "Not if you're trying to get a peaceful night's sleep . . . Jeeesus!"

An hour later we are propping up the bar in my quarters. I don't drink a hell of a lot but when I do I like to be on my feet. I built the bar myself out of stripped pine. It's the right height and has a footrest. It's a civilised watering hole. Newman and Allen stayed for one drink and then took off into town – probably chasing tail. If we do the job they want to come on the "Nimitz" with us; nurse us and the Ultras right off the deck; fine tune the engines and every other square inch of them. Without looking at Komlosy I remarked that it might be difficult. The brass get nervous about having civvies around. Komlosy had said simply, "Don't worry, guys. If they go you'll be there."

133

We are on to our third Scotch. Komlosy is in a strange mood. At one moment introspective and appearing sad, at another excited and enthusiastic. He's in total awe over what he's just seen. I'm pleased with the exercise but I don't tell him what he didn't see. One of Sacasa's squad overshooting and almost having contact with the side of the chancery. Moncada's squad arriving more than a minute late. Also Gomez's. They were too high when they switched on their lights. Overall the operation ran about four minutes over. But it was good for a second effort. In ten days they'll be precise. I don't tell him this because I want him to go back and tell the President that we're already dazzlingly brilliant. I want this job so bad it really hurts. I want to ride a winner. Just once. Right now Komlosy's in one of his enthusiastic moods.

"Silas, there's one thing I don't understand."

"What's that, Mike?"

"Well, it was dark. But dammit, it wasn't that dark. There was reasonable visibility and I knew they were coming. I was watching for them all round. But I didn't see them until a couple passed right in front of my nose. Silas, I've got twenty-twenty vision!"

I pour him another three fingers of Scotch.

"Mike, I'll tell you. There have been tests – field tests – that have proved that someone searching the sky for aircraft almost never looks higher than an angle of forty-five degrees. They never look straight up. So my guys come in high until they're directly over the target. Then they spiral down right over your head. With an Ultra that's particularly effective because there's no sound."

He sips reflectively. "Yeah, I see that now. Let me ask you something else. Couldn't you use more men? I mean wouldn't that give some more insurance?"

"No way! More risk of early detection. More risk of confusion. More complications. More isn't better, Mike."

He nods. "Okay. Hell, after watching that tonight, I'm not gonna argue with you."

"So what are the chances, Mr NSC? What are the chances we get it?"

His mood changes visibly. He swirls the amber liquid in his glass, draws a deep breath and exhales slowly.

"The President's already impressed with you. He was a mite thrown by your list of disasters. He's been asking the brass some embarrassing questions. He'll be even more impressed after I report tomorrow on what I've seen tonight. If the operation goes ahead you've got a better than seventy per cent chance of getting it . . . if it goes ahead."

His last sentence is spoken gloomily. His glass is empty. I pour more Scotch.

"But why shouldn't it, Mike? It's the obvious option."

He snorts. "Yeah, but the options are all fucked up."

I sense that he might open up. I've got to be careful not to push. I go over to the stereo and put on a tape – Thelonius Monk being cerebral.

Back at the bar I roll my eyes and with my best Uncle Tom voice say, "Wail, Ah's jest a souldjer. Life's real simple; git mah orders and 'bey them . . . most times."

He looks up and grins. He's already on the threshold of being drunk.

"Yeah. You know, Silas, right now I envy you. Watching you today and tonight I really envied you. You're a pro doing just what you like – what you're brilliant at."

"You're a pro yourself, Mike."

He sighs. "Yeah, and I've got a job that's mighty complicated but should be logical. Silas, you don't know fucking politics – it's a slippery heap of shit."

"Well, I can guess but surely politics doesn't come into this?"

He smiles and it turns into a grimace. "You know about a guy called Conrad Tessler?"

"Sure, big industrialist cat. Power behind the President. Financed him from the early days. Got him made Governor and then President."

"Yeah, well he's got three sons. The eldest works with him in the business. The second he put into politics. The youngest, Arnold, he put into the CIA. He knows that information is power. Well, Arnold is one of the hostages."

"Ahah! I'd seen the name and didn't connect it."

"No, the media is co-operating and playing it low key."

"So Pa Tessler is worried that a rescue attempt could endanger his little boy's life . . . an' he's putting pressure on the President?"

Without waiting for me to do it he pours more Scotch. His hand is a little unsteady.

"Silas, pressure is an understatement. He must have pointed out a hundred times that although it took fourteen months, the Teheran hostages got home unharmed. He's mighty persistent and mighty fond of his little boy."

My anger rises. "And the President's bending under this pressure? Is that what you're telling me? In spite of his own convictions — it's obscene!"

He shakes his head. "It's the power of politics wielded over generations, but don't be down-hearted, Silas. There's another complication — a beauty — and it's pulling the President in the other direction. It's really a beauty."

I keep quiet, willing him not to stop now. He lights a cigarette and blows smoke into his glass.

"Our Ambassador there, Peabody. He's an expert on Cuba . . . advises the CIA. It so happens that there's a big operation under way soon against Castro. It involves people high up in the administration. Peabody advised on it. He knows the names."

"Okay. But he's hardly likely to spout them out to the Chamarristas. An' they wouldn't dare torture him."

He's got both elbows on the bar now. He's nodding his head. "True, but along comes another complication. They owe Cuba an enormous debt. They've given Castro access to him."

"How?"

"We have a dozen agents in San Carlo including the one in the compound who we've finally made contact with. We also had a guy at the airport. He managed to get some photos of disembarking passengers on some of the planes that flew in after the takeover . . . before we imposed the blockade. They took a few days to get through to us. One of those photos showed the face of a man called Jorge Calderon . . ." He bends his head back, stretches his neck, then looks me straight in the eye. "Top interrogator for Cuban Intelligence. Apparently a very effective guy."

I'm beginning to feel glad I'm only a soldier; but also I'm pretty intrigued.

"And this Calderon is in the compound?"

"He comes and goes every two or three days in the back of a provisions truck."

"Can't our guys knock him off?"

"He's guarded day and night. Besides Castro would probably send in someone else."

"Okay, but even he's not gonna be torturing an American Ambassador . . . or is he?"

He shakes his head. "No, he's using psychology. That's his forte. He's humiliating Peabody. Keeping him isolated in the guardhouse. He's almost naked. There's no sanitation and all they feed him is garbage once a day."

"Bastards . . . ! But Mike, an Ambassador has to be top material. That's not gonna make him crack."

He sighs again and lights another cigarette.

"A team of psychologists and psychiatrists were given in-depth profiles on Peabody. Every single thing we know about him. They reported yesterday and alarm bells have been ringing in Washington ever since."

"That bad?"

"Listen, buddy, that guy had some kind of tragedy decades ago. It turned him in on himself. He never married . . . has no friends . . . few acquaintances. He's got a brilliant mind and he buried himself in books and his work. Even wrote a few himself. His anti-communism has reached obsessional level . . . and in his personal habits he's turned fastidiousness into a fetish. Our experts think that he's prime material for the skills of a man like Calderon. The report concluded: 'Continued exposure to such conditions of detention together with intense psychological pressure could have a detrimental effect on his mental state.'"

A long silence, then the clink of glass as Komlosy pours again.

I remark, "The President has quite a choice to make. Does he lose sleep over it?"

He smiles. "I doubt it. He's developed 'switching off' into a fine art. But one thing's for sure, he doesn't want to jeopardise that operation. Sometimes I think he'd rather knock off Cuba than Russia. To him, having Castro dirtying our doorstep is a perpetual insult."

"What will he decide, Mike?"

"Nothing."

"Nothing?"

His smile is devoid of humour. "Not for five or six days. During that time the CIA has another operation running. A lovely little operation." He's looking morosely into his glass. "I tell you, Silas, if I don't develop the President's 'switch off' techniques soon it could have a detrimental effect on *my* mental state."

"What are they gonna do?"

Abruptly he shakes himself.

"Hell! What's happening to me? I'm known as a close-mouthed guy. Here I am shooting my mouth off like a kid to a favourite uncle!"

Very quietly I ask, "You're worried about my security, Mike?"

He cups his chin on his palms. His twenty-twenty vision is getting a shade myopic.

"No way, Silas. But you know I shouldn't be telling you any of this."

I take a slow breath. "That's so. But if the President decides on the rescue, I'm likely to be the first guy floating in there. Maybe the first guy to die."

Another long silence, another cigarette lit. He's reached the point when he wants to share the secret – I hope.

"Okay . . . Using the agent in the compound they're going to try to poison him?"

"The Cuban?"

"Peabody."

For a moment I don't believe what I've heard. I look at his face; at his eyes. I believe and I want to throw up. He pushes himself erect. "I'm going to take a pee."

The whole obscene thing churns around in my skull. When he comes back, walking a bit unsteadily, I say angrily,

138

"Are you telling me that the President of my country authorised the murder of one of his own Ambassadors?"

He affects a shocked expression, shaking his head vigorously.

"No, no, no. God no!"

"Then the CIA are doing this without authorisation?"

Again the head shaking and the parody of shock.

"No, no, no."

"Mike, you're not making sense."

"But I am." He leans over the bar. "Silas, did you ever hear of a man called Thomas à Becket?"

I don't hide my sarcasm.

"Sure, why, din that ol' cat play tight end fo' the Dallas Cowboys?"

Suddenly the myopic look is gone. He straightens up and says stiffly, "Sorry for the condescension ... Anyway he was a great nuisance. The king, in front of his knights, and in exasperation said: 'Won't someone rid me off this cursed priest,' or something like that. The knights give each other knowing looks and go off and kill Becket. The king is horrified ... or professes to be. That's why in CIA parlance there's what's called 'Becket approval'. In this case there was a meeting. They waited for a key sentence or phrase. They spelled out the painful alternatives. There was much soul-searching and references to the realities of geopolitics. Eventually they heard the key sentence. Something like, 'Sacrifices for freedom and our way of life' ... Becket approval."

"It stinks!"

"I agree."

"You were at the meeting?"

"Of course. I argued against it ... every way I could."

I look closely again into his eyes and again believe him.

"Did you talk to him afterwards? Try to get him to stop it?"

"Sure."

"And?"

"He'd switched off."

While I'm thinking about that he says, "To get to be

President you have to do some rough things . . . and when you get there, things get rougher."

"Yeah . . . When does it happen?"

"They have to get a special poison down there. They figure five to six days. Believe it or not they use nicotine – pure and concentrated. One drop and you're dead in five minutes."

"I hope the bastards fail!"

"So do *I*." He looks at his watch. "God! I must get some shut-eye."

He drains his glass and looks at his cigarette. "Fucking nicotine!"

He grinds it out.

JORGE
San Carlo
Day 9

There's an on-shore wind and from the north-west the big rollers sweep in and crash on to the beach below, sweeping in from Cuba. It's only five hundred miles away. It tugs at me. For two days I had talked of Cuba, stayed in the compound for two days and argued, cajoled, threatened. It came to nothing. It was a road I had to go down. After hearing that tape I had to examine the possibility.

I am standing on the balcony of the hotel room. It is early evening. The light is soft. The sunsets here are like Cuban sunsets. Sudden, dramatic, vivid. Then darkness coming down like a warm black sheet. I am experiencing unhappiness. Not sadness, that is not the antithesis of happiness. Sadness is melancholy, unhappiness is mental discomfort. For a few minutes I indulge myself in semantics; then invariably I think of Peabody – part cause of my unhappiness. I cannot break him intellectually or logically. He is not my superior but he is my equal. After the tape, we talked for hours. On reflection I talked more than him. That was part of his skill. I talked more than I expected but it was also part of my purpose. An attempt to draw him close to me. So close that he would be vulnerable. He turned questions back on me. I found myself talking of my father. How I grew to hate him. How he wore his pride and selfishness like a well-tailored suit. How he reacted to the loss of unearned privilege like a child. How he turned his resentment into a weapon against my mother. Of course I used the parallel of capitalism. My father sucking off the milk of capitalism and then wailing like an infant when the milk dried up. But as I talked, I felt personal emotions. When I talked of the joy when he was able to leave for Spain, the joy was rekindled. When I recounted hearing the news of his recent death in a drunken car crash in Madrid, I felt again the indifference.

Peabody prodded at me. He pointed to the gold signet ring on my finger and asked: "But was not that your father's?"

I told him no. From my grandfather and then I talked about him. Also a capitalist with vast landholdings. But not a man to wail when matters went against him. A good man, whose wisdom might have allowed him, had he lived, to accept that change that had to come.

When I asked about his own parents he talked briefly of them as though they had been inanimate paintings on a wall. There was no feeling in him. No passion. They were just a mother and a father; like a left and a right foot.

But mostly we talked ideology. I reminded him of his last words to Vargas:

"The world of extremes is not flat. It curls around and melts into itself."

I took that as my theme. I explained that we, in Cuba, were not North Koreans or Albanians or even Russians. We pursued socialism hand in hand with humanism. I related my own life and experiences to illustrate my thesis. I pointed out our achievements and contrasted our society with what had been before. I searched in his eyes for a spark of sympathy – or even understanding. There was no spark. I reminded myself that this was the man who had once loved passionately. Who had recently damned the excesses of Vargas. Virtually called him sub-human. I played the tape again in front of him. Listened to his words; of children killed in blood lust. Of how an innocent killed as a communist will create five communists. Then with a chill I realised that the words coming off that tape were devoid of emotions. He was simply setting out conditions to force a dictator to be a more acceptable loan recipient.

Now, for a moment, I'm close to despair. I have one formidable weapon. But if I misuse it it's gone for ever. But to use it I need to draw him close; to depend on me. There must be a way. I think again about his trips to the airport. Scores of them. There was surely a vital reason. He spent hours. Last night I pored over an airline ABC trying to find a pattern. Trying to get a glimmer of who he was waiting for – or watching for.

The door slides open behind me and I feel the cool of the air-conditioning on my back. She comes up beside me and rests her elbows on the rail. The sky is turning red – and tinting the sea. It reflects on her face. She is the other part of my unhappiness. I think I love her, and the terrifying realisation is that she senses it. I am shamed by the absurdity. I know what she is. Moment by moment I can see the unsheathing of her claws. She showed the tips of them last night.

Bermudez has taken to having working dinners late into the night. He gathers his acolytes around him like an inner court and they eat and talk – or mostly listen to him. Roberto Bermudez who would be the new Fidel. Last night we were invited – as we are tonight. He enjoys his power and enjoys showing it off. He also competes with me for Inez. It is at once subtle and direct. He defers to me in a way so respectful as to be on the brink of parody. He calls Inez "comrade" with the inflection of a sensualist. She responds with a prurient twitch of her lips and a flick of her eyes in my direction. And I feel pain. Me! And because of the weakness of feeling pain I feel agony. Fidel was right. I should have listened to him.

"Don't you think it's exciting, Jorge?"

"What?"

"What we are seeing. What we are part of. The transformation of a country. Being at the centre. Knowing what is being done – being planned. History is being made."

Irritably I say, "History is being made in Cuba. You never took much interest there."

"Ah, it's different. This is young. This is now."

"It could also be very short. Bermudez is losing his sense of proportion."

She puts a hand on my arm.

"Jorge, you are just irritable because of the American. Because he is not easy for you. You must try harder. Roberto was saying last night how much he hopes you succeed. We must go soon or we'll be late."

I say gently: "Inez, I have to think a little more. Go inside and wait for me. I will come soon."

She squeezes my arm and kisses me on my ear. She never wears perfume but the scent of her skin is in my nostrils. And the sense of my shame is circling in my guts. I wrench my mind away, back to Peabody. I must get it off the witch in the room behind me. I try to concentrate again about his trips to the airport. They have assumed massive importance. I try so hard to concentrate but the image of her face intrudes. The image of her looking at Bermudez. Her mouth smiling at him. Hell! The sheer loneliness of jealousy.

Wait! Something has happened in a back recess of my brain. The loneliness of jealousy? The loneliness of envy?

She is expunged.

I know!

I am flooded with excitement. The doors of my mind fling open. I am Jorge Calderon! I turn and slide open the door. She is not in the room. I call, "Inez!"

She appears in the bathroom door.

"I'm going to the compound."

Her eyes glitter.

"Now? We must be at the palace in half an hour."

"Fuck the palace. I'm going to the compound. I must."

She walks forward stiff legged.

"Well I'm not staying here alone. I'm going to the palace!"

I pick up my bag. "Do what you want."

As I reach the door she says defiantly, "You will be sorry, Jorge Calderon."

She is standing legs apart, all claws showing. Her eyes radiating a single simple message. I am not unhappy. I am unbelievably sad.

"Yes, Inez. I will."

Peabody is surprised to see me, but I think not displeased. He comes gingerly out of his cell. His grey beard is growing down more than out. It makes his face appear much thinner. His shorts are wet and I comment on this. Immediately he is hostile.

144

"I washed them in the pitiful amount of water that remains after I drink and wash myself!"

There follows the whole litany of complaints and protests in his own name and his Government's. But I sense this time the words are said for form rather than purpose. I have ordered coffee and while we wait I give him the usual assurances that the other hostages are in good health. To his questions about the outside situation I am vague. Of course his Government has imposed sanctions and frozen assets. I don't mention the blockade or the sudden diminished activity of the 'Nimitz' and its aircraft.

The Mestizo boy brings in the coffee. As Peabody takes his first sip he cannot keep the anticipation out of his eyes. I study him. Am I right? Was my moment of intuition correct? If so this old man in front of me is about to have his brain exposed as in a lobotomy, and will I be able to prepare him for the final phase? If I'm wrong he's going to regard me as a fanciful idiot, and my task will be a thousand times harder. It's a risk that's been thrust at me. But first I have to get him in the right mental state. I want him confident and enjoying himself. I know how to do it. I will play the game to his strength.

I start an ideologue again, taking up where we left off before. But this time debating from the points of view of several Latin American writers.

We argue for an hour. I keep my voice modulated and my manner relaxed – none of the vehemence of past sessions. He is on strong ground, at least in his view, and obviously begins to enjoy himself. I throw Marquez at him. He counters with Borges. I thrust with Galeano and he parries with our own Cabrera Infante. After an hour he is on top, and knows it. He starts turning Marquez and even Llosa against me. He is a master in this field; able to quote whole pages from memory, and of course is remarkably adept at interpreting a thesis to favour his own philosophy. He even smiles on two or three occasions as he makes a telling point. I judge that the moment is right. He has the air of a professor who has just delivered a successful lecture.

I shout for more coffee. While we wait and while the

Mestizo is in the room I keep a deliberate silence, pretending to read something in one of my files. I am tense, vividly aware of the importance of the moment. As he raises his mug, I say very casually, and still looking down at the file, "Peabody, I know why you made all those trips to the airport."

I look up. The mug is suspended in mid air. There is a startled look in his eyes. Time is also suspended. Then his eyes drop to the file, and the startled look is gone. He visibly relaxes. The mug travels up and he drinks. He thinks that what I know is in the file. He is aware that such knowledge can be in no file. He sips again, puts the mug down and patiently waits for me to make a fool of myself. I close the file and in a sombre tone say, "I would not have believed that a human being, so intelligent, so widely read, so aware of the world, could be . . . so lonely."

He pulls his head back; his whole body shrinks away from me. His eyes narrow as if in pain and I know that I'm right. My own emotions are a blend of elation and pity. As I look at him, the elation fades.

"Peabody, you did not go to the airport to meet or watch for any particular person. Your visits coincided with the flight arrivals from Madrid and Rome. Latins are emotional people . . . You went to watch the passengers being welcomed . . . Parents greeting children . . . and children parents . . . grandparents . . . wives . . . husbands . . . and lovers. Peabody, for a brief time each week you were on the fringe of emotion and love. You sat and watched those people embrace, and kiss, and sometimes cry with joy. You never went to the departure hall. You never went to see the tears of sorrow."

He is staring down between his thin knees. No artist or sculptor could create a vision of such melancholy.

"Peabody . . ."

He lifts his head. His eyes are wounds in his face.

"Peabody. You who knows everything, who knows exactly how the lives of human kind should be arranged. You who are so strong to need no one. You had to creep close to the aura of love between strangers; like an animal creeping near

146

to a camp fire at night; hidden by darkness. Frightened of the fire but from a distance absorbing a hint of warmth."

His head sags again. I push my chair back and stand up. Slowly I walk around the desk and come close to him. He stays completely immobile. I cannot see his eyes. I bend my knees and crouch beside his chair. He turns his head and in his eyes I see a pleading. It could be for me to vanish into the air. To vaporise for ever. It could be a plea for something else.

His hands are resting on his knees. I reach out and cover one of them with mine. I can feel fine bones under dry skin. Many seconds pass. He doesn't move. Then in a choking whisper he asks, "How could you know that? How could you have guessed?"

I have no simple answer. I came to the knowledge through no logic. How did I guess? I realise that I had to be able to feel as he feels. There has to be something in me that is also in him. I guessed because in spite of diametrical differences we have, in our cores, stunning similarity. I tell him.

"I guessed only because I must have the same capacity to isolate my intellect from my emotions. To stoke the fires of one and smother the other. You took that capacity to an extreme. But you are more than twice my age, have travelled a longer road, have smothered until there is barely an ember still alive. I tell you now that it frightens me. If that can happen to you, so it can happen to me."

I would never have believed I could utter those words, still less that they are an exact expression of what I feel. I am confused by this. So confused that at first I don't notice. Then my eyes focus and my skin feels. He has moved his other hand and covered mine with it.

I am numb with emotion. I recall my grandfather dying. I was a child and unhappy. For hours I would sit by his bed trying to give him comfort. My hand, like now, would be between his. I drew more comfort than I gave.

I look up at Peabody's face. There is no change of expression. But he knows what has happened and so do I. From the beginning I had to set out to do it. Set out to crack through his exterior and expose to himself what is inside.

147

I have succeeded brilliantly; but not how I imagined. In cracking him I have cracked myself. Does the influence of Inez have anything to do with this? I must leave here now and think.

I withdraw my hand and straighten up.

"Peabody, I will come to see you in two days. Until then try to think on something. Try to imagine that if a man warps his true instincts and for years presents a false face to the world, then the whole philosophy of that man could also be warped and false. Try to think on that and let us talk about it next time."

We are looking at each other. He smiles faintly and stands up. At the cell door he turns. "Calderon, understanding me is one thing. Using that to extract information is another. Good night to you."

He goes in and closes the door.

As I cross the compound I try to decide when to use the concluding weapon. It will be devastating. I know he is close to being ready for it. Maybe the next session or the one after. I decide on the one after. I will leave him alone for two days. I had been looking forward to the moment; anticipating it. Now I'm deferring it; all anticipation gone.

Fombona is talking to the guard at the entrance to the residence. I tell him, "I'm leaving in the morning."

He shakes his head. "There's no deliveries tomorrow. You'll have to go the day after."

"What are you talking about?"

He is grinning. "The deliveries tomorrow have been cancelled."

"By who?"

He shrugs insolently. "Someone outside. Don't worry, you won't go hungry, we have plenty of food."

I realise Bermudez has sealed me off here. He is too subtle to move on Inez tonight. It would be crude. He knows crudeness will turn her away. He also knows that his isolating me here, his cleverness over me, will attract her. He understands her character.

Anger and frustration threaten to overwhelm me. The ape Fombona must know what's behind this. There's no way I can leave the place except in the back of that van. I know there's a radio link with Bermudez, but because of NSA eavesdropping, only to be used in dire emergencies. I don't care.

"Fombona, I will use the radio."

His foul grin widens. A shake of his head. "No chance. Orders are total . . . and they came from our leader."

Another rage of frustration – and jealousy. It's a humiliating emotion. I stamp it down. As I go through the door I tell Fombona, "If your leader calls, tell him he's going to regret this."

PEABODY
San Carlo
Day 10

I know about the "Stockholm Syndrome" – about captives
being drawn to their captors, sufferers to their tormentors. I
think about it for a long time, trying to analyse my feelings
objectively. It is difficult, alarming and sometimes painful to
probe my own emotions, to face weaknesses the existence of
which I had never admitted. In looking back over four
decades I can only see the arid flatness of an emotional
desert. But since I had created it, surely I wanted it? And
wanting it, how could I be so devastated to have it shown
me? Now I recognise the truth. I never did want it. I built it
from bitterness and sustained it with false pride. I decide
that what I am going through has nothing to do with the
"Stockholm Syndrome". Certainly I have drawn close to
Calderon but the reality is that from the beginning he
affected me in a remarkable way.

Throughout the early sessions my rage at him was always
overlaid by fascination. I count my scratch marks on the
wall. It was only ten days ago that he sat in his chair looking
at death down the barrel of Fombona's gun as though he was
examining a rare and exotic flower. When I threw shit on
him the only thing he wanted to do was kill me, yet his
expression showed nothing and when he talked his voice was
natural. He has an intellect and the gift to express it the like
of which I have never experienced.

I analyse myself again, try to decide whether it is
admiration that has drawn me to him.

It is not. I have admired many men and women for gifts
both natural and acquired, but never been emotionally
drawn to them. It happened because, like nobody else, he

150

understands me. I suddenly realise with a shock that the emotion I'm feeling is paternal. He understands me in the way a son will sometimes understand a father. More mental confusion as I try to work out how this happened. But then I decide not to care. Enough analysis.

It is just after dawn. Natural light is replacing that from the bulb. I wonder again what is happening in the outside world. He was deliberately vague. Maybe that will change now. A rescue plan must be in process. The Special Forces will be training. Even with satellite surveillance alone they will know the disposition of the hostages and guards. The chances of success must be good. They will surely have learned from the Teheran attempt, and the "Nimitz" is only a few miles away. For a moment I yearn for the comfort and dignity of my home. Then I think about the Tessler factor and imagine the mogul applying the pressure. Will the President resist it? My thoughts switch to Calderon again. If he is in the compound when the rescue is attempted he will be killed or captured. I picture his face at that moment. It will be calm, even sardonic.

Such an ability has a profound influence on others. I remember my sole attempt about ten years ago to break out of my chains of loneliness. How I could have used such an ability then!

Emma Grayson, a widow in her early forties, who worked in an office down the corridor from mine, a slender woman with lustrous black hair, not beautiful but a fine distinctive face, always modestly but elegantly dressed. She was an analyst of Latin American affairs and spoke excellent Spanish. For more than a year we merely nodded acknowledgment when passing. Then one morning she tapped hesitantly on my office door. She had a copy of my latest book and, shyly, asked me to sign it. As I did so I was very conscious of her standing beside my chair. The aura of subtle perfume. From the corner of my eye I could see the soft swelling of her breasts under a pale blue cashmere sweater. I felt sudden physical stirrings long dormant. During the following weeks she often dropped by my office, usually with a request for help in a

151

difficult translation. After a while I realised that these were mere excuses. She was showing an interest in me and was looking and waiting for a response. I was in a quandary. That small part of my brain which, over the years, had still stored emotion and affection hammered at me, told me that this was a rare opportunity. We had much in common. Her work gave us shared interest. She had a good dry sense of humour, happily devoid of facetiousness. She came from a good family, was intelligent and neat about her person. Finally, I felt a rare and strong physical bond. Slowly, very slowly, I convinced myself there was another route than the one I had so rigidly mapped out. Weeks passed while I built up resolve and then one morning I went down to her office determined to ask her out for dinner. I paused at the door feeling callow, then drew a breath and tapped. She was talking on the phone in Spanish with much animation. She waved me to a chair and as I sat down the words she was saying penetrated and translated themselves and chilled my whole body. "Yes, darling, I will try to make it by eight o'clock." Then I noticed the new ring on her finger. The old ones were gone, the thin worn gold one and its partner with the tiny diamond. The new one sparkled with the brilliance of large diamonds and emeralds. She had ended her conversation and hung up and was looking at me quizzically. I managed to stammer "Congratulations must be in order . . . I mean, best wishes . . ." She had smiled. "Thank you, it was quite sudden, you know him . . . Jaime Cortez." Yes, I knew him, First Secretary at the Spanish Embassy, silk smooth, urbane and very wealthy. How could I have been so stupid and presumptuous? Again she was looking at me quizzically and I realised that I needed a reason for being there. A moment of panic, then I noticed a magazine on her desk. "I just wondered if you had read the article on El Salvador by Montez, it is very good . . ." She shook her head and smiled. "I have been very busy. Of course, I will have to leave the service. Jaime is being appointed Ambassador to Uruguay next month. There is so much to do." I had risen and headed to the door mumbling words and good wishes for the future and wondering again at my presumption, but my final glance at her face gave me pause for thought. In her eyes was a definite message. "You were slow, Mr Peabody. Too slow and too timid." That evening I went to the airport and again a couple of days later. The diversion was there but I was back on the well-trodden path.

Calderon, you would not have been slow and you would never have been timid.

I hear the sound of the outside door and clomping of boots. His boots. He walks with a heel-sliding swagger that I find comic. I get up as the key turns in the lock. He said two days. What is he doing here and why so early? The door is pushed open. I hear him clomping to his chair. There's a little water in the bucket. I splash some on my face and go out.

His face is different. Something is missing. His eyes are not alert as before. It's as though they look in rather than out.

"You said you weren't coming for two days."

He shrugs and continues looking at me silently.

"And why so early? It's barely dawn."

"I couldn't sleep. That bed of yours is too soft."

"You said before it was comfortable. You can switch it with that palliasse in there if you like."

He doesn't smile. His fingers are tapping on the desk. He drops his eyes to a burn mark beside them. He is obviously troubled and for a moment I think events are moving. Maybe freedom is on the way, but then he says, "Peabody, were you ever jealous?"

"Jealous?!"

He looks up, his eyes are now defiant. "Yes. Jealous."

"You mean over a woman?"

"Of course."

"Sure."

"Often?"

I think about that. Christ, it was so long ago.

"I guess a few times."

"Why?"

I can't help but laugh. From anyone else it would be a ridiculous question, but he gives it the weight of earnestness. I answer, "It's human nature to be jealous. With some it's a disease. Others feel it less. I guess some very few never feel it. What's all this about? Are you jealous of someone?"

He ignores the question. His fingers are tapping faster. "When was the first time you were jealous?"

"Listen, Calderon, this is stupid."

He looks up. "Tell me . . . please."

He spoke the last word softly, almost painfully. It's the first time he has used it with me. He is surely troubled. I'm shocked again to feel paternal instincts. Here is this near genius complete in himself, struggling to discover what jealousy is, or is not. I delve into my memory and am astonished to find a crystal clear picture of her face.

"I was fifteen. So was she. I dated her a couple of times. We were in high school together. She started dating a football jock who was seventeen and dropped me."

"You loved her?"

"Hell no. I thought I did at the time."

"Thought you did!" He is genuinely puzzled. "It makes no sense. Either you did or you didn't."

"Not at all. I thought I was in love three times before it finally happened and I found out what the word really meant."

"When you met Amparo?"

"Yes."

He stops tapping and runs his hand through his hair, which has lost its usual studied disarray. It is now merely unkempt.

"I don't understand, Peabody. You were not genuinely in love with that first girl, but you were jealous about her. That's not logical."

I smile. "Logic, love, jealousy. They don't make a good triangle."

"True, but genuine jealousy over a woman can only be caused by genuine love. So if you only 'thought' you were in love with that girl maybe you only 'thought' you were jealous. What about the others?"

"What others?"

"The other two you thought you loved. Were you ever jealous over them?"

154

Again I go back over the years and again I'm surprised how clear the memory is.

"One, yes. We dated for five months and then I found out that she had been seeing another guy for at least the last two months. I was very angry . . . and yes, I was jealous."

"And the other one?"

"No. After two months with her I broke it off."

"Why?"

"Why? Why am I telling you all this?!"

"Please."

That word again.

"She had bad habits."

"Oh yeah!"

"Not like that . . . she wasn't too clean . . . personal hygiene and so on."

For the first time he smiles slightly. "She sure picked the wrong chap to be dirty around. But, Peabody, what you're saying is that it's possible to be genuinely jealous, without being genuinely in love. That's like a Zen monk who after years of study can drink tea from an empty cup and truly slake his thirst."

I consider that. There is a similarity.

"Yes, of course. The emotion of jealousy in that context can be falsely stimulated. But you'll only ever know that by hindsight."

I feel as though I'm helping a child put together the pieces of a picture puzzle, though God knows I'm hardly a qualified expert. He sighs and asks, "Did you fuck that fifteen-year-old girl?"

"No. Morals were a little different then."

"But you did the others?"

"Yes . . . But, Calderon, don't think that jealousy over love has to have a sexual element. There's certainly a possessive factor though. Don't confuse it with envy."

He shakes his head. His eyes are focussed inwards again. He scratches his nose thoughtfully and says, "I know you don't like to talk about it, but how long had you known Amparo before you got this revelation of genuine love . . . ? I'm not being sarcastic."

Strangely I find I don't mind thinking or talking of her.

"After about a month. At first I was attracted by her beauty, and her manner. Then after we had been out a few times I got an idea of her character. Then it just happened."

"Suddenly?"

My mind goes back to the exact date. June 19th, 1958. I describe what happened. "We were sitting in a small bar in a side street off El Prado. A guitarist played softly in a corner, the lighting was subdued. She was wearing a blue and white blouse with a high collar. It was just a bit like a scene out of those corny movies they used to make. The guitarist finished a song. There were about a dozen people there. No one clapped. She started clapping defiantly. The others joined in. The guitarist smiled at her gratefully. She turned her head and smiled at me – and in that instant I crashed into love."

As I finished the story he looks morose.

"That sudden?"

"Yes."

"Had you made love to her?"

I feel ridiculously grateful that he hasn't used the four letter word.

"No. The first time we made love was an hour later."

He sighs as if this information adds to his problems. My curiosity is acute.

"What's it about, Calderon? You've been here less than two weeks. Have you already fallen for a local girl?"

"No." He shakes his head sadly. "I brought my problem all the way from Havana."

"You brought a woman with you? Castro allowed that?!"

His smile would have looked well on a skeleton.

"Fidel warned me about her."

I can't help being intrigued.

"Castro knows her?"

"Knows about her. He let me have my way, but he warned me."

"She's so bad?"

"She's not like those girls you dated back in medieval days."

"What has she done?"

He looks at his watch and sighs. "About now, it's just possible that she's climbing out of Bermudez's bed. If not, it's a certainty that by tonight she'll be climbing into it."

It's as though I'm hearing a précis of an unwritten Shakespearian tragedy. Certainly the characters are rich enough. Certainly the one in front of me is brought low from a tower of confidence. Stabbed through by a woman! But there's a flaw in the plot. I point it out.

"You said it's possible she's been with Bermudez. If it's not certain, why don't you go and try to stop it?"

His expression instantly changes. Sadness becomes hatred.

"Because that bastard, that pocket pint-sized little prick has cancelled the delivery van today! I can't get out until tomorrow or even communicate."

A nice twist. The bard was on form. Calderon is breathing more quickly. In this session his poker face is absent. If Bermudez could see his expression at this moment it might well dampen his ardour.

"This woman is very beautiful?"

"Very."

"And very bad?"

"A witch."

"And yet you are jealous over her, which by your convoluted logic means that you must genuinely love her."

"That's what I'm trying to find out."

"Dammit, man. If you're not sure then you don't really love her. Believe me. And your jealousy is nothing more than envy or anger that another man is using your possession or taking it from you. Especially a man like Bermudez. He's charismatic."

"So am I."

"He's got power . . . if only temporarily. Is she a communist?"

He laughs bitterly. "Communist! I told you, she's a witch – an animal even."

"So why did you get involved?"

He looks me direct in the eye.

"Peabody. I know you and I guess you know me. You can work it out."

I can for sure. This is the man whose sole reaction to possible death is fascination. He enjoys going to the edge. This woman must be something else again to pull him so close to it. But I'm still puzzled.

"Have you been in love before?"

"No."

"Been jealous before?"

"No."

"Are you being honest with yourself?"

"Yes I am." He sighs in disgust. "I'm attractive to women. I've got power with them. I've known many. You've slept with three in your whole life. I've lost count. Sometimes . . . occasionally . . . well . . . very occasionally, a woman has left me for another man. I never felt a twinge of jealousy . . . or envy."

I believe him and I'm intrigued as hell that it should have finally happened. I'm just wondering if he really loves her when he says flatly, "I'm indulging myself. I don't just think I love her. I know it. Peabody, how could I fall in love with an animal?"

"I can't help you there. I'm not an expert on bestiality . . . So what are you going to do? I mean you don't even know for sure if she's done it . . . or will."

"I know. She knows. He knows."

"So?"

I watch his face resume the normal Calderon expression. He's probably holding a low pair but it could be four aces.

"I'll work it out. Anyway I'm not here to talk about damned women."

"Calderon, I'll tell you the perfect way you work it out. When you get out of here, take her straight to the airport and fly home with her; meanwhile having given the order for me to be taken from this cesspit and reunited with the other Americans."

"I can't. There's no planes."

Ah! The power of a woman. He's so unsettled he's slipped and shown his low pair. "No planes." So there's a blockade

158

as I suspected. I'll bet he wants to chew his tongue into mincemeat. He tries to recover.

"Peabody, listen to me. I'll do better than reunite you with the others. Give me one name and within half an hour you'll be freshly bathed and shaved; wearing your finest clothes and sitting at your dining room table eating a sirloin steak from your own kitchen, along with deep-fried onion rings and a mountain of french fries. Think about it, man. One name!"

I have to force my senses not to take in the sight and aroma of the dish. Coldly I tell him, "When I leave this room it will be to total freedom or to rejoin those Americans who are my responsibility. Do you really believe I would betray my country for a piece of meat?"

He smiles and shakes his head. "No. But if you thought about my final words last night you would give me the name. You know it's morally the right thing to do."

I shrug negatively. He leans forward and says with great intensity, "It's morally the right thing! You don't have to speak. I will list the possible names. When I come to a correct one, just tap your finger. Peabody – just tap your finger!"

"Calderon, Judas had more imagination . . . and you are the one with the finger-tapping habit."

SLOCUM
Fort Bragg
Day 14

The phone rings. I'm in the bath. It always happens. It bugged me enough in the past that I rigged an extension right on the wall next to the taps. Now it's useless. The technicians came in yesterday and fixed up a little black box. You get a call, you flip a switch and no one understands the conversation except the legit caller and called. But there's no little box on the goddam extension.

I heave myself out of the bath, wrap on a towel and drip water through to the study. It's Komlosy. I tell him severely, "You got me out of the goddam bath."

"Tough shit. You switched the gizmo thing on?"

"Sure."

" 'Kay. Decision was taken. If the nicotine operation fails, the rescue goes ahead – soonest. You and your brownies have been selected."

A surge of relief – and anxiety.

"When will we know?"

"It happens within forty-eight hours. We'll know a day later."

"Bastards."

"Yeah. When will you be ready?"

"Three hours ago."

"But it's only been twelve days. You said you needed three weeks."

"I was pessimistic. My brownies got all their badges. They even learned how to light a fire without a zippo."

"Zippo? Silas, you're dating yourself."

"Thank God for that. What's the next move?"

"Sure you're ready?"

"Listen, Mike. You were here five days ago. Since then we've hit the compound fifteen times. War is like a football game. You train your guys 'til they're perfect. Then you stop, or they go downhill. My vampires made the perfect raid three hours ago."

"Okay. When we know, General Simmons will make arrangements to transport you to the 'Nimitz'."

"General Simmons?"

He laughs. "Yeah, General. There's been a lot of back-stabbing going on. The brass were profoundly displeased that you and your boys were selected. The President felt that Simmons needed a little more astronomy to combat the flak."

"How much astronomy?"

"Three stars."

"Jesus Christ in pink!"

I'm astonished. That promotion is unprecedented. I hear tinny laughter. The little gizmo box does funny things to voices. He asks, "How much dialogue have you had with Simmons?"

"Very little. I need something, I call him, he delivers."

"Silas, the delivery's been tough. You should know that Simmons has faced every bureaucratic obstacle since Hannibal requisitioned all those elephants. You know about him?"

"Yeah, he quarter-backed for the Dolphins."

He gurgles. He sure is high. "Silas, when Simmons met a block he'd call me. I had to call the brass and they pissed me about. Two days ago I blew up in front of the President. He issued an order that in future Simmons call *him*. Simmons does. The President likes him. They both collect Remington sculptures. This morning Simmons called in after a certain two star General had tried to fuck him up. I was in the Oval Office. It was historic. I've never seen the President do it. He got so mad he went black in the face. Silas, you'd have been jealous. Then he picks up the phone and calls Grant. Very brief conversation – one way. Quote: 'Brigadier Al Simmons is promoted to three stars. You better start looking over your shoulder.' End quote."

"It's beautiful. What about the Tessler factor?"

Even with the distortion I can hear the relish in his voice. "Ah Tessler! The word is that the Pres told him, 'You had your pound of flesh. The whole carcass you don't get'!"

Cautiously I ask, "There's no chance this nicotine thing can be called off?"

His voice sobers. "No. The Pres is being macho but he's still playing the odds. Anyway, get ready to move. And, Silas, if you go in, it has to work, or Simmons will be busted to something lower than PFC and you'll be cleaning latrines."

"What will you be doing, Mike?"

"Being cleaned by you . . . Got it?"

"Got it."

"I'll be in touch."

The phone goes dead. I hang up, flip off the gizmo and pad back to the bathroom. The water's cooled. I run the hot tap and climb back in. I always think better in the bath. Once, between shampooing my hair and washing my crotch I worked out an entire campaign to subdue the Warsaw Pact.

I bring myself back to reality. If they kill Peabody, the chance is off. I will the guy not to be killed. I do more. I lie there with water up to my chin surveying the twin islands of my knees and I put the "hex" on the bastards trying to kill him. The "hex" is a mental spell. It makes things go wrong. Eve put the "hex" on the apple. I learned it from my grandpapa and he used to kid me that his grandpapa brought it all the way from the Gold Coast. My grandpapa once sold a Chevvy to a guy who found a legal way not to pay him the full amount. He "hexed" that Chevvy. Inside of a month the fuel pump packed up, the clutch seized up, the cylinder heads screwed up and a door fell off. The guy sold it for junk. When it was being junked the hydraulic press blew a leak and didn't work for a month. To "hex" a Chevvy is difficult, but to "hex" a guy is easy.

You put a picture of him in your mind and then you make him grow hair. All over. Stiff straight hair like a lot of little spikes. Even his toes have to grow hair. After a while he's a hairy ball. He looks like a porcupine at the wrong end of the evolution cycle. A guy with that appearance can do nothin'

162

right. I've seen newspaper pictures of Douglas Baker, director of the CIA. I conjure him up. He's got a big nose and ears that stick out. I start him into growing hair. It takes a while. Meantime I think about the job. I want it real bad. I go back through my life. It's like walking along a sandy beach at high tide. Every time you turn around, your footprints have been washed away – you were never there.

The CIA director's sprouted a mass of hair. All that's showing are the tips of ears and his nose. The hair is ginger coloured. He looks grotesque. Any guy looking like that has got to screw up.

I've also seen photos of Peabody. I conjure him up: a tall elegant cat. Don't worry, Peabody baby, that hairy prick Baker will fuck up for sure.

Jorge
San Carlo
Day 15

I study the photograph trying to imagine how it was. How she was. It is not difficult. Once again I go over my strategy. It must be exact. He is ready and, in normal circumstances, I would be fully confident of success. But nothing now is normal. I am in a strange delirium. It is necessary that I hurt him. Hurt him so deeply that he will reach out to me for comfort. But I have no passion for it. Also in this strategy I have to lie just a little. This should not be a problem but it is. In past sessions, when I told him the truth he believed me. I sensed it for a certainty. Is the opposite true? It is a frightening possibility. I must, in my voice and demeanour, be brilliant, at my very best. I must be better than when I broke Cubelas. But I hated Cubelas. The hatred was the adrenalin for my effort. Peabody casts over my energy only a soporific.

I hear the key in the door and slide the photograph back into the file. She comes in with the face of a child entering an unguarded chocolate factory. A face redolent with physical satisfaction and seeking its mental counterpart. She leans over and kisses me on the corner of my mouth. The witch has not even bothered to bathe. I smell his cologne.

"You should have come, Jorge. It's a beautiful *finca*. The furniture is from Spain . . . antique. Even the handles for the doors."

It comes out even before I can think. "And I suppose the bed was a Castilian four-poster."

She smiles. Pretty white teeth, perfectly shaped, lips curving into an arc of derision.

"You are so clever, Jorge. Eighteenth century. It is said that Queen Isabella slept in it."

164

Yet again the jealousy makes me nauseous. I must not show it. She is trying to prise it out and expose it for my humiliation.

When I returned from the compound yesterday she was pretending to be asleep but her eyelids were fluttering like butterfly's wings. I adopted a nonchalant attitude. I raged inside but I said nothing of my forced containment in the compound. It confused her. She was so sure that finally I would lose control. I contained it with great difficulty. I must continue to do so or I am lost.

"Five thousand hectares, Jorge. All coffee. It covers hills and valleys."

Keeping my voice neutral, I remark, "And doubtless Bermudez will now turn it into a commune for the benefit of the poor workers who slaved on it for years."

Her black hair swirls as she shakes her head. "Roberto has decided that the *finca* will become a state guest house."

I laugh bitterly. "Presumably for the sole benefit of the heroic leaders of the revolution."

She flounces away to the window and over her shoulder says, "Don't they deserve something? Roberto fought for years. Endured great suffering. You think the people will begrudge him one *finca* out of thousands? He has given them freedom."

I desperately want her to understand. In the understanding maybe she will turn away from him. I know it is not irrevocable. She came back today. She is using me against him, just as she does the opposite.

I tell her, "Inez, freedom is equality. There cannot be oppression if there is equality. This country has had a history of oppression just as ours did. Bermudez overthrew that, but I tell you he will recreate it under a different name. It has happened so often before. The heroes become the new dictators. I have been in Russia. They have two peoples. Those who are inside the power system and those outside. There is no equality. Those inside have cars, colour TVs, coupons to special shops. They are proud of it – this corruption. Those outside spend half their lives queueing for a piece of meat. Bermudez will run down that road. I smell it

165

on him already. Ask yourself this: a quarter of a century ago Fidel made his revolution. Does he live in a palace? No, he lives in a small apartment. He owns no great estates . . . no *fincas* with antique furniture. After all these years, he works every day, sometimes sixteen hours . . . for the revolution . . . for Cuba. Now, Bermudez, in less than twenty days, is casting his eye over the country like a vulture. He wants a billion dollars from the Americans. How much will the people see of it?"

She turns and climbs on to the bed and sits cross-legged. There is malevolence in her eyes.

"You are jealous of him. You think you are so clever but he is cleverer. You are the same age, but he has already conquered a country, is already the leader of his people. He is clever, Jorge. Did you know that he sent General Lacay chasing after Cruz and his brigade? But he sent him as the nominal head of a Chamarrista column. And he promised that on his return he will be nominated as President for the coming elections. The old fool believed him. Here in the city he promoted close sympathisers to the second rank of the old National Guard. Soon the old officers will have lost control. Lacay will have an unfortunate accident and Roberto will oversee everything."

"He told you this?"

"Of course."

"He is a fool."

Her eyes flash in anger. "A fool! And what are you? You talk of what he has done in less than twenty days. What have you done? Has your American talked? No! Have you got one name? No! Roberto says that if after twenty days you have failed, then he will do it. He owes it to Fidel."

"What the hell are you talking about?"

She sees my fury and leans forward, feeding off it.

"Just that. Roberto thinks you are soft. Why spend twenty days?"

"You told him? About the twenty days?"

"Of course. Why not? Should it be a secret from him? He wants what you want. He knows exactly what you are doing. He gets reports."

"And he said that? After twenty days he will do it? How?"

She looks down at her vermilion finger nails, relishing her knowledge.

"How?!"

"He is clever. He expects the American allies will soon offer the aid package; there is much talk already the crisis will be over. If he tortures Peabody then there will be a worse crisis. They will invade. But he knows this information will only come from torture. So he will do it . . . Fombona will do it. Without leaving marks. Then they will give Peabody an injection. He will die. They have the drug. Vargas used it. Maybe the Americans gave it to him. It will seem like a heart attack. Even the best doctors cannot tell. They will be very sorry. Express much regret. Deliver the body with full honours. Roberto knows that Fidel will be grateful."

The scenario rips through my mind. I consider the angles. What would Fidel's reaction be? He would go with the odds. He is truly desperate for that name. The Americans have tried to kill him a dozen times. He would find no compassion. He would balance the danger. After all, the Chamarristas would do it, not him. For him it's a windfall. I could persuade him otherwise but I'm impotent. There is my radio contact from here but even if Bermudez would allow me a transmitter everything would definitely be decoded by the NSA computers. There is no friendly Embassy yet established with secure communication. I'm on my own. So is Peabody. He must talk within four days. I believe her. Bermudez would do it. He is drugged by his triumph. He walks above the ground. He even fucks this woman of mine. Everything falls at his feet. I know the experience. I admire and loathe him. His confidence will kill him. I tell her,

"Peabody will not talk under torture."

"Fombona tells him different."

"Fombona is a fool. So is Bermudez."

"He gets what he wants!"

She is wearing a thin cotton blouse. One nipple indents the cloth. She sees my eyes on it. She raises her right hand and circulates a finger at the centre of her other breast. The other nipple thrusts out.

"He can just look at me and bring out my little penis. You could never do that. He's a wonderful lover . . . superior to you."

I'm in the cage with nothing. She smells the odour. I grasp for control.

"So why are you here?"

She swings her feet to the ground – struts over and stands close to me.

"Jorge Calderon, you are finished . . . a failure. I like strength. I move from weakness to strength. Something went wrong with you. Just in the last few days. I don't know what. Maybe with the American. Roberto says the American is stronger than you. I came to get my clothes. A car waits. Jorge, you are . . . boring."

She spits in my face.

Control is gone. Some seconds pass. I hardly hear her screams. I don't hear the door opening. I only feel the throat under my thumbs. I don't hear their shouts or feel their hands pulling at me. I only see her eyes blazing triumphant in her reddening face. I pull away a hand and smash at it and feel a bone crunch. Then I am stunned with a blow to my head and she pulls away. I am lying on the carpet – my cheek is on it. She is laughing. My bodyguards help me to my feet. They are mumbling apologies, explaining that they could not let me kill her. She is sitting on the floor, her back to the foot of the bed. She is no longer beautiful. Her nose is twisted. Blood drips from it, unchecked, down her chin and on to her blouse. She is sobbing in triumph. I have a terrible pain in my head. I stumble as I walk to the table and pick up my files. An eternity passes while I fumble them into the bag. A bodyguard tries to help and I strike at him. They both stand clear as I walk carefully to the door. I don't look at her, but as I leave, her laughter sears my ear drums.

The Mestizo is again in the truck. He looks once at my face and turns away. My hands are still shaking – and my brain. I feel the lead of shame in my belly. I have grown so weak that I can no longer control myself. Peabody will look at me and

168

guess; will know that I've been beaten by that woman. He will not be impressed by me. Not after that. How can I make him believe even a small lie, now that my "essence" has gone?

By the time we reach the compound I'm more composed, but not enough to face him. I go straight to the residence; to his private suite. First I take a shower and reflect on the irony. He threw shit on me and I kept control. She threw words at me and I cracked.

After the shower, I go into his sitting room. There's a cocktail cabinet against the wall. I find a bottle of Royal Salute. Typical of him. He drinks little, but when he does it must be the best. I taste the whisky and for a moment consider getting drunk. No . . . no more weakness. I have to get my "essence" back. The only way is through Peabody. He must give me a name. Bermudez will be waiting. The witch will be waiting. Of course Fidel will be waiting. If I fail and Bermudez succeeds than I am finished in all their eyes – and my own.

I drink the last of the whisky and resolve that I will succeed. I will never lose control again. Quickly, I pick up my bag and walk to the guardhouse. I send the sleepy guard away, take out the file and unlock the door. I am sitting behind the desk looking at the file when he moves out and stands opposite the desk. I look up and my resolve is washed away. He is watching me, his head slightly on one side. There is concern in his eyes. Concern for me. I suddenly know what I feel for this man. It goes far beyond affection. It goes beyond what I felt for my grandfather. This man, this capitalist prude is closer to me than anyone I've ever known except my mother. It's not love. I can't find an expression for it. I don't want to.

"What happened to you, Jorge?"

My name "Jorge". It sounds so natural, this first time he uses it. It's unbelievable! I'm close again to losing control. I have to swallow hard.

"I tried to kill her."

Without taking his eyes off me he carefully sits down.

"What did she do?"

169

"Nothing unexpected. She left me for Bermudez. Her going was in keeping with her character. She was vicious. I allowed it to affect me, as she wanted. I was stopped from killing her. She enjoyed it."

After a thoughtful silence he says, "The same way that you enjoyed the risk when Fombona almost shot you on that first day."

He remains perceptive. Strangely, such a man understands people like myself – and like Inez. I give him his prize.

"Something like that."

"And when two people like that are together one loses and one wins."

"Yes."

"You fell in love . . . so you lost."

In a dozen words he has painted the exact picture. He makes more brush strokes. "And this loss is your first. Devastating. You never conceived it possible. You imagined yourself different from other mortals."

I am pinned and squirming. He has peeled me open like an over-ripe banana.

His voice changes tone. I feel like a boy as he gently says, "Jorge, bless your luck. Had you gone on that way your character would have fossilised . . . like mine. If that witch took away your arrogance . . . or made you aware of it, then she has done you a service beyond imagining. She may just have turned you into a human being."

It's all going wrong. I know what I have to do and I sit and listen . . . and believe. I want to sit and listen and talk for hours; and maybe find the paths I have never seen. Maybe learn to love someone other than an animal. Maybe understand that being the best is not always best. I cannot do it now, at this time. I have to save my confessor, and by saving him inflict him with his own tragedy. With an effort I put coldness into my voice. "Peabody, my situation is immaterial. We both indulge ourselves with emotions. Now circumstances have changed. It is vital, both for me and for you that you give me the name I want."

Very quietly and very firmly, he states: "Whatever happened and whatever comes, I will never do that."

170

I have difficulty looking at him. I centre the file in front of me – position the weapon exactly between us.

"Peabody, you know that name . . . and the others, because you advised the CIA. You advised them because over decades you built up a hatred for my country . . . and my leader. A hatred based on a tragic incident. That incident never happened."

I look at him now. He is puzzled.

"Never happened?"

"No. Amparo Flores did not die in a Cuban prison twenty-five years ago. She died in the finest Cuban hospital two years ago . . . ironically from cerebral thrombosis."

Tension is immediately in the room. The link between us is broken. All feeling for me leaves his voice.

"That's a foul lie to utter."

I now have to make my little lie. He will not believe yet. His memory will scream "lie", but then I have the next stage – and that must convince. With genuine sorrow I tell him: "A month after she enrolled at Havana University, Amparo Flores became an agent for Fidel Castro. She was a fervent believer in the revolution." I tap the file. "Her first assignment was to seduce a Colonel in Batista's National Guard and discover troop dispositions for defence of the city. She carried it out brilliantly. Her second assignment was to seduce the Political Councillor at the American Embassy . . . and influence him to the cause."

He is shaking his head, puzzlement still in his eyes. Puzzlement caused by these words coming from me. This lie being uttered by me. We are so close now. He must ask himself how I attempt such a cheap, unworthy trick. I force myself on.

"She also carried out that assignment brilliantly." Emphatically I tap the file. "You became almost an advocate for the cause. You fell in love with her." Again I tap the file. "You told her much about American policy – even as you argued against it. To keep you forthcoming she agreed to a betrothal. Peabody, when Havana abruptly fell to Castro her relief was boundless. Her assignment was over. But at the time, Castro did not want to alienate you or any other

171

Americans. He persuaded her to continue the assignment. Even urged her to marry you and go on supplying information and influence. She tried for another month. But then it was too much. She had met Raul Gomez who had fought with Castro throughout the struggle. They fell in love. You will know his name. He is now Assistant Minister for Agriculture. It was arranged that she would be arrested as a subversive. In due course her death was announced. In reality her name and papers were changed. She married Gomez secretly. Meanwhile you had predictably gone crazy and eventually had to be recalled."

He is a bearded statue, carved into the chair. I pause now, waiting for him to react. Needing him to react. To set himself up for the next lunge. He speaks and his voice is still puzzled.

"You cannot be telling me this. Not you. Stop it."

One small part of my mind revels in my skill. The rest is in pain. Another tap on the file. It is easier now. I am able to tell the truth.

"She worked as a teacher. In '63 she had a son – Luis. He went on to become a doctor. I know him. In '66 she had a daughter – Pilar. She is also a teacher . . . I know her."

His mouth opens and then closes. He is breathing deeply. He shakes his head again.

"Jorge, don't make these lies. They will change nothing. Why try to smear her memory? She never deserved it. I don't deserve it."

The moment has, at last, arrived, accompanied by ghouls dressed in black.

I open the file and slide out the photographs. Eight by ten enlargements. I push the first one over. Amparo Flores aged twenty-seven sitting in a chair smiling at the camera. She is holding a baby. Beside the chair is a boy of three clutching her arm.

I watch as he looks down at it. I wait, judging the moment, then reach out and place the second one on top: Amparo Flores aged thirty-nine. She is smiling at her tall, teenaged son who proudly holds a small silver cup won in a school athletics contest.

Peabody is frozen, but an aura of pain is emanating from

172

him. Very slowly, unwillingly, I reach forward and complete the pile with the last photograph: Amparo Flores aged forty-five. She is sitting at a restaurant table wearing a white dress, her hair piled high on her head. She is still remarkably beautiful. Her husband, Raul Gomez, is on her left. On her right sits Fidel Castro looking down at her appreciatively.

Still he doesn't move or utter a sound. This has to be the moment. Irrationally, I'm aware that if he actually survives this moment he is a dead man. To live he has to talk. For this reason, not thinking of myself, I concentrate all my skills. I must break through his silence. I must nudge him over the top and down to me. As though talking to a victim I quietly say, "You know these photographs are genuine. No science can fake her face or her expression . . . Jason, we did not kill her . . . you built a philosophy on a lie . . ."

Still not a flicker from him. His eyes are riveted on the photograph. On the only woman he ever loved. The only person he ever grieved over. On her, on her husband, and on Castro.

The moment is balanced. I dare not say another word. Doubts are building in me when the sound comes: a sob. Then another. Slowly he moves; his shoulders shake. There are drops wetting the gloss of her likeness. His head sinks. I watch in a storm of emotions as he slumps across the desk, as his sobs cry out for an explanation. I have won. He believes everything. This man who hasn't wept for an eternity, who for decades has hermetically sealed his emotions, has cracked open. I feel no elation, but strange and deep relief. I want to reach out and help. To absorb and take away at least some of his pain. I cannot. I must end it now. The sobbing has stopped. His cheek is lying on the photographs, his arms around his head. I repeat my words.

"Jason, you built a philosophy on a lie. Your logic was warped by hatred. It's over now. You know that. I'm appalled by what you've gone through. Not just now, but all those years. You've been forced to live inside that lie. It's over now."

I reach out and grip his elbow. "Jason, after that pain you can be yourself again. What you were thirty years ago. What you were trying to be with Vargas. You can find the ideals and emotions that you smothered . . . Jason, give me a name. Let it out of yourself . . ."

He raises his head. I am looking at a bearded skeleton. Cubelas looked like this when he finally talked. I wait for his quivering voice. I wait for the words.

They come in a whisper, but without a quiver. "Jorge, whatever I became after that lie, whatever I've done, whatever is done to me, I will never give you a name. I know the names; all of them. I will not betray them. I will not betray my country. Whatever that lie did to me. No matter what road I went down. I know that my country, for all its ills and mistakes, is a force for good in this world . . . I will not betray it."

The words, the quiet conviction of them, the astonishment of hearing them from a broken man, snap my control. I scream at his gaunt face.

"You are stupid! You are dumb! Just a stupid, dumb American!"

Through the haze of my rage his whispered words come back. "In a dictionary, dumb is defined as mute; silent. When it comes to betraying my country I'm proud to be dumb."

PEABODY
San Carlo
Night 16

I have lost the sense of time. Was it ten minutes or an hour ago when he stood up and walked out? He left his files on the desk. I can't find the desire to look at them. I sit in this chair and look at the wall. I sat for a while before a guard came, took away the files and locked the office door. It never occurred to me to walk out into the compound. I have nothing left now. Not even a memory.

Not so. I have the names and I must cling to them. They are the only threads to my sanity. I think about sanity. I'm aware of how close to the edge I am. I may have even dropped over. What a pathetic waste I've been, shuffling around on this earth. Half my life an idealistic fool; the other half a puritanical fop. Because a woman looked at me in a bar one night.

Shame and frustration well up as I recall my little story about falling in love; my homily about jealousy. But inside him, he was not laughing. How could that be? He knew everything, even then. Christ, I am so confused!

I hear the key turn. He comes in briskly, but his attitude is more resigned than confident. Over the past days I have been sledge-hammered into mental change. So has he.

He sits down and with an air of conclusion says, "Jason, it is time now to face reality. Your position is not good. I am going to tell you the situation. You are going to consider it and then reach a decision. There is no more time for sparring. I am going to talk to you and for your sake you must believe me."

My mind is a desert. Suddenly the palliasse becomes an inviting option. But there is a different intensity in him now. I try to concentrate.

"Why must I believe you?"

"Because of your very life. Listen, I accept that whatever I do I'm unlikely to get a name from you. What I do now is not a trick. Not part of an interrogation. What I do is for you."

"Then why do it?"

He is as numb as I. It shows in his eyes. He says, "I don't want you to die."

"Why?"

He turns his head and looks at the wall, makes a decision and says, "Because I cannot bear that thought . . . don't ask me more, please."

I don't ask. I know why. He feels as I do. I find myself clawing back to sanity.

"Why should I die?"

He tells me with precision.

"I told Inez that I was giving myself twenty days to break you. She told Bermudez."

"Inez?"

"The witch. Bermudez has delusions. The power has affected him. He's decided that after twenty days, if I don't have a name, he'll set Fombona on you and extract it . . . by torture."

His words are incredible but he states them with conviction. Before I can react he says, "First listen. The situation out there is changing fast. Bermudez is overwhelmed by himself . . . don't think it's my jealousy talking. He wants that name as a gift to Fidel. He also wants it to make me smaller. I cannot communicate safely with Fidel. I only have a radio code to give him a name or names."

I should be suspicious but I'm not.

"If you could communicate, what would he do?"

"My guess is let it happen. Jason, over the past twenty-odd years your people have tried to kill him time and again. Kennedy authorised it for sure. So did Johnson and Nixon and I wouldn't doubt those that followed. You know this better than me. Fidel knows what 'Operation Cobra' implies. He will take whatever information he can get . . . and not worry how he gets it."

176

The realisation is reaching me, but something is wrong. I concentrate again, then ask, "How can you believe that Bermudez would allow me, an Ambassador, to be tortured, knowing the consequences when my Government finds out as they surely must?"

Dismally, he completes the picture.

"I told you, he's deluded. Otherwise why would you be here now? I told Fidel, Bermudez is crazy. He'll let Fombona torture you without leaving a mark. Fombona will know how to do that. Afterwards they inject you with a drug. It will appear that you had a heart attack. This is feasible, Jason. I know about the drug. It exists. Afterwards the 'militant students' will make a regretful announcement and hand over your body to the 'authorities', who in turn will beat their breasts and give it back to your people."

With a chill I realise he's telling the truth, but still the whole scenario is preposterous. My sanity is firmly in place.

"Jorge, my people will know. Doesn't Bermudez realise the consequences?"

He sighs. "I told you, he's deluded. As a Marxist he shouldn't believe in God, but he does. He worships his maker . . . himself."

I think about torture. How would I react? I try to imagine the pain. Once when hiking in Maine, I slipped on a loose rock and fell down the side of a hill breaking my leg. I was alone and had to hop and drag myself to the nearest road, more than a mile away. The memory of the pain washes over me. Can it be worse than that? In a stark instant I realise that the pain alone will not constitute the torture. That will come from its being deliberately inflicted by another human being; by a human being who will draw pleasure from it.

He is watching. His eyes see into me, into my thoughts.

"Jason, this is not a trick. You must believe me. You must give me a name. I will send the coded signal and you will be safe. I cannot protect you if I don't have that name."

I can picture Fombona's face as he listens to my screams. For one wild moment a name, then more, are rushing from my brain to my lips. In the next moment my conscience

catches them. I shake my head. "I cannot do it, Jorge."
I am surprised by how much conviction I hear in my
voice. Apparently he is not. He merely nods thoughtfully.
There is a long silence while I contemplate my short future
and how I will face it, then he says firmly, "They will not
torture you."

I feel a surge of relief, mingled with anger. It was a trick
after all and I nearly fell for it. I burst out: "That's a filthy
thing to do."

His smile is wan. "They will not torture you because I will
leave here in the morning and signal Fidel two coded names.
Those that I suspect the most: Pineda and Samarriba."

Those eyes are totally alert as he says the names. While I
keep my expression neutral I marvel at his perception. One
of them is correct. I shrug negatively. With resignation he
continues. "With the names, I will signal the words: 'Hold
until my arrival.' Fidel will do that. He will not let anyone
else interrogate them. I will go overland to Managua and
then fly to Havana. Of course I may be right in my guesses.
Then so much the better. If not, I will drag out the interrogations. When you are free – and I think it will not be too
long – then I will release them and tell Fidel the truth and
take the consequences."

Fombona's image fades from my mind. I am almost
paralysed with gratitude. I manage to ask, "What will be the
consequences?"

He smiles and it lights the room. "I don't know, Jason. I
know Fidel well but I cannot imagine what he will do. It will
give me much to think about in the coming days. I will have
to be a brilliant lawyer and argue my own case."

I have a feeling of helplessness. He is destroying his own
life to save mine; and telling me about it with a smile. I
search around in my mind.

"Jorge, if you are right, and if I get out of here soon, there's
a way I can help. So far, we didn't manage to overthrow or
kill Castro. I can tell you that we're no longer trying to kill
him. That policy's changed. But the CIA still has a strong
presence in Havana. There's a good chance they could get
you out. You could have a new life in the States."

He smiles again. "Thanks, but no. My failure here hasn't changed my convictions. I'll go on with my old life . . . wherever it leads. Anyway forget that. Things are about to change. I feel it. Like they used to say in your old westerns; 'It's too darned quiet out thar.' I think there will be some action soon. You will lead your life – I will lead mine."

JORGE
San Carlo
Night 16

He looks dubious – even disheartened. Not for a second did I consider his offer. Whatever has happened, or is to come, I, Jorge Calderon, will not run from it.

There is a tap on the door and I call "Enter."

I know it is the Mestizo boy and I know what he brings. I had ordered it in the residence kitchen half an hour ago.

The boy approaches nervously, puts the tray on the desk between us and then scuttles out. I watch Peabody closely. His eyes are fixed on the tray and its contents. There is a look of disbelief on his face. His brain is refusing to accept the message from his eyes. It is as though he is studying a mirage. Then literally, his nose twitches. His doubts are washed away. No mirage could give off such an aroma.

On the tray is a large oval plate from the residence. In the centre of it is a juicy sirloin steak, slightly underdone. It is flanked by twin hillocks of french fried potatoes and deep-fried onion rings. Beside the plate is a wine glass, a bottle of vintage Robert Mondavi and a corkscrew with a silver handle.

He is running his tongue across his lips. He cannot shift his gaze from the plate. I say, "When you finish that you can go to the residence. The water in your bathroom is hot. Your soaps and shampoos are all there."

With a visible effort he raises his head, looks at me and nods. Then he reaches for the bottle of wine and the corkscrew.

I find my own gaze transfixed on the steak. Perversely I realise that it's a symbol of my failure. It lies there glistening in its juices – a carnivorous mockery of my ineptitude. I feel a rage building in my guts. He is very carefully removing the foil from the bottle. Holding it still so as not to disturb the wine.

The rage is moving up to my chest as he eases out the cork, unscrews it and raises it to his nose. Satisfied, he places it on the tray, picks up the bottle and half fills the glass. He swirls the wine a little, then lifts it to his nose. I can practically feel the bouquet going all the way down to his toes. My own rage has risen to my head. He takes a sip, nods in satisfaction and then says apologetically, "Jorge, I forget myself. Won't you join me? Call for another glass."

My rage explodes. I hear my voice screaming at him.

"Fucking hell! You sit there like you're in some private fucking club in Washington! You can't wait to bite into that steak but you fart about opening the wine and sniffing it like it's liquid gold, and preparing yourself to eat like a fastidious cat pawing at a cockroach. Fuck you!"

I lunge forward and pull the tray across the desk. Some wine spills from the glass. I can still hear my voice – words tumbling out in frustration.

"Fuck you! I'm the one who's going to suffer. I don't get a name – you don't get a fucking steak!"

I grab the knife and fork, cut a piece of meat and raise it slowly to my mouth. It's red rare and dripping juice. He stares at it with awful fascination. At the first bite my rage is washed away; also my self-pity. What have I been reduced to? I chew mechanically, swallow and quietly tell him, "Don't worry. I indulge myself. That was the last edge to my spleen."

I push the tray back.

He is watching me suspiciously. I gesture reassuringly at the plate. Quickly he picks up the knife and fork, cuts a slice and pops it into his mouth.

But wait! It is not delicious. I have a bitter aftertaste in my mouth and my gums begin to feel numb. Suddenly I feel the pain – like a white-hot knife being plunged into my guts. I realise in an instant. Poison! The Mestizo boy! He asked me twice in the kitchen,

"It's for the Ambassador? The American?"

And when he put the tray down his hands were shaking. He's been out of the compound. Someone got to him. Another searing spasm of pain, then I realise that Peabody is chewing. I scream.

"No! Wait! Don't eat!"

He pulls back in his chair, suspicion and consternation in his eyes. He chews rapidly. I hurl myself across the desk scattering the plate and wine, smashing into him with my forearm. He goes over backwards with me on top. I hear and feel the back of his head crack on the concrete. He lies stunned while I push fingers between his teeth, praying that the meat's still there. It is at the top of his throat. I pull it out and throw it across the room. The wine bottle has rolled to the edge of the desk and is spilling its contents. I grab it. His eyes are open now, looking up at me in shock. I push the neck of the bottle against his lips and hiss at him,

"The meat was poisoned! Wash your mouth out. Don't swallow! Wash and spit out."

He sucks the wine in. I roll away from him with spasms of pain spreading out from the centre of my body. My knees come up to my chin. I have never known such pain. I realise with cold clarity that it's the prelude to death. I force a finger down my throat trying to vomit but it's too late.

He is beside me, an arm cradling my head; his voice urgent.

"I'll call someone. They'll get you to hospital."

I shake my head. "I'm done, Jason. It was meant for you. The Mestizo boy. Your people tried to kill you."

I can feel death coming. It marches in time to the spasms. He sees it also. His eyes are wet. I have to tell him.

"Jason, I lied . . . listen to me. You have to know . . . Amparo loved you. It's true she didn't die in '59. True she married Gomez . . . true she died two years ago . . . but she loved *you*, Jason. She would have married you . . . wanted to. Fidel wanted her to . . . and keep passing information . . . he had a hold over her . . . but she was ashamed at already betraying you . . . could not go on . . . so she chose the other way . . . but she loved you . . . it's the truth, Jason . . . believe me . . . I lied, I had to . . . but please believe me now."

182

Through the agony I feel his other arm come around my shoulders. He holds me tight and says, "I believe you, Jorge."

I see his face through the haze and it shows that he does believe me. The pain, like guilt after a confessional, seems to be washed away. I'm aware of my limbs moving but I cannot feel them . . . I can only feel his arms holding me . . .

His body convulses. I draw him closer. His face against my chest, my arms holding him. More convulsions. I put my lips by his ear. I can hardly talk but I force the words out.

"You are as my son . . . Jorge . . . you are as my son."

His fingers grip me as a vice. I am sobbing in time with his convulsions. Suddenly, abruptly, he is still.

I hold him as time passes. I know he is dead. I think about natural justice. Is there ever a jury? What judge pronounces the sentence? What fingers manipulate our lives? Just twice in over sixty years I felt bonded to another human being. Always so brief and then taken away. I run my fingers through his hair, straightening it. Yes, it needs more lemon juice. It is damp. My tears have made it damp.

There is a noise at the door. I look up to see a face. It disappears. I hear shouting outside. Within a minute Fombona crashes in, sub-machine-gun pointed. Others crowd in behind him.

"What happened?"

I resolve, at this moment, not to speak another word. Even if I have to be mute for the rest of my life.

They have to prise him out of my arms. One of the guards punches me in the face and Fombona hurls him across the room in anger.

"Don't mark him! I don't want a mark on him!"

They take Jorge away and leave me lying on the floor. Time passes. I hear a distant, single shot. More time and then Fombona comes again. He walks past me and opens the cell door.

"Get in there!"

I decide not to move. There is a pause and then I hear him move. I feel his fingers in my hair and I scream at the sudden agony as he drags me across the floor and into the cell. I look up at him standing at the door. His face radiates anticipation.

"You will scream some more, pig. Tomorrow I get some equipment here and you scream and scream . . . and you will talk."

The door closes.

I will not talk.

SLOCUM
Fort Bragg
Day 17

I wait beside the Grumman Trader. My brownies plus
Newman, Allen and all the equipment left three hours ago,
just before I got the call to wait so that Komlosy could brief
me personally. I'm coldly excited. I've been this way for
eight hours since Komlosy's tinny voice came through the
gizmo telling me that the other operation fucked up and
we're going in. The old "hex" worked. I sent vertical mental
thanks to the Almighty – and my old grandpappy who is
surely up there with Him. I'm excited but also very pissed
off with Mother Nature and a lady called Olga. She's a
hurricane which at this time of year has no business lurking
around between Venezuela and Haiti. The met. boys just
shook their heads in puzzlement and gave me the comforting
news that it's been thirty years since a hurricane was in
that area so late. Olga is capricious. For twelve hours she
moved north-east out of contention. We all breathed easier.
Then she stopped, went around in a little circle and headed
north-west. Not good but not catastrophic. She would have
hit East Jamaica and then Cuba and serve the bastards
right; but after six hours she slowed and is now heading
south-east of the "Nimitz". She keeps that up and Olga's
gonna be a goddam problem. Grant and the brass must be
wetting themselves with delight. They know that our Ultras
can't operate if the wind is gusting over forty-five knots.
Right now it's up to thirty over the "Nimitz" and if Olga
keeps coming it's gotta get worse.

I'm putting a "hex" on Olga but it's not easy to make a
goddam hurricane grow hair. I'm working hard on it when I
hear the chopper. It lands about a hundred yards away.

186

Komlosy and Al Simmons step down. Simmons is holding on to his newly braided cap. Komlosy's holding on to his hair. As the chopper's rotor stops I walk over to meet them. I shake Komlosy's hand and grin at Simmons. He's got his stars up and is a bit self-conscious. I ask, "Do I have to kiss your ass now, Al?"

He grins. "Hear this, you black mother – you ever come near my ass an' I'll post you to Alaska with nothin' more than a jock strap!"

Komlosy's very uptight. "What about this goddam hurricane, Silas?"

I try to be reassuring. "The met. boys say it's gotta start moving soon, probably north-west which would be just about okay. If she heads towards the 'Nimitz' we could have a three to four day non-operational period."

"Damn!"

I point out, "Sir, for a lot of that time under such conditions not even choppers could operate. I'm sure Grant has gone into an 'I told you so' mode, but hell, under his plans they wouldn't even be ready for another couple of weeks. You should point that out."

He smiles. "I didn't have to. The President did just that. I guess I'm on edge because it's all so imminent. Anyway three or four days is not that vital any more. By the way Al has a personal message for you."

Simmons is a tall gangly cat approaching sixty. He has straw-coloured hair and a face that looks as if he's always about to tell a joke. At this moment he's very serious. So is his voice.

"Colonel, the Commander-in-Chief asked me to convey his entire confidence in you and your men. He is sure that as a result of your forthcoming action our citizens will be safely returned and our country's honour upheld. He is looking forward to welcoming you and your team at the White House."

I've got a goddam lump in my throat! I'm trying to think of a suitable solemn reply when a jeep pulls up. Simmons says, "I'm going to pick up my kit. I'll be back in ten minutes."

He climbs into the jeep and as it pulls away I ask Komlosy, "What happened to the other operation?"

He grins. "Apparently they poisoned the wrong guy. Our agents report that the Cuban was delivered to the morgue . . . stiff."

"And what about our agent in the compound?"

He loses his grin. "Silas, we have to assume he's dead. He was a young Mestizo who worked in the kitchen."

I'm puzzled. "But why would he take that risk? He must have known what would happen."

Komlosy nods solemnly. "He knew. He was one of twelve children. Very poor family. We guaranteed to get his entire family out of the city and into the countryside . . . and then to a new life in the States . . . he sacrificed himself."

This news gives me pause for thought. Komlosy reads the thought and says, "You're thinking about those explosive jackets. If that kid died for his family then maybe Bermudez did find twenty-seven fanatics who would die for his revolution."

I speak emphatically, partly to reassure myself. "No way, Mike. Those jackets are dummies. Anyway whether they are or not doesn't change the plan. We go in assuming they're real. We neutralise the fanatics first."

He nods thoughtfully and then muses, "Silas, you pull this one off an' there's no limit to how far you can go. You know that."

I voice some thoughts that have been in my mind for the past few days.

"We'll pull it off, Mike. You can call it ego but this is the first operation that I've conceived totally myself and that I'm going to lead myself. But after it's over I'm thinking of taking early retirement."

His face shows his surprise.

"Why would you do that? Hell, you're only forty-six. You don't want to be a General?"

"No, Mike. I've been in this army since I was eighteen. There's bin good times an' bad. I don't regret any of it. I came from nothin' and the army gave me a good life, but this operation is my swan song. I want to do somethin' else."

"What?"

"Don't laugh, but I'm gonna be a rancher. Never spent much money – saved most of it. Coupla years back I bought a small spread in Wyoming. Not big, but enough for me. It's tucked in right under the Rockies. It's got a pineboard cabin on it – not much but comfortable. I'll get a couple of bird dogs an' walk behind them of an evenin'."

He's got a smile on his face.

"What's so goddam funny?"

It widens to a grin. "I'm picturing you as a cowboy. Where are you gonna find a horse big enough to lump you around?"

I'm stuck for a quick retort and he turns serious again. "Silas, you're an enigma. Have you got any real close friends?"

"What would you call a friend?"

Thought lines appear across his forehead and I sense I'm going to get a deep answer. He starts slowly.

"Silas . . . I guess a friend is, well . . . the rare person who can listen to your problems without getting even the slightest satisfaction from knowing they're happening to you and not to him. Someone who's comfortable with you in a silence . . . I guess a real friend never competes with you . . . someone who knows how and when to take . . . not just to give."

"That's real poetic, Mike."

"Yeah. Do you have any friends like that?"

"Nope."

"Not ever? I would have thought that army life generated those kind of friendships."

I feel the incongruity of the situation. I'm about to step into an aircraft and go off and risk my life and he's waxing philosophical. I like the guy but he makes me a little uncomfortable.

"Mike, army life does just that for most people, but I guess I'm a loner."

He's looking puzzled, almost hurt.

"But not one friend? It's not natural."

I sigh. "There was a guy once. We got kinda close . . . real close. I guess he was a bit like a younger brother."

"What happened?"

"It was in 'Nam. He got taken out by one of our own air strikes. A pilot fucked up and got his co-ordinates wrong."

"Were you very cut up?"

"Sure. I was the guy who called in the air strike."

He looks thoughtfully out across the airfield. A pair of F16s are taking off in tandem; there's a red glow from their afterburners. I recall other times when people got philosophical when they were seeing someone off into action. Someone who might not come back. They get a strange urge to bond themselves; to associate with the fear or the danger ... or the thrill. The F16s leave behind a growing quietness; and a kind of vacuum around us. Softly he asks, "Black or white?"

"What?"

"That solitary friend."

"Black."

Again silence, then, "You think real friendship can ever bridge that barrier?"

My answer comes easy. It's the product of a lifetime's cogitation.

"Nope."

He smiles but there's no humour in it. "Silas, that's cynical. You're not telling me there are no close friendships between people of different colours."

"There are exceptions that prove the rule."

"But why should there be rules?"

Again I'm feeling uneasy, wanting Simmons to return and end this dialogue. But Komlosy's expression is earnest. I try to make him understand.

"Why should there be colour? Why should I be black and you white? It's God or nature ... or whatever. Maybe over a few million years – or sooner, if the goddam geneticists get their way – it will change and we'll all be a pale mud colour – or somethin'. Meanwhile because we're different, we think different. Not better or worse ... just different. The kind of thing you were talking about ... that kind of a bond. People look for that among their own kind. It's natural."

190

He shrugs resignedly and I sense an air of disappointment.

"But Mike, like I said, there are exceptions."

He smiles wryly. "Sure."

With relief I hear the jeep coming. It swings around in front of us and Simmons climbs out. The driver quickly runs round to get his kit bag but Simmons waves him away and lifts it out himself. Three stars are not about to change that cat. He walks to the Trader, hefts his bag inside and then comes over.

"You ready, Silas?"

"Yessir, General."

He gives me a look that says, 'Don't sass me just because I've got some stars up'. I'm gonna enjoy teasing this cat. He shakes Komlosy's hand warmly.

"Mike, thanks for everything. Sleep easy. We'll be back with them real soon."

Komlosy slaps him on the shoulder. "Good luck, Al. You've done a great job getting it all set up . . . just a great job."

Simmons glances between me and Komlosy, then turns away saying, "I'll see you in the plane, Silas."

Komlosy holds out his hand. I grip it and say, "Mike, thanks for giving me the chance. I won't let you down."

He smiles. "It's kinda odd being thanked for giving a guy a damned good chance to get killed." His smile fades. "I just wish I could share the danger with you. I'm gonna feel damned helpless just sitting behind a desk."

His emotion is tangible, and it's communicated to me. His Adam's apple bobs as he swallows. I feel a surge of affection for him. Lightly I say, "Remember that ol' cat Milton? Used to be a runnin' back fo' the Packers 'fore he took up on that poetry. He once wrote, 'They also serve who only stand and wait', or somethin' like that."

He smiles and suddenly we're embracing in a bear hug. His fingers dig fiercely into my shoulders. Close to my ear he says quietly, "Silas, know this. If ever I'm in a hole like those hostages there's no one in the world I'd rather have come to get me but you."

I slap him on the back and turn to the plane. I must be getting goddam soft. I can't say anything because I'm scared my goddam voice will quiver!

Al and I are the only passengers. We sit in companionable silence while the Trader climbs to cruising altitude. He's probably thinking about the mission. I'm not. My head is full of the recent conversation with Komlosy. I sure can bullshit sometimes. Such bullshit that I damned near believe it myself. Why do I always have to project the big black tough guy image? The lone old bull elephant wandering majestically through the goddam jungle. Majesty – shit! May's words come back through twenty years carried on the end of a branding iron to singe themselves on my brain.

"Silas, I don't understand it much either. I know you love me an' I sure love you. But Silas, I need you and you don't need me. It's taken me two years to face up to that. You don't need me or anyone else. I don't want to be a dependent woman all my life. If we have children they'll look up to you and need you. But that need won't ever come back. I've got to find a man who needs me . . . just as much as I need him."

I can see her face as she spoke those words. Earnest, sad, intelligent and beautiful. I took it on the chin like a big tough bull should and pushed along through the jungle. It took five years 'til I woke up one night and realised that I'd rather have May than a super-tough image. Five goddam years! I traced her to a suburb of Fort Lauderdale. She had married an engineer just six months after our divorce came through. I had to know, so I took some furlough, flew over there and hired a car. I located her house and cruised by it a few times. It was a nice home. Single storey, brick built, with a big, well-kept garden. The husband had to be at work so I parked at the corner and told myself I ought to go over and visit. Hell, why not? Just kinda say hello and ask how she'd been. Nothin' wrong with that. I sat there for an age tellin' myself there was nothin' wrong with that, but unable to get out of the car. Then she came round the back of the house pushing a pram. She walked down the drive and crossed the street right in front of me. She didn't notice me. Her whole attention was on the occupant of the pram. She was heart-stoppingly beautiful – and transparently happy.

So I went and crawled back under my tough bull image and let all those thoughts wither away until my mind was like an elm tree in winter.

Friendship. What the shit do I know about that? Guys as tough as me don't have friends. That emotional junk is for softies. So what about Luther? Sure he was a friend and knew it, but tough old Major Silas Slocum never gave a damn thing away. When that half-assed pilot rocketed Luther I collected a body bag and stuffed in all the little bloody bits and pieces I could find. The old bull never showed a sign. I heard the whispered comment by one of my men as we choppered back. "Sheeit! Slocum could have bin in a restaurant stuffing leftovers into a doggy bag!"

But my men weren't there when the tough old bull was in his bunk that night and couldn't understand the tears that wet his face and the pain that cut through his heart. And the many nights that followed and the final resolution that, for a guy like me, having a friend was an emotional liability I didn't need.

"Silas, you're looking glum. Somethin' bothering you?"

The words snap me out of my reverie.

"Nossir, General! It's just the light flashin' off all those stars kinda dazzles mah eyes."

"Cut the crap, Silas. You were responsible for my getting them. You bring those hostages out and you'll have one too. Ease up on me, okay?"

"Okay, Al. The crap is cut. I'm glad you got 'em; you sure as hell deserve them."

I don't tell him about my thinking of retiring; nor about the ranch. I'm in no mood for more explanations. Fact is the whole idea is terrifying. Trouble with me is that if I take a decision I gotta go through with it. For sure, tough guys don't go back on decisions. I remember buying that ranch. Heard about it from a soldier who came from the area. The old owner had died and the bank had taken it over. The bank manager was one of those types who walk across broken glass to prove how liberal they are. I went to see him in full uniform, complete with fruit salad. He was impressed to all hell and I got a good deal on the ranch. I had no exact idea when I'd leave the army but decided it would be before I was fifty. The ranch is in a mainly white area. I found one old black guy, out of work for a few years, to look after the place. He told me that the white community – the ranchers and the farmers – were cut up about my buying the place. Explained kind of apologetically that basically they were good people but farmers and the like were inherently conservative and a black rancher in their midst was hard to take. There wouldn't be any trouble but I was likely to be socially ostracised.

I had grinned and told him I didn't give a flying fart. But since then I've changed my views. I bought a lot of books on ranching and subscribed to several magazines on the subject. It quickly came home to me that ranching involved a mite more than sitting on my homestead patio with straw in mouth and cold can of beer in hand watching my contented cows chewing the goddam cud. Like everything else, technology has come swinging in to baffle simple straightforward guys like myself. These days a rancher needs to be a mixture of biologist, veterinary surgeon, artificial inseminator, nutritionist and computer programmer. The cowpoke bit has been elbowed on to a back burner. I'm sure gonna need friendly help from people who've spent their lives at it. And there's another thing. I might not have friends in the army to fit Komlosy's parameters, but I enjoy sitting around in the mess of an evening chewing the fat with a few of the guys about the day's events, and trading a little professional small talk. For sure I'm gonna want to do that in my new profession, but how? If those guys won't even talk to me it's gonna be a lonely existence. I take a little comfort from the thought that if I pull those hostages out unscathed I'm gonna be some kind of a hero. I don't give a shit about that but it might soften the bigots up a bit. The thought brings my mind squarely back to the operation. From now on there's gonna be no extraneous thoughts. Forget everything else, Slocum. Be a soldier now – only a soldier.

PEABODY
San Carlo
Day 18

I try to imagine describing it to someone. How to convey the
bodily agony and the mental degradation. The terror to the
mind so finely tuned to every flayed nerve ending. Fombona
is a master of the putrid practice. Torture stretches our
species' depravity beyond any possible comparison. No
other animal on earth contemplates it. The evil of sadism is
confined to mankind and as it oozes through the veneer of
culture like a foul fungus it mocks all pretensions of moral
ascendancy over other creatures.

I have read many descriptions by people who have
endured torture, and their reactions. I realise now that it is
like reading the attempted description of an incomparable
odour. Imagination is meaningless.

It starts in the mind. Trepidation rising to panic hardly
conveyed my feelings as I waited for him to return with his
"equipment". Sleep was impossible. I sat with my back to
the hard wall and tried to prepare myself. Solzhenitsyn had
once written on the subject. His thesis was relatively simple:
first imagine that you're dead already. There's nothing
anyone can do to a dead man. Assume that your life is over
and finished and therefore expect nothing. You become an
inanimate object impervious to the will of others. Simple.
Solzhenitsyn, I have news for you. Your thesis gave me a
crumb of comfort during the night of waiting, but a fraction
of a second after Fombona began, your theory was dust
beneath the convulsive ripple of agony. Maybe you could do
it. Maybe your mind is so staggeringly great you could
convince your body that the pain is illusory; that the nerve
endings are deluding themselves. I am a mere mortal. I'll

know I'm dead when the pain stops. I'll be convinced then.

The night passed with dreadful speed. Shortly after dawn I heard the squeak of the gates and the motor of the truck and Fombona's voice shouting orders. Minutes accelerated into seconds. I could feel my heart and the coppery taste of fear on my tongue and gums. Then the key turning and Fombona at the door with a smile on his face and pleasure in his eyes.

He supervised the installing of the "equipment" with the air of a house owner arranging the deployment of a new suite of furniture. "Over there," he commanded as two guards struggled to get a heavy canvas-covered object through the door. Grunting with exertion they manoeuvred it near to the far wall. Fombona eyed it critically.

"Bring it out a bit . . . a bit more. Careful, you fools! Don't damage my beauty."

There followed a high, small-topped table, a canvas bag, several rolls of thick black cloth and two large buckets of water. He had the table positioned beside an electric socket and the bag, buckets and cloth put beside it. The guards were dismissed and the door closed. The key was not turned. An irrational moment as I contemplated trying to run for the door. Then the icy reality of my situation prevailed.

Fombona was standing in the centre of the room watching me with his head slightly on one side. Anticipation radiated from him.

"Okay, pig. Here's how it is. You give me one name or in a few minutes you start to experience pain that you never knew existed."

I took a long, slow swallow and shook my head. Immediately I saw the relief in his smile.

"Good! Then you will give me all the names. Every one of them. Believe me, pig."

I held up a hand and was relieved to see it was not shaking. Also that my voice was clear of any tremor.

"Listen, filth, I know the outcome. If I talk I die immediately. Calderon told me. An injection – simulated heart attack. Not a mark on me. Your promises of relief if I talk will convince me of nothing."

He is not at all disconcerted.

"So talk now, pig, and you won't have to go through it. No pain – nothing. You can go back to join the other pigs."

"Lies! If I give you a name I'll die anyway. Those cretins Bermudez and Castro won't want it known that I've talked. They'll want the operation to go ahead so they snuff out other dissidents. If I talk now I die anyway."

He chuckled. "You're a clever pig. No matter; you will talk, and soon." His voice becomes conversational. "A few weeks ago we caught a captain of the National Guard. I and my friend Umberto interrogated him. After two days I brought a handgun into the cell. I told him there was just one bullet in the chamber, then I handed him the gun. Umberto and I were two metres away in front of him. He knew he could kill either one of us. He also knew that the other one would continue the torture . . . so he put the gun to his own head and pulled the trigger."

My face must have showed something. The swine laughed and said, "Of course there was no bullet." He laughed again. "He died after six days and all those days he begged for death . . . you will beg for that needle and believe me it won't take six days . . . it won't take two. Those names will be your passport out of hell. You will give them to me with joy in your voice."

He turned away rubbing his hands. "Let us prepare. I will introduce you to 'El Abrazo' – the embracer."

Theatrically he pulled off the canvas cover. I stared at it with morbid fascination. It was like a great wooden barrel sliced lengthways and mounted on a stand. Its dark surface was broken by gleaming metal studs spaced about four inches apart. There were leather thongs hanging from the corners. He ran his hand over it affectionately.

"This is not the natural colour of the wood. It's been stained by the blood of hundreds. Men, women, even children. Vargas used to watch . . . sometimes take part. But he was not good. Too impatient. I am not impatient, pig."

He fetched the rolls of black cloth and started draping them over the studs, musing. "What a pity I am not allowed to let your blood add to the stains . . . How I would like to see your blood. If I were allowed to mark you I would strap a funneled cage of hungry rats to your ass. They would gnaw their way up your rectum and into your bowels and eat you from the inside out. You will not bleed now, but I promise you it will not be comfortable riding 'El Abrazo'. The two of you will become intimate."

I could feel my limbs going rigid with fear. Of course the mental torture had already begun. He was working trepidation up into terror. He walked to the door, opened it and beckoned. There was a brief, whispered conversation. Then he turned back grinning. From the canvas bag he lifted a black metal box trailing three wires. One ended in a plug. The other two, longer and thicker, were each attached to a silver-coloured crocodile clip.

Still grinning, he held the apparatus up for my inspection. With a strange clarity I noted the single switch and the dial with its graduated colours: vectors of yellow, blue, green and red.

"Excellency, meet 'El Rompecabezas' – the tickler." He nodded with his chin to the barrel. "'El Abrazo' and 'El Rompecabezas' are partners. One lovingly embraces . . . the other tickles." He put the box carefully on to the table and pointed. "The switch turns on the current. The dial is a rheostat. The yellow sector gives a moderate current. It increases through the blue and green. Red is usually fatal." He smiled. "This time we will be in the yellow zone nudging up towards the blue. Next time we will go higher . . . much higher."

By this point I was mentally numb. I had one wrenchingly hopeful thought that this was all a slowly building bluff to terrorise me into talking; but it quickly faded. It was all part of the torture.

He plugged in the box just as there was a tap on the door. A guard came in carrying a large tabby cat. I recognised it as belonging to Mrs Walsh. She had brought it with her from the States. Its legs were bound back and front by cloth. The guard handed it to Fombona and then stood by the door watching with interest. Fombona held it gently and tickled it behind the ear and crooned soft words. It visibly relaxed. In the small room I could actually hear it purr.

"A little demonstration," Fombona said, watching me closely.

I had decided, with Jorge lying dead in my arms, that I would not utter a single word. I knew what was coming but he would not get the satisfaction of hearing me say a thing.

With the cat in one hand and the two thick grey wires in the other, he moved to the barrel. Gently he laid the cat on the curved black surface and again tickled it behind the ear. It lay still while he carefully attached the crocodile clips. One to the tip of its ear and the other to its tail. He moved back to the box and set the dial at the beginning of the yellow zone. His fingers moved to the switch.

"Watch, pig!"

I wanted to close my eyes but could not. I heard the sharp click of the switch. The cat jerked upwards, its hair straightened and it was like a hedgehog; emitting an unearthly shriek. It rolled down the side of the barrel as Fombona quickly turned the dial through into the red zone. It was so stiff it bounced as it hit the floor and then lay still. Fombona shook his head.

"Can't have noises like that. The other hostages might get the wrong idea."

He pats the obscene box happily. "But 'El Rompecabezas' is functioning well, and impatient to make your acquaintance."

He looked at the guard and gestured. The guard walked round the barrel, unclipped the cat and picked it up by the tail. It swung grotesquely as he carried it out leaving an odour of singed hair.

Fombona reached down into the bag and took out several rolls of bandages and put them on the table. Then he pulled out a white bundle and unrolled it. In my mental state I didn't comprehend at first what it was. Then he slipped it on – a doctor's coat. He smiled at me and again reached into the bag. This time it was a stethoscope which he hung around his neck with a broad grin.

"Doctor Carlos Fombona at your service, Excellency. I

was in fact a medical student for a year. Not a good one but I learned a few things. For a man of sixty-three you are in good health but sometimes 'El Rompecabezas' can upset the heart. You will be glad to know that I will keep monitoring yours."

He gestured at the barrel. I forced movement into my legs and edged away to a corner. I had a sudden inspiration. They would have to force me. I would fight like hell and they would have to mark me – bruise me. That would be evidence. Retribution would come to all of the bastards. I clenched my hands into fists and crouched, filled with rage and terror. Fombona shrugged and shouted an order.

Four of them crowded into the cell. Fombona said harshly, "Whoever marks him will follow him on to 'El Abrazo'."

They approached cautiously. One of them held a grey blanket loosely over one arm. They were very practised. I was not. One made a feint for my left wrist. I lashed out at him, striking only air and losing my balance. Then darkness as the blanket enveloped my head, and arms clasped me. I kicked out and connected and there was a grunt of pain and then hands were gripping my waist and ankles and I was helpless and the terror was rising.

I was lifted and laid down on my back. I could feel the studs under the layers of cloth and could imagine the pain had they been unpadded. The blanket was pulled away and there was light and Fombona's face leering over me.

"First his ankles. Hold him tight."

I felt something being wrapped around my left ankle.

"Bandages," Fombona remarked. "They will stop the leather from chafing your delicate skin."

I had an inconsequential realisation. Fombona, who normally spoke with grunts and words of one syllable, was now articulate. His pleasure at the proceedings had made him so.

I kept still as they bandaged my ankles. It lulled them and, as they fumbled with my right wrist, I abruptly jerked it towards my face, turned my head and bit deeply into the arm of the guard holding me. He screamed shrilly, pulling away and leaving skin on my teeth. I saw his other wrist raised and

200

then a crack as Fombona smashed the side of his hand across his face. I heard him hit the floor with a thud and Fombona's growled order, and a slithering as they dragged him out. They were no longer lulled and quickly finished the bandaging. I gasped in pain as my arms were forced backwards and down over the slopes of the barrel, and Fombona murmured, "Wait, pig. Just wait."

With the thongs tied, I was stretched as though on a rack, and after only seconds began to feel the aching pain spreading; moving from my arms into my shoulders and across my chest and back. I heard Fombona dismiss the guards; the tramp of feet and the closing of the door. Silence. It was about to happen. The pain in my arms and shoulders was almost unbearable. Desperately I tried to prepare my mind. Repeated to myself that I would not utter a word, no matter what. I could hear and feel my short breathing, every sound magnified in the stillness, but suddenly his face was above me and I had not heard him approach. He must have moved like a cat. The associated thought made my breathing even faster. I thought again of Solzhenitsyn's thesis. I was dead already. I'd ceased to exist. Nothing mattered.

The end of the stethoscope was swinging gently, inches above my nose. I was mesmerised by it. Then he moved. Its round flat end was lowered on to my chest with his finger on it. A horrible parody: he listened intently, moved it a little and listened again. His lips were pursed in his broad dark face; cruel eyes narrowed in concentration. There were fine beads of sweat on his forehead below the black brush-cut hair. He nodded slowly.

"Good. Beating fast but sound. A good heart. It will stand much."

He disappeared from my view. I strained my ears for a sound but heard nothing. Then a slight scrape and suddenly my chin was pulled roughly back and fingers were digging in on each side above my jaw, forcing open my mouth. Something hard was pushed in between my teeth and below my tongue. I gagged as I tasted rubber.

"A bone for the dog." His voice was very quiet but very

201

clear. "To stop you biting your tongue . . . and to muffle your screams. Now we make it secure."

He pulled my head up by my hair. I could feel the cloth strips being pulled tight under my ears and fingers fumbling at the nape of my neck as he tied the knots. The rubber tasted foul. I could hardly move my mouth and had to breathe through the nose.

Another mind-screaming hiatus. I closed my eyes, squeezing the lids together, praying for strength. I felt something on my belly and my eyes unwillingly opened.

He was standing on my right: white coat, stethoscope still hanging. In his left hand he held the two thick grey cords. I strained my head up. He was swinging the cords slowly. The crocodile clips were softly caressing my belly. I looked up at his face. It was horribly serene.

He moved, laying one cord across my chest and taking the other further down. I put my head back trying to control the shaking in my limbs. I felt his hand on my right foot and the grip of metal on my big toe. I strained against the leather, and rivulets of agony travelled up and down my arms and shoulders. I was secured like a pin-stuck butterfly. I was dead. Nothing mattered.

He was at my left arm. The clamp of metal on my thumb. I lay still. He was alongside me again, talking in a soft, intimate voice.

"We will begin. Only the yellow sector. In later sessions we will go higher. Remember that. The clips are on easy places. Later it will be different. They will be on your penis, your lips, your tongue. Even in your anus. After those sessions you will know that this one was nothing."

His fingers were on my body; just the tips, moving lightly across my belly and chest as he talked; like snakes sliding over my skin.

"I want no names now. Don't try to tell me names. This is only to introduce you to 'El Abrazo' and 'El Rompecabezas'. Don't spoil it by trying to tell me names . . . listen for the click."

The fingers were gone. The scrape of a shoe and then silence. I drew a breath and held it – and held it and held it.

Then the air had to come out. It whistled loudly down my nostrils – but still I heard the click.

The pain was a memory of a millisecond after it ended. A memory enclosed in a scream. A searing, cold memory.

In Brazil I once saw gold being smelted. A huge vat of yellow viscous heat. Someone dropped into such a vat would have the same last memory, and be lucky it was the last. The scream ended. I felt it dying in my raw throat. The utter relief of ended pain highlighted the memory. I was sobbing in my throat. I could feel my teeth embedded in rubber. I could feel every square millimetre of my flesh shrieking from shock. The lesser pain that followed – torn muscles from the spasms – was a relief; a pleasurable comparison.

Then he was bending over me, the flat of the stethoscope on my chest. I couldn't see. Sweat stung my eyes. I turned my head and shook it, trying to stop sobbing. He listened for a long time and then straightened. My vision cleared. He was smiling as though at a recovering patient.

"Good. Your Excellency has an excellent heart. Strong enough to take you to the very bottom of hell . . ."

Of its own volition, my skin cringed against his stroking fingers. "That was only two seconds . . . a little introduction. Next time it will be longer. Maybe five seconds, maybe ten . . . maybe longer . . . listen for the click."

I tried to shut my ears again. I waited and waited and waited, my body quivering. It came loud as a gun shot. Then again. One searing spasm – a scream building and then relief. I heard him chuckling. He was beyond evil. He wanted no name. Nothing but the pleasure.

For half an hour he tortured and teased. The agony was matched to the degradation. At one point he splashed me with water from a bucket explaining in that sick, intimate voice how it improved the contact and overall effect. He could have been describing the allure of a new perfume.

When it was over and they lifted me limp from the barrel his attitude reverted. I was a pig again. He watched as they tied my hands and feet with cloth and informed me that nourishing food would be brought. They would spoon-feed me. If I refused it he would put a tube down my throat and force-feed me. He wanted me healthy. With a sneer he informed me that the next day was to be the twentieth day – the Cuban's twentieth day. Where the Cuban failed he would succeed. On that day I would go on to "El Abrazo" and stay there. I would come off dead – after I talked. From the canvas bag he took a plastic box, opened it and showed me the contents – a hypodermic needle glistening on a bed of cotton wool.

"That is your release, pig. That is your passage out of hell. By this time tomorrow you will beg for it."

I took the food. A rich vegetable and meat soup. The guards had been ordered not to say a word to me. It was a relief. No words from them. No words from me.

A guard was always in the room sitting on a chair by the door. Eyes always on me; changing every two hours or so. Fombona is taking no chances that I will mark myself.

I woke about an hour ago, astounded that I had fallen into sleep. Now I wish I had slept longer. I lie on the palliasse in the centre of the room, the silent guard eight feet away. My body aches – throbs. Every rhythmic pulse sends the message up to my brain: "No more! No more of that."

There is a faint light at the barred window. He will come again soon. Hopelessly I try to think of something else, but always the barrel and the box and the wires push out other thoughts. I pass through moments of enraged bitterness. What are they doing about me? Those bastards back home? First they try to kill me – then they just leave me here. For Christ's sake we've got over three million people in our armed forces. Why can't even a few of them be here? What the fuck are they doing?

The moments of bitterness come and go. So do moments of profound self-pity. Also, at times when I can force away thoughts of the coming torture, I review my life – both with bitterness and self-pity. What a mockery of a life. Almost all of it wasted. I made a smartly pressed suit more important in my life than a caring thought; a perfect cup of coffee superior to a human emotion; a vintage claret preferable to love. Too late now. The twentieth day has dawned.

My heart shudders at the sound of the outer door. But the footsteps in the office are not his. I know his footsteps well. The door opens and a guard enters carrying a bowl and spoon. The other guard pushes me into a sitting position and they squat beside me and spoon-feed me like a child. I swallow painfully but absently. My throat is still raw from the screaming. The screaming is automatic . . . psychosomatic . . . thoughtless. I am trying to come to terms with the coming ordeal. Come to terms with death. I am arranging mental building blocks to create a fortress in which to face death. The blocks are a jigsaw. Who do I know who has actually looked at death in the face? On the last spoonful the blocks fall into place – the jigsaw complete – Jorge. I will face death like Jorge!

"Fombona said he is coming soon. Be patient."

The squatting guard is grinning at me. He will get no words from me. I will be as Jorge. I clear my throat and spit the phlegm straight into his monkey face.

He leaps up with a curse and swings back his boot. I don't move as the other guard screams: "No! Fombona!"

Slowly the boot is lowered. He looks across at the barrel and then down at me. He wipes a hand across his face and his voice rides on waves of hatred.

"I pray for your pain – may death be a slow messenger!"

What would Jorge have done? I smile at him and nod as if in thanks. He turns away clutching the bowl, his eyes baffled. I feel the power and understand it. The secret is to be better – superior to the one who threatens or torments you. That was Jorge's secret. He believed it until the witch destroyed him. I will believe it now. No witch will destroy it – and no warlock in the guise of Fombona. If I have to die then I will die in the manner of Jorge: with contempt for the inferiors who torment me.

He leaves me for several hours – I cannot count. The guards change frequently. He thinks he is torturing my mind. He is wrong. My fortress is built. I am not at peace, but I am no longer terrified. His mental dominance has withered. When finally I hear his footsteps I push myself to a sitting position and face the door. It opens, and as our eyes meet I send him a silent message. "Not one word, filth." He pauses as though receiving the message, then advances, followed by his piglets. I offer no resistance as they lift me but I manage to hold my knees back. As they manoeuvre me towards the barrel I jack-knife my feet out. One piglet was careless. I feel my heels crunch into his testicles and he goes down with a squeal. Fombona laughs and I smile at him. The laugh fades and he looks puzzled. I am superior. They are careful now of my feet and my teeth. They are preparing me for death but they are careful of me. Even when I am strapped on the barrel they are careful of me. Jorge, if you could see me you would laugh with pride.

We are alone. The rubber is against my teeth. He shows me a knife and then moves down. I lift my head and watch as he cuts away my shorts. I am naked. He looks at me and I look back steadily. For a moment he is out of my vision, then he reappears holding the crocodile clips; trailing the fat, grey cords. I feel his fingers on my penis, then the clamp of the metal. He laughs. "Puny. Very puny. We'll liven it up."

No words. I just look at him.

He brings up the other clip and fastens it to my lower lip. Again he moves out of sight. I hear the scrape of the bucket and a moment later the shock as the water sluices over me.

I blink it from my eyes and snort it from my nostrils. He is standing over me. Again the chameleon change. His voice soft, almost seductive. "Excellency, it is noon on the twentieth day. It goes on now until you call for the needle. No respite. We start on the blue sector. Every once in a while I will take out your rubber bone. You have five seconds to ask for the needle – then it goes back. Later we will move to the green zone. I promise you, Excellency, by midnight you will ask for the needle."

Once more his fingers are caressing my body, but my skin doesn't cringe: I am superior. He moves away saying, "Listen for the click, Excellency."

I set my mind. I listen for nothing. I try to imagine Jorge standing in the corner watching. You would have saved me from this, Jorge. Watch me bear it.

The click explodes in my mind. Agony, agony, agony. A life in a molten vat. A never-ending scream.

Over. My body is quivering uncontrollably, my mind screaming at me. A thousand times worse. A million times. What can be superior to that agony? In a mist I see Fombona crouching over me listening through his tubes to my racing heart. He straightens. The mist vaporises. He is nodding in satisfaction.

"Excellent. It will take you easily into the green. Maybe to a little of the red. Listen for the click." He moves away.

God, Jorge, what would you be thinking now?

I know – "Fuck you, Solzhenitsyn!"

SLOCUM
USS "Nimitz"
Night 20

On boarding the liner *Queen Mary* in New York, Mae West was reported to have asked the Captain: "When does this place get to Europe?"

I get the same kind of feeling whenever I'm on one of our big carriers. I'm standing on a city of over six thousand people. During dinner I asked a naval officer next to me how he got over to people, who didn't know, the sheer size of the carrier. He had replied seriously, "I just tell 'em that our bakery produces three thousand loaves of bread a day. They kinda get the picture."

I'm standing under the island beside the folded wing of a Tomcat. It's a dark night just after eleven o'clock. There's not a lot of activity on the acres of flight deck. I came up here to be alone for a while and to try and control my frustration. It's chipping away at me like a goddam woodpecker. San Carlo and the compound are just twelve miles away. I'm facing towards it swaying a little in the gusts of wind caused by that contrary bitch "Olga". She's slide-assing around down south. I restrain the urge to go to the met. office again. Those guys are already pissed off with my badgering. But being alone is doing nothin' for my frustration. They're loading a Tomcat on to the port side elevator so I walk over and get a ride down to the hangar.

The great cavern is filled with noise and movement. There are mechanics working on a couple of A6s and more on a Sikorsky Sea King. The Ultralights are in three groups at the far end. They look like a flock of black crows crowding together for protection amongst eagles and hawks. My boots clatter on the steel floor and the mechanics look up and watch me pass. Extra silencers are being fitted to the Ultralights and I'm glad to see a lot of my guys there including all four squad leaders. Newman and Allen are also there covered in oil and enjoying themselves hugely. I nod to Greg Dobson, the ship's chief engineering officer, and remark, "A little different to what you're used to."

He grins. "Sure is, Colonel. Never even seen one before, but I tell you they're engineered real good."

Newman picks up a black, round object from a bench, hefts it in his hand and says, "Just baffles and an expansion chamber, but it works like a dream and weighs in under two kilos. No one's going to hear you out there. Greg and his boys have done a beautiful job. Greg, if you ever return to civvy street, you come and work with us – you hear."

Modestly Dobson says, "Well we got access to some real light alloys – come on, let's fit the last of them."

As he turns away, the Tannoy blares, "Hear this, hear this, Colonel Slocum to report to the Admiral's sea cabin."

The message is repeated as I hurry across to the elevator. I make my way through the maze of corridors feeling a little apprehensive. Admiral George J. Barnet could be a clone of General Mathew Grant and at our first meeting gave the impression that the presence of me and my men and our flying machines caused him extreme pain. What does the cat want of me now?

The senior met. officer is sitting on a chair outside the cabin with his chart case between his knees.

"What's goin' on?"

He gives a "search me" look. I tap on the door, hear the barked "enter" and go in.

The Admiral's sitting at the head of the table. The "Nimitz's" Captain is on his left and next to him is the Executive Officer. Al Simmons is sitting on the Admiral's right. They are looking mighty serious. The Admiral indicates a chair at the front of the table. I sit down and shoot Al an anxious look. He sighs and says to the Admiral, "Allow me to do this please."

The Admiral looks unhappy but nods. I'm suddenly relieved that Al's three stars make him senior to the

Admiral's equivalent rank. There is a little pile of signals flimsies in front of him. He shuffles them for a moment, sighs again and says, "Silas, there's been a development . . . an ominous development. As you know, the Agency has an increasingly strong presence in San Carlos. Reports are flowing into Langley in growing numbers. We have a lot of the official buildings in the city under surveillance. Well, two mornings ago an open truck was observed pulling into the police compound on Avenida de Santanda. A large object and several smaller ones were loaded on to it. Fortunately before the object was covered by a tarpaulin it was photographed. It was identified a few hours ago as being an instrument of torture known in that area as 'El Abrazo' – the embracer. Victims are strapped on to it in a very painful manner and then abused."

As he pauses and takes a sip of water I feel myself going cold.

"We also have the army barracks under surveillance – where the delivery truck to the compound leaves from. The truck carrying 'El Abrazo' went directly to the barracks, backed up to the rear of the delivery truck and its load was transferred." He takes another sip of water, picks up a signals flimsy, reads for a moment and continues, "We have the compound under comprehensive satellite surveillance. Agency analysts went back through the photos for that morning. The delivery truck usually goes straight to the chancery building and unloads there. On that morning it was photographed backed up to the guardhouse door. Several men were pictured manhandling from it a large object. It corresponds in size with 'El Abrazo'."

There's a silence while I try to get to grips with this information. Then Al's glum voice drones on.

"Our analysts conclude that there's a ninety per cent possibility that our Ambassador to San Carlo is currently being tortured. In that event it is one hundred per cent certain that the torturer is the leader of the so-called 'militant students': one Carlos Fombona. He's an expert and a known sadist. The National Security Council is in session and waiting for our recommendations."

For a moment I think of Komlosy in that drab room and then rage threatens to overwhelm me. How can the bastards do that to my man? – My man! Sure I care about the others but Peabody's goddam special. First they abuse and humiliate him. Then the goddam shrinks decide that he's a loser. Then our own spooks try to poison the poor bastard. Now they're fucking torturing him! He's just a dozen miles away. Frustration wells up in me and then subsides as I realise what I have to do. The ship's Captain is talking.

"I just don't understand why they'd do that? Why take the risk? They must realise the consequences."

Simmons says curtly, "They have compelling reasons but that's classified. Our analysts surmise that afterwards they'll fake death by natural causes. It's . . ."

I break in flatly, "So we go and get him out – now!"

The Admiral grimaces. "You seem to forget hurricane 'Olga' and the attendant weather conditions out there which exceed the flying parameters of those contraptions of yours."

I retort, "We'll go anyway. Enough of us will get through to do the job."

He shrugs cynically. "You hope."

I lean forward to deliver a few selected words but Simmons cuts them off.

"Colonel! First we rapidly examine all aspects . . . then we forward a recommendation to the NSC who passes it on to the President for executive decision." He turns to the Admiral. "We should get an update from the met. officer."

The Admiral nods and while the Exec. fetches the met. officer I say, "I'd like to have Newman and Allen sit in on this."

"Civilians?!" the Admiral barks incredulously.

Good ol' "no shit" Simmons answers for me.

"They're the world's top experts on those contraptions, Admiral Barnet. They're conversant with all aspects of 'Operation Vampire' . . . they are on this vessel by executive order."

Al's normally humorous face is as hard as his voice. Barnet stares at it, then shrugs and nods. As the met. officer

211

sits down and pulls out his charts, the Exec. picks up a phone and gives the order.

They arrive in about three minutes. I'm relieved that they've taken their oily overalls off, but they still look scruffy as all hell in their denims and creased shirts. They look about as out of place in this cabin as spare bridegrooms at a wedding. They sit down with expectant faces. Newman says "Hi" to the Admiral. He looks pained. But the Captain, a tall lugubrious cat, is trying not to smile. As I quickly bring them up to date, their faces turn sombre. Then the met. officer takes over with his weather charts.

"Olga" is round and fat and furious. Although she's lurking some 180 miles south of us, the lines of her outer, circling winds pass over our position. They vary from forty knots to gusts of close to sixty.

Allen and Newman start shooting questions at him. He's disconcerted. "Well yes, with the high over northern Brazil she could drift south . . . then again maybe not. The patterns over the eastern Atlantic could exert an influence."

They're both leaning forward over the chart. Newman traces a finger down through our position and through the coastline of San Carlo. He glances at Allen who nods and murmurs, "Yeah. But hairy as hell."

They resume their seats and the Admiral asks, "So?"

Newman takes a deep breath and succinctly spells it out. "Our Ultralights would not normally operate in wind speeds over forty knots – fairly constant knots. We've got up to sixty. My guess is that 'Olga' will drift south-west to the Brazilian high . . . but slowly. It could be two, even three days before the wind drops and steadies. There's one factor in our favour. The wind is tangentially on shore." He looks at the Captain. "I understand you can get this tub up to thirty-six knots?" The Captain smiles and nods. Newman smiles back. "Okay, so you steam down wind but even picking the right moment it's going to be a very dangerous take off . . . very." He looks at me. "Then because of the Russian spy ship sitting out there the plan calls for a sea-skimming flight for the first five miles with the 'Nimitz' in between to block off their radar." He shakes his head. "Those waves out there are gonna cause all kinds of low level turbulence. A split second's loss of concentration over those five miles and you're swimming . . . if you survive the impact. Then you climb. With that wind behind you'll have a surface speed of around seventy-five m.p.h. That helps your glide ratio. It would be about fifteen to one. So you'd only have to go up say 4,000 feet, but even at that height you'd be riding a roller coaster." He winces. "And then the landing – enclosed area. You just have to land into the wind. Get a gust at the wrong moment and you get flipped like a tossed coin. You could be losing men from take-off to landing."

The Admiral cuts in. "Would you dare to try it, Newman?"

Allen starts laughing. "You don't know this idiot, sir. If someone dared him, he'd fly right through the centre of 'Olga' playing a saxophone."

Simmons takes over the debate. "What losses would you expect, Larry? Give me a percentage."

"Al, that's unfair."

Simmons shakes his head. "Decisions have to be taken . . . it's an unfair situation both for the Vampire force and for our Ambassador there. Give me a percentage."

Newman and Allen look at each other. There's a painful, drawn-out silence. Then, still looking at Allen, Newman says, "They're good. Damned good, most of them . . ."

The quiet, reserved Allen says starkly, "Between forty and fifty per cent."

Sadly, Newman turns to me and nods.

Allen goes on, "And I wouldn't let Brand go . . . or Kerr . . . no way. The others are naturals. Those two are proficient by effort alone."

Simmons is now very assertive. He says to me, "You can expect to lose up to half your men before you hit the compound. That leaves you with ten."

"No, Al. I've got five reserves and I'll take them. After dropping Brand and Kerr I'd have twenty-three at take-off. Minimum eleven or twelve in the compound. It's enough. We've planned for it. Rehearsed it."

"Don't count on it, Silas. If the decision is taken to go, then it will have to be volunteers only."

"Like hell it will, Al." I can't stop myself rising – or my voice. "If I order them to go – they'll fucking go!"

He's also on his feet, his eyes and the stars on his epaulettes glittering.

"Sit down, Colonel!"

There's a silence while we glare at each other. Abruptly the Admiral dismisses the met. officer. As he gathers his charts and heads for the door, I sink back into my chair. Still standing, Simmons says, "Larry, Bryan, I'd appreciate it if you'd wait outside a while."

"Sure . . . sure."

As the door closes behind them he pours it over me. The cat really is pissed off.

"Hear this, you overgrown lump of shit. Who do you think you are? Your head is getting as big as your ass. You think I'm some fucking Corporal. Forget these fucking stars! Forget about court martials! You talk to me like that again and I'll kick your balls right up into your goddam skull – where they belong! You got that, Colonel Slocum?"

I crack it out. "Yessir!"

The navy brass are looking at each other in bewildered astonishment. Annapolis this ain't. Without taking his angry eyes off me, Simmons slowly sits down. The Admiral coughs discreetly and Simmons glares at him. The Captain is studying his fingernails. The Exec. is examining a speck on the table. Simmons's breathing slows. He turns to the Admiral.

"Okay. I'm gonna call the White House and put the situation to the NSC. There is no way that with those projected losses this can be anything but a volunteer operation." Without looking at me, he snarls, "I suppose the ape over there personally volunteers."

"Yessir!"

Is there a hint of a smile on that long face? If so it's disappeared. He asks me sharply, "And what if, before you get to the compound, you take sixty or seventy per cent losses? You'll be under your minimum. If you go on, you could foul it up for any future attempt."

My mind races.

"No problem, sir. A minute before arrival over the

214

compound we'll break radio silence. Even if we're picked up they'll never get warning to the compound before we're inside. We'll do a count. If we're less than ten we'll turn back – try to reach the carrier . . . or else ditch in the sea."

He gives me a very hard look. I bounce it back.

"General Simmons. If we're less than ten we'll turn away."

Another long stare then he turns again to the Admiral. "Okay. Then I propose that if we get the go-ahead . . . an' if we get enough volunteers, we proceed as soon as possible this night."

He waits for a response. The Admiral is in a bit of a daze. He blinks a few times and says, "Uh . . . yes. You don't think they'll want to try something else?"

Simmons shakes his head. "No. For sure they'll be hustling up 'Delta' force and might even fly them in tomorrow for back-up. But because of the special circumstances, and national security, my guess is they'll risk a try with 'Operation Vampire'. Now could I be patched through to the White House, please?"

The Admiral gestures at the Captain, who picks up a blue phone in front of him. In less than a minute Simmons is talking to Komlosy in the Sit. Room. He is beautifully terse as he maps out the situation. Then he answers a few questions.

"Yes, Mike." He rolls his eyes. "Yes, you could say that Slocum is eager to go . . . I don't know, we'll find out in a few minutes . . . yeah, just as soon as they can get suited up . . . Like I said, forty to fifty per cent . . . sure – has to be a volunteer job . . . I'll hang on . . ." He cups the mouthpiece and says to the cabin in general, "The President's in the Sit. Room. We'll get a fast decision. Colonel, he wants to know how soon you can go."

I ask the Captain, "Are you still steering that figure-of-eight pattern?"

"Affirmative."

"When will we next be going directly down wind?"

"Jimmy?"

The Exec. picks up a phone, punches a button and repeats

my question. After a very short wait he hangs up and says, "At zero ten hours." He glances at his watch. "That's in forty-three minutes."

I say firmly, "That's when we're going, Al."

He holds up a hand and says into the phone, "Yeah, Mike. Okay. Got it . . . yeah sure. Listen, if all goes well they'll take off in about forty minutes . . . sure, will do . . . I'll get back to you right away."

He hangs up, looks at me, sighs and says, "Slocum, if enough of your men are suicide-prone, you have the President's order to go and get our people out."

A surge of relief followed by anxiety. I'd picked a bunch of wildly diverse individuals. Some for sure will go. But will it be enough? If even half a dozen opt out it'll be a non-starter. I shrug off the thought.

"Most of them are in the hangar, sir. I'll have the others sent there . . . let's find out."

The Admiral decides to stay in his cabin. He has the air of a man overtaken by events. But the Captain and Exec. are keen and helpful. Simmons and I follow them through the maze.

Newman and Allen, who had been lounging outside the Admiral's cabin and presumably hearing everything, trail after us. I turn and give them the thumbs-up sign. They nod. There's little humour on their faces. Better than anyone they know the dangers of flying Ultralights in extreme conditions. Out of the side of his mouth Al says, "You asked for it back there, Silas."

"I know. Sorry, Al."

"Okay. I know how wrapped up in this you are. It's become totally personal with you. But hear me, Silas. When we get to the hangar, you don't say one word. Understand?"

"Yessir."

As we enter the hangar, the Exec. shouts an order and all the work stops and there is an immediate silence except for our footsteps. My guys are lined up in front of the Ultralights with the four squad leaders in front. Captain Moncada shouts, "Ten-shun!"

There's a ragged clatter as twenty-four pairs of boots hit

the steel. I wince; this mob is not exactly a drill instructor's dream. We line up in front of them with Simmons in the centre and slightly ahead. He says loudly, "At ease."

Another ragged clatter. He looks along the row of faces: at the different colours and expressions; then in a quiet, clear voice he lays it on them. He keeps it free of all emotion. No calls to patriotism; no stress on national security. Just the torture of our Ambassador; their instructors' assessment of up to fifty per cent projected losses; a total volunteer operation. No man will ever be looked down upon if he decides not to go. With those projected losses everyone would understand. It's not a suicide mission but comes very close to it.

I think: Shit! He's practically talked them out of it. Some of them are glaring at me. I stare straight ahead. In his strange, high-pitched voice, Moncada asks, "Sir, may we be addressed by Colonel Slocum?"

"You may not."

They are all looking at me now. There is a pause before Simmons says, "I can tell you, though, that Colonel Slocum has volunteered." Another pause, then he commands sharply: "Ten-shun!"

Yet another ragged crash. I'm so wound up with tension that I hardly notice. Enunciating every word, Simmons commands, "Volunteers take one pace forward . . . hut!"

No drill sergeant working with them ten hours a day for a month could have produced a movement with more precision and unity. Twenty-four left boots come forward. Twenty-four right boots come down beside them in a single reverberating crash. Twenty-four pairs of eyes looking straight ahead. One pair of eyes is threatening to water. I swallow and get a grip on myself. Tough old bulls don't show that they're churning up inside with relief, pride and affection.

I sneak a glance at Simmons. He's nodding thoughtfully and slowly; beyond him the ship's Captain is shaking his head in awe.

Simmons cannot totally keep the emotion from his voice. "I'm sure your Commanding Officer is proud of you. So am I . . . and your country will be. Good luck! Go ahead, Colonel."

I look at my watch and step forward.

"Okay. We have only thirty-five minutes to take off. There's much to do. The plan will have to be modified. Under these conditions we'll be taking the back-up men . . . with the exceptions of Brand and Kerr."

"Why?"

The question comes bluntly and aggressively from Brand; a squat white guy who even in the army has managed to keep his lank black hair long enough to cover his ears and forehead.

I try to make it easy. "Your instructors have assessed the flying abilities of all of you. It was decided that anyone with a liability factor of over fifty per cent should not be allowed to go."

"Why?"

I sigh and forget the diplomacy. "Don't be an asshole, Brand. You and Kerr are not natural pilots. You worked damn hard and made yourselves proficient but conditions out there call for more than that. You're not going."

He leans forward and looks at Kerr down the line. Kerr is young, lanky and fair-haired. He's tough as old boots but he looks like he just came off the farm. He doesn't ever use many words. Now he just nods and Brand says doggedly, "We're going, Colonel."

I get mad. "Brand, you're not going. You'll damned well obey orders!"

"Fuck orders. We're going."

I'm shouting. "You're staying on this ship if I have to beat you unconscious!"

He takes a step forward. "Go ahead, Colonel. You're tough, but a lot of guys have tried that and failed."

From the corner of my eye I note that Kerr has also stepped forward. In exasperation I look at Simmons. He just shrugs. It's up to me.

"Okay, idiots. If you want to kill yourselves, that's your problem." I glance at my watch. "We're losing time. Be at the briefing room in ten minutes."

PEABODY
San Carlo
Night 19

He no longer bothers to check my heart. He no longer strokes me with his fingers. He no longer talks to me in seductive tones. All that stopped after he moved the dial up into the blue sector. I have beaten him but will die anyway. There is a guard helping him now. He crouches by my head. After every shock, every convulsion, he pulls the rubber from my mouth, puts his ear close, then he shakes his head, forces the rubber back in and it starts again. I have been slipping in and out of consciousness. They are blessed but frightening moments. Once as I regained my senses I heard the guard's excited voice, "He murmured something! A name!"

Instantly Fombona is over me, his face eager and sweating. "What name?"

"Jorge, comrade. Twice."

For a moment his face was puzzled then it suffused into anger and he twisted away muttering, "That fucking Cuban!"

The dial was turned higher and the agony increased.

Twice he brought the plastic box and silently showed me the hypodermic. Twice I managed to introduce Jorge into my body and mind and I smiled and closed my eyes.

He was right after all, that Solzhenitsyn. The time does come when the agony only happens to the body. The mind is dead and cannot be manipulated.

My body rises again and ripples as a new shock passes through. My nerves shriek. The scream comes; but from throat muscles, not the mind. My mind defends itself and I pass out.

I come back slowly. Voices murmuring. Fombona talking to the guard. A baffled, surly voice.

219

"Go now. Sleep. I am on the edge of the red. I will give him half an hour's rest. At midnight I start again. If he doesn't talk by half past midnight, I give him the needle anyway."

A half hour's rest; a half hour's torment; death. A timetable to peace. Jorge, I go with you.

The briefing was short. The changes to the plan minimal. I
am now going to land behind the west end of the residence.
I will take with me our best pilot, a Puerto Rican called
Rodriguez. I will also have Brand and Kerr follow me in if
they get that far. They will then move directly to the front
of the chancery while Moncada's squad approach from the
back and sides. Rodriguez will follow me to the guardhouse.
After I secure the Ambassador he will guard him while I join
the main assault. Castaneda's squad will assault the apartments where most of the guards should be sleeping. Sacasa
and his men will cover the residence and act as general
trouble-shooters. We went quickly through the much-
practised radio procedures. I am Vampire One, Rodriguez
Vampire Two and Brand and Kerr Three and Four.
Moncada is Green One, his deputy Green Two and so on.
The colours blue, yellow and red and the various numerals
were given to Castaneda, Sacasa, Gomez and their men.
These call signs could have sounded boy-scoutish but conditions being what they were they had the ring of gravestone
inscriptions. When I finished, the Admiral stood up and, in a
firm clear voice, said, "You are courageous men, and true
Americans. I'm proud of you. The support of this ship and
all ships in the battle group is right behind you. Good luck!"
    He sure meant it. The back-up has been outstanding.
After my men left to suit up I spent a few minutes going over
timings with the leaders of the three groups: the A6E
Intruders and helicopter gunships who would "sanitise" the
area around the compound; the evacuation helicopters; the
signals officer; the officer in charge of the rescue of any of my

ditched men and finally Simmons, who was co-ordinating the whole operation. Then the talking was over.

We're all grouped in the lee of the ship's island. It towers darkly above us. The Ultralights are in position, held by sailors at each wing tip. Their canvas wings are flapping and shaking in the gusts. They look about as sturdy as butterflies.

We use the buddy system: the men in pairs checking each other's equipment. It's much practised and goes rhythmically:

"Knife. Check.
Stun grenades, 4. Check.
Flare grenades, 4. Check.
Frag. grenades, 4. Check.
S.M.G., safetied. Check, check.
Suppressor. Check.
Mags, 6. Check.
Helmets, transmission off. Check, check.
Hand and leg cuffs, 5 & 5. Check, check.
Dinghy. Check."

"Check, check, check." I'm the odd man out and have to do it alone. I'm feeling the loneliness – the weight of command; suddenly aware that I got all those guys into this hairy scene. Quickly I think about what they're doing to my man over in the compound, and the bile surges up reassuringly in my throat. I look at my watch. Five past midnight. Everyone's ready. The black guys are moving around slapping black ointment on white faces and trying not to look superior. My four squad leaders are in front of me. I remember Wellington's words when he once reviewed some of his troops:

"I don't know what they'll do to the enemy, but by God they frighten me."

They're a murderous looking quartet. Webbing festooned with grenades and spare mags. Sawn-off shot-guns slung over shoulders. Black faces. Knives in boots. S.M.G.s swinging from one hand. Black goggled radio helmets from the other. They're waiting for final orders. There aren't any. Hard and mean as they are, I sense they're also waiting for a few words of reassurance. I want to hug all four of them and tell them it's gonna be just fine, but I'm the tough old bull.

"So if you bums are ready, pile your boys into their kites and let's go do it."

I see the flashes of white teeth in the darkness as they turn away; and know I have judged them right. The young flight deck officer is at my shoulder.

"Four minutes, Colonel."

I nod and pick up my S.M.G. and dinghy and helmet and call loudly, "Let's go!"

We move out on to the flight deck and into the wind. The Ultras are facing the bow, spread out across the width of the great deck in five flights. Mine is at the front. Newman and Allen are moving between the machines like mother hens checking their chicks. They come over and slap me on the shoulder and wish me luck. I nod at them and move on. I do a quick check of my Ultralight. The wings, struts and wires. Everything okay. I drop my helmet on the seat and sling my S.M.G. over my shoulder and tie on the dinghy. I pull the helmet over my head and check again that the radio transmission switch is off. The microphone is an inch from my lips. I pull down the infra-red goggles and everything is suddenly brightly pink. Next I pull down the dark visor and everything is black; but it will enable me to keep my eyes open and see everything when the flare grenades are burning and blinding the enemy. I lift it and turn. Rodriguez is directly behind me, already seated. On either side of him are Brand and Kerr. Newman is checking Brand in and Allen is hovering over Kerr. They're worried sick about those two. Moncada's flight of seven Ultralights is behind them. I gave him extra men. With me diverting first to the guardhouse his role is vital in securing the other hostages. Behind him is Sacasa's flight of five, the Castaneda five and finally, at the back, Gomez's flight of four.

I have momentary doubts. Should I have given Gomez more? He has to take out the M.G. emplacements on the roofs

223

in the compound. That role is also vital. Fuck it; everything is vital! Besides, he and his three men are crack pilots and more than likely to make it.

They're all seated. I raise both my thumbs. The signal to start engines. Apart from the two sailors holding the wing tips there's also a third sailor at the front of all the machines. They will signal as each engine is running smoothly. There is hardly any noise but one by one their right arms go up. I do a count: twenty-four. All on go. I duck and swing myself into my seat, get as comfortable as my bulk will allow, and switch on. I feel rather than hear the engine kick into life. I ease up the throttle while the sailors take the strain, quickly check the few instruments. Tachometer, wind meter, compass, temperature gauge and glide indicator – A-OK. I glance at my watch. Midnight ten. Time to go.

In front, to my right, is a perspex dome and under it the head and shoulders of an officer. As far as possible we're following normal launch procedures. As soon as I'm set and ready I snap off a salute. He hits a button. If I was in a Tomcat it would be the catapult firing button and I'd be airborne in half a second and doing 160 knots two seconds later. This time it will be a button that changes a red light to green. Then I go with my flight. The other flights follow the same procedure. I look first left and then right at the sailors holding me in check. They're just boys, eighteen or nineteen years old. They both mouth the words "Good luck". I nod back.

Now I concentrate on the wind and abruptly I'm scared. Is the fear for myself or of failure? Angrily I think of my man over there; the fear goes and with one hand on the throttle, I concentrate again. A strong gust and then another and then a lull. My right hand begins to move and then stops; another gust. Four, five, six seconds, another lull. Fuck it – let's go!

I snap the salute. The green light's on. I pour on the power and the machine surges forward. I'm airborne! In a near panic, I struggle with the handlebar controls to stop myself drifting to the left. The bow of the "Nimitz" slides away beneath and I'm looking at a very angry, white-topped sea. The machine bucks upwards and then sinks sickeningly. I feel spray on my hands and I'm looking at the foaming top of a wave right in front of me. I haul back on the bars and climb again. I could be having a bad time in a rodeo. I work the machine a bit higher and it steadies for a while. Christ, what's happening to the guys behind?! I twist my body and crane my neck around and I'm plunging again sideways. Down on the right handlebar, ease it back. Shit, Newman was right. This is a fucking roller coaster! Why did I let those assholes Brand and Kerr talk me into letting them come along? I should have beaten the bastards senseless. I'm not going to risk another look back. Every goddam gramme of concentration is needed to keep this thing and me in the air.

But I'm forced to concentrate on other things. The plan is to stay at one hundred feet for the first five miles but that really is suicide. I take a decision and fight the thing up to 500 feet. It's no less turbulent but the sudden down drops are now less likely to be fatal. If anyone survived behind me they'll follow me up. Screw the spy ship's radar!

It's getting a bit easier. I'm getting used to it and I'm not snatching at the controls; anticipating instead of just reacting. I check my watch and then my surface speed. It's bouncing between seventy and eighty knots. I work it out. Shit. In three minutes we start the climb. What will it be like up there? The met. officer and Newman and Allen forecast a little less turbulence. We'd decided on a ceiling of 3,500 feet. I decide to start a gradual climb now. Slowly the altimeter winds up. At 1,000 feet conditions are definitely better. The roller coaster is just a little smoother.

At 2,000 feet I can see a darker line on the purple horizon: San Carlo. I'm going to make it. I pray that there are at least nine others behind me. I reach 3,500 feet and ease the throttle. We also decided that with the conditions and the effectiveness of the silencers we could motor in close to the coast. It takes shape rapidly. A few lights show up. There's a ninety per cent blackout due to no oil getting through the blockade; but I know that the outer floodlights on the compound walls are operational. I search for them. They must be visible by now. Nothing. Then it's there on my vision's periphery, way out to the right. The wind has carried me down further south than expected. I turn and start crabbing up to the north, fighting against the handlebars. My excitement climbs as the light forms into a square. I can make out the dark blobs of the individual buildings inside the walls. There it is! The guardhouse. I'm so intent on it I almost forget. I can see the waves pounding on the shoreline below. It's time. My guts feel like a block of ice as I reach up to my helmet and flick on the transmit button. Please God, let there be nine behind me!

"Vampire One to Green One, come in."

I count the seconds. Three – four – five. I want to scream and then loud in my ears:

"Green One to Vampire One. We are three."

With me that's four. Nerves racing, I call:

"Vampire One to Blue One. Come in."

Instantly: "Blue One. We are two."

Shit and hell! It only makes six.

"Vampire One to Yellow One."

Sacasa's voice crackles in.

"Yellow One. We are three."

Jesus, only one to go!

"Vampire One to Red One."

Gomez's accented voice will be easily recognisable. I yearn to hear it. I don't. It's another voice.

"Yellow Two. We are two."

It's the voice of Hal Lewis, Gomez's number two. Gomez must have bought it. But we are eleven. We go in. I don't have much hope for Brand and Kerr but my "ace" Rodriguez must have made it.

"Vampire One to Vampire Two."

Seconds pass. Nothing. I repeat.

"Vampire One to Vampire Two. Come in."

A dour voice crackles in my ears.

"This is Vampire Three. He didn't make it. Neither did Vampire Four."

Such is war. My "ace" dipped out and ol' duffer Brand survived. Well, we're eleven. My civvies were right. We lost fifty per cent plus one. But we're twelve and we're goin' in. Simmons on the "Nimitz" will have monitored the radio and by now will be talking to Komlosy in the White House Sit. Room or even the President himself. As we cross the coast, I consider whether to juggle my remaining men around. I decide against it. The biggest problem is the Red squad. With Gomez and one other gone the two left are going to have their work cut out silencing the roof-top M.G. emplacements. But Lewis is a good man; so is Spooner, the other survivor.

The compound is below me on the left. I reach for the engine cut-off and say, "Vampire One. Engines off."

It takes me a few seconds to get used to the machine in the glide mode, then I'm spiralling sharply down, fighting the handlebars and praying that we all get on the ground in one piece. It comes rushing up at me. I'm lifted by a gust and strain against the handlebars. As I cross the south-west corner of the wall my eyes are fixed on the rear of the residence. For a moment I marvel at the skill of our Seabees. I practised this a dozen times on the mock-up at Bragg and it looks exactly the same. Concentrate, asshole! I'm too fast – too low! I ease back the bars. The canard wing lifts. I slow and crab sideways. The building looms in front of me. I correct and I'm down and rolling, pushing out my right leg on the nose wheel bar, turning into the shadow of the wall. A second of relief and self-congratulation then I'm scrambling clear, swinging the Ingram S.M.G. off my shoulder, cocking it, and straining my ears. Not a sound, not a whisper . . . yes, a whisper. A dark pink blob glides past me. It's Brand. He's overshot. His left wing is dangerously tilted only a foot off the ground. I draw in my breath as he corrects and the machine bumps on to the ground with a squeal. He comes to a stop six feet from the back wall of the residence. While I listen for any alarm his squat figure jumps off and pulls the Ultralight close in under the wall, then he's shuffling towards me in a crouching run.

I punch him lightly on the shoulder. He grins. His hair is falling over the top of his infra-red goggles. For a crazy moment I think he looks like Ringo Starr. We creep to the corner of the residence. The guardhouse is about fifty yards away to our right and beyond are the main gates. I can just make out two figures slumped against the wall beside them. I tap Brand on the shoulder and point. He taps me back in confirmation. Far to our right are the blocks of staff apartments. On top of the nearest one I can make out the hump of an M.G. emplacement, exactly where it should be. I hope that Lewis and Spooner are circling slowly down ready to take it out. Two hundred yards in front of us is the chancery building. As I focus on it two diamond shapes glide down behind it. Okay. Away to our left there's a scuffling sound and a couple of bumps. There's nothing to see. It must be Sacasa's squad going behind the apartments. Time to go. Instead of taking the long way around hugging the compound walls I decide to risk going direct. Everything's gonna cut loose any second and when it does I want to be at the guardhouse with my man. We set off in a fast crouched duck-waddle. Half way across a goddam Ultralight crabs in across the wall, straightens up and lands right in the middle of the compound, coming to a stop on the edge of the Ambassador's swimming pool. Who the hell is that? Never mind. He's down and there's no alarm. As we reach the back of the guardhouse I turn and see a figure detach itself from the Ultra and scuttle away towards the apartments. We creep round one corner of the oblong building and up the other. I put my head round. Next to the door is a figure sitting slackly in a chair with his chin on his chest. I move back and my heel comes down on Brand's boot. He moans softly. I tap him on the chest and point with a curving motion round the corner. Then I hold up one finger and parody a sitting man with his chin on his chest. He nods and reaches down and I see the pale pink gleam of his bowie knife. I move clear and he slithers round the corner like a squat lizard. I'm right behind him as he glides up, slips a hand behind the guard's neck, clamps it across his mouth and pulls up and back. There's no sound as the knife slices through the jugular. He lifts the body clear as it kicks and twists. There's a soft grunting and coughing and then it slackens. Brand lays it quietly on the concrete. I make a sign to him to guard my back and then gingerly turn the door handle. I open it a crack, slide the barrel of the S.M.G. in and nudge it open.

228

The room is lit by a single bulb. It's empty except for a desk and two chairs. On the far side is another door with a key in it. My man is in there.

Suddenly from behind that door I hear a muffled but unearthly sound. A sound out of hell. My skin prickles. I move quickly. My rubber boots hardly make any noise on impact with the concrete. I put my ear against the door. There's a voice: muffled, but I can make out the words.

"Talk, pig! Talk to me! Give me a name!"

I turn the knob, kick open the door, and raise the S.M.G.

It's a tableau. A high barrel-shaped thing; a thin, naked man strapped over it, his face a mask of agony. Standing over him is a big beefy guy with short black hair, wearing a white coat with a goddam stethoscope round his neck. He's holding a syringe in front of the agonised face. My thumb flicks the S.M.G. on to single shot. I hear my voice.

"You want a conversation? Talk to me, bastard!"

His mouth opens and my bullet cracks right into it, slamming his head and body back. I'm seeing things through a red haze and it's not the goggles. They're pushed up over my helmet. His head is on one side, a bloody hole at the back where the bullet exited. The body is still twitching. I line up the barrel and suppressor: phut, a bullet in his belly. Phut, a bullet in his balls. He's not twitching any more. I hear my voice.

"You just had your last words, prick – from an Ingram Ten sub-machine-gun. Rot in hell!"

I turn and the red haze lifts and urgency washes over me. Peabody's narrowed eyes are watching me, but he seems far away. There's a wire attached to his lip from a crocodile clip. Another attached to a fold of flesh behind his knee. Gently I remove them. I slip out my knife, move round and cut through the leather bindings. He moans terribly as the pressure is eased. Then I bend over him.

"It's over, Mr Ambassador. I'm taking you out and home. First I gotta see about the other hostages. I gotta leave you here, two or three minutes. There'll be a man at the door guarding you. Two or three minutes an' I'll be back." His eyes are glazed. "The other hostages, sir. I gotta go."

229

His eyelids flicker and his head moves slightly. I squeeze his shoulder and he winces and moans and I want to punch myself in the face.

"Sorry, sir – I'll be back."

I race through the outer room flicking the Ingram on to automatic. Brand is crouched at the door scanning the compound. I pull down my infra-red goggles.

"Anything?"

"There was movement by the apartments. I guess the Blue squad."

"Okay. I'm heading for the chancery. The Ambassador's secure but in bad shape. Guard this door and don't move, no matter what happens!" I point to the two sleeping figures by the gate. "Take them out as soon as it starts."

I tap him on the shoulder and, in a crouch, head across the compound thinking that everything is going pretty damn good.

Of course just then everything starts to unravel. There's a shout from near the chancery; the rapid coughing of an Ingram on automatic; and then a piercing scream. I flick on my transmission switch.

"Vampire One to Base. Sanitise. Repeat, sanitise. Ambassador secure. Confirm torture. Going into chancery now. Over."

Simmons's voice crackles straight back.

"Base to Vampire One. Sanitising."

It's happening now. There's a splintering of glass. Loud shouting in Spanish. Explosions from the chancery. The lights come on in the sky. Their beams wobble across the compound. Shit! In these wind conditions they're never gonna be able to keep them steady. On the roof of the chancery I can just see the long barrel rearing upwards. The lights lead to the target. I scream into the mike, "Lewis, Spooner, switch off your lights!" One goes out immediately. The other is slow. The M.G. on the roof clatters and the light twists and then goes out. Three seconds later there's a rending crash behind me. I turn and see the Ultralight: a crumpled heap with a dark nucleus.

I'm twenty yards from the chancery. A series of "crumps"

and then a blinding white light from the windows and door. I snap down the dark visor and can see again. There's a short flight of steps to the door. I take it in one leap. Moncada is screaming, "Americans lie down! Americans lie down! Don't move." I swing right into the reception area and it's all in front of me. About forty people. With the exception of Moncada and his man next to him they've all got their hands over their eyes. Some of them are sinking to the ground. A kid in jeans has pulled his tee-shirt up over his head. He's holding a little box in one hand and with the other frantically twisting a dial. A surge of relief. The explosive jackets are fucking dummies! Moncada fires and the kid spins away screaming. Another guard, one hand over his eyes, the other groping behind him at his belt. I line up the Ingram, flicking on to single shot. Phut! The hand leaves his eyes and clutches at his chest as he goes over backwards. His pistol clatters to the floor. Moncada is shouting in Spanish,

"Hands on your heads or you die. Hands on your heads!"

My eyes sweep the room. All men. The hostages are all down. The flares are fading. I turn and race back through the door. Two guards on the stairs, both with pistols, both firing. The sound of an angry wasp passes my head. I flick to automatic, dive forward, roll out and squeeze the trigger. They're punched back up the stairs and then roll slackly down.

The door in front of me is open. I run through it discarding the empty mag. and clicking in a fresh one. The plan of the building is stamped on my brain. Through another door, down a corridor. I can see the light of the flare grenades and two seconds later I'm coming through the door. The third man of Moncada's squad has his back to me. There's a number 'Ten' stitched to his battledress so I know that he's Sam Shaw, Moncada's number two. He's got the situation under control. But totally. The seven women are lying on the floor, their hands covering their faces. Two of them are moaning in terror. Another sobbing. The seven female guards are also on the floor. They are not covering their eyes from the glare. They don't have to; they are all dead.

Shaw spins as I come up beside him. With his visor down

he looks like something out of space. I guess I look the same. The glare is fading. We both push up our visors. His lean tanned face is troubled.

"I was alone, sir. I couldn't take any chances. I took 'em all out."

"You did right, Shaw. The plan called for three men. You did right."

I can hear the clamour of heavy machine-guns from above. The roof-top emplacements are still in place. I can also hear the faster staccato rattle of unsilenced Ingrams. Silence no longer needed, the suppressors have been discarded. In the background are the deeper sounds of cannon fire and the constant rolling rumble of explosions. The A6s and helicopter gunships from "Nimitz" are making sure that not even a mosquito gets close to the compound. It's reassuring but I've got a hell of a problem. The light in the room now is normal – only from the electric bulbs. I say, "Ladies, you can uncover your eyes now and get up." Slowly, apprehensively, they lift their hands from their faces and start to scramble to their feet. They look with shock at the dead bodies. Urgently I say, "Ladies, I'm Colonel Slocum, US Army. We've come to take you home. Your menfolk are all okay, but it's still very dangerous here. I want you to shuck off those jackets and follow me. Keep low." They're looking at me with dazed expressions. "Come on, ladies. Move! Quick!"

A little bird-like woman with mussed-up grey hair starts taking off the dummy jacket and also taking charge. "Come on, girls. Irene, Julie, let's go."

I tell Shaw, "Go ahead. Scout to the main entrance and then stay there keeping watch."

He moves off in a shuffling run, and I follow a few seconds later with the women crowding behind me. We pass him lying at the door. Infra-red goggles over his eyes staring out over his S.M.G. into the darkness. As we enter the reception area five of the women rush past me shouting out names. I guess the other two are secretaries. There's an emotional moment as they greet their husbands and then Moncada's shouting at them.

"Get down! Get down, all of you. Stay on the floor!"

They sink down clutching each other. There's a babble of voices directed at me. I hold up a hand.

"Listen. Everyone's safe. The choppers will be coming to take you out soon, but there's still fighting. You've got to stay here on the floor 'til we clean it up. Captain Moncada here and his men will look after you and lead you to the choppers. Do exactly what he tells you."

A voice calls, "What about the Ambassador?"

"He's sick but safe."

A small cheer goes up. To my left Moncada's other guy is snapping hand and leg cuffs on to the quiescent guards. He calls out, "Colonel, throw me your cuffs."

I unclip them from my webbing and toss them over. There's still a hell of a row outside and it's not just coming from the sanitising. There's at least two heavy M.G.s still firing inside the compound. I flick on my transmitter.

"Vampire One to Base. Come in."

"Base to Vampire One. Go ahead."

"Hostages all safe and secure in chancery. Ambassador in poor condition but alive and secure in guardhouse. There are still active, enemy, heavy M.G. emplacements on roof-tops. Over."

Simmons's voice comes back laden with excitement and relief.

"Well done, Vampire One. You want an airstrike on those roof-tops?"

"No fucking way, Al. No airstrikes!"

"You're sure, Silas?"

"Damned sure. We'll do it ourselves. Meanwhile keep the Evac. choppers in hold just off the coast."

"Okay. Good luck."

I've got to get a situation report. I decide to dispense with the goddam code words. First I want to find out who it was that crashed in the middle of the compound.

"Slocum to Lewis. Come in."

"Sir, this is Spooner. Lewis bought it."

"Okay. Report, Spooner."

"Sir, I got the M.G.s on top of the chancery and

apartments but then I took fire from the residence and crash landed by the swimming pool."

"Are you okay?"

"Broke my right leg. But I'm by a corner of the residence. I've got a clear field of fire across the compound to the west of the chancery. Ain't no one gonna cross there."

"Good man. We'll get to you real soon. Castaneda, report in."

"Castaneda. Apartment building one cleaned out. Fifteen enemy dead, twelve captured and shackled. No friendly casualties. Cannot cross to the chancery, we're pinned down by two M.G.s on the residence roof."

"Okay. Well done. Stay put. Sacasa, report in."

"Sacasa here. Apartment buildings two and three secured. Twenty-two enemy dead. Three captured. Legrand got hit by fragments from his own grenade. Chest and shoulders, but he's walking. We're also pinned down by those M.G.s."

"Okay. Stand by."

It's a fucking problem. Maybe it's logical to call in an air-strike. We've got no one in the residence, but I'm damned if I'll do that. Spooner's right on its corner and the chancery is only two hundred yards away. I'll do the job myself. A voice is calling from the floor, "Colonel, Colonel."

It's a tough-looking cat with a crew cut. "Gunny Sergeant Cowder, sir. Marine Corps. I have fifteen men here, sir. We'd like to help."

There's not much they can do but his face carries a yearning expression. He's had the sense not to get in the way up to now.

"Okay, Sarge. We've no weapons to spare but collect what you can find from the guards. Put yourself under command of Captain Moncada."

I tell Moncada to use them to enhance security of this building and to keep a look-out.

Now I've got to get up on that residence roof. As the Marines clamber to their feet I call out, "Where's the Embassy admin. officer?"

"Here, Colonel . . . George Walsh."

234

He's a middle-aged, round-faced guy. I ask: "Is there any way up on to the residence roof apart from that access hatch?"

As Walsh shakes his head, Moncada says, "That would be suicide, Colonel. They'd have it covered or even booby trapped."

Suddenly Walsh's face lights up.

"Wait. Sure there is. There's a ten inch drainage pipe up the back wall to a gutter."

"That's not on the plans."

He shakes his head. "No. The day after Ambassador Peabody arrived there was a tropical downpour. The normal drainage couldn't handle it and there was an overflow. The Ambassador's lounge got a little flooded. He ordered extra drainage immediately. It wouldn't show on the plans."

"That's my man."

From Moncada I take extra mag. for my Ingram and three more frag. grenades, making my total seven. I switch on the mike and say, "All units, I want blanket fire aimed at the residence roof-top in sixty seconds from now. Keep it up for thirty seconds and then quit."

I flick off the switch and tell Moncada, "If I buy it, you better call in an airstrike."

"Yessir. Good luck."

I move to the door and wait beside Shaw. Abruptly the barrage starts. I leap down the steps and start running. I don't look left or right. Just watch the corner of the building looming up. Thirty years ago at school I ran the hundred yards in just under eleven seconds. I reckon I'm goin' slightly faster now. There's a wanging sound off to my right getting closer. The bastards up there are traversing towards me. I strain to move my legs faster and then dive and roll. I smash into something soft and it screams.

"Who's that?!"

"Spooner, sir. Sorry . . . my leg."

"Hell, I'm sorry. Listen, there's a drain pipe back there. I'm going up it. Can you cover my back?"

"Sure thing, Colonel. Just drag me over there to the corner."

I move him the ten yards as gently as I can but he still murmurs through his teeth in pain. Man, is this kid ever gonna get a medal.

The covering fire eases up and then stops. I move down the building and locate the drainage pipe. Perfect. It's bracketed into the wall at about five-foot intervals giving excellent hand and foot holds. The sanitising aircraft are dropping flares outside the walls. They light the place up too much for my liking. I flick on the transmitter.

"Al. Come in."

"Yes, Silas."

"I'm goin' up on the roof. There's too much light. Can you ask those guys in the A6s and choppers to hold up the flares for a while?"

"Sure thing. Watch your ass."

"Will do."

Within seconds it starts to darken, but I can still see very clearly through the goggles as I inch my way up. As I reach the top, I consider asking for more covering fire but decide against it. A stray bullet could just as easily knock me off as them. I get a grip on the gutter and it squeaks but there's still a lot of noise all around the compound. I raise my eyes over the gutter and sweep the roof-top. They're at each end. On the left I can see the shape of a head above the sandbags as one of them looks down into the compound. The head turns and I duck down again. I consider the position. The two emplacements are about a hundred feet apart. As I go for one I'll be exposed to the other. Simple: I got to take 'em out; one immediately after the other. Slocum, asshole; it would have been simpler to bring another guy with you. But no, you just gotta be the tough ol' bull. Well, let's get on with it.

I wait for a series of explosions and heave myself up and over the gutter. It squeals. I roll over and scramble to my feet darting a look left and right and reaching for a grenade. It's in my right hand and the pin out. I transfer it to my left hand and reach for another one. As I pull out the pin there's a shout from my left. I lob the grenade, transfer the other one to my right hand and drop to the ground. The explosion compresses my ear drums. I don't bother to look. I can see the barrel of the other emplacement swing towards me. Still lying, I lob the other grenade at it. Shit! It hits a sandbag on the side and bounces over the roof. I hear the explosion as I scramble to my feet grabbing for the Ingram. The M.G. barrel is coming into line. I run towards it holding the Ingram high; squeezing the trigger and spraying bullets like a hose. There's a scream and then the heavy hammer of the M.G. He's high. I can feel the bullets whipping over my head. Still fifteen feet away, he's got time to correct! I'm gonna damned well die! Ten feet. I feel something like a branding iron across my side. Then I'm diving over the sandbags with an empty Ingram. There's two of them. One slumped with blood on his face, the other lunging back from the M.G. and grabbing for a pistol at his belt. My shoulder smacks into him. We sprawl on the concrete. He's getting the pistol closer. I smash the short barrel of the Ingram into his face. Then again. I'm in a rage. I pick him up and throw the bastard off the roof. There's a shot and a bullet thuds into a sandbag next to me. I crouch and swing around. The other emplacement has been blown apart but there's a guy lying behind a single spilling sandbag. He's resting a pistol on it – pointed at me. I check the M.G. beside me. It's pointing at the sky. There's a gleaming belt of bullets feeding into it. I crouch behind it, get my hand on the grips and lift and the barrel swings down. Another bullet thwacks into the sandbags in front. He's in the sights. My thumb clamps down on the firing button and stays there. The bastard's sandbag disintegrates and so does he. I hose the pieces right off the goddam roof.

It's done. I wait a second while my breathing settles to something approaching normal; then flick the transmission switch.

"Vampire One to Base. Compound totally secured. Send in the Evac. choppers."

Al's exultant voice vibrates in my ears.

"They're on their way, Silas. Well done. See you soon."

I can hear cheering from the direction of the chancery. I say into the mike, "All units: lay down the landing flares. Moncada, get our people ready. Bring them out when the choppers are on the ground. Women first. Then the men. Then the Marines. All other Vampires stay in position and provide cover. I'll bring out the Ambassador myself. Keep on your goddam toes. We're only home and dry when we're on the 'Nimitz'."

I flick off the switch and take a deep, deep breath. Yeah. Time to go an' fetch mah man.

PEABODY
San Carlo
Night 20

The black face is over me again. So very black and shining wet. Is it another dream? Is it real? I've been slipping in and out of consciousness. It's as though I've been sleeping through a thunderstorm. He's talking.

"Sorry, sir. It took a little longer than I thought. The other hostages are all fine, sir. I'm taking you out of here now."

He's black. Why is he black? Everything is black. His helmet. Strange glasses pushed up on it. Black clothes. I hear another voice.

"Choppers are down, sir. Women are movin'."

Women? Is it really happening?

"Sir. I'm gonna carry you. It's gonna hurt some. You'll be in the sick bay on the 'Nimitz' within minutes."

Ah . . . the "Nimitz". The good ship "Nimitz". I feel his arms working under me. He lifts. Yes there's pain. But it's sweet pain. I know so much about pain. I'm in his arms. I'm a child. I move my head and rest it against his shoulder. I try to speak. I must have made some sound for he lowers his black ear next to my face.

"What . . . what's your . . . name?"

"Slocum, sir. Colonel Silas Slocum. United States Army."

We're moving now. He's so gentle. So very gentle. I have to say something else. My throat hurts but I have to say it.

"Colonel . . ."

The ear again in front of my face even as we move.

"Don't . . . don't leave me, Colonel. Stay with me . . ."

There's a loud noise. Something spinning above me. Voices talking. Faces looking at me. I snuggle closer in his arms and hear his voice . . . very husky.

"I won't leave you, sir. You're my man. I won't leave you."

It's all right. Everything's all right. I let myself slide into the peace of senselessness.

*   *   *

I'm conscious again. I see a white coat, a stethoscope, a syringe. The scream tears at my throat, echoing in my ears. A startled face receding. A furious voice.

"You stupid bastard! Wait!"

Black Slocum again bending over me, holding my hands. Eyes full of care.

"Don't worry, sir. It's not the other one. He's dead, sir. Dead, dead. I killed him myself. This is a doctor. He's going to give you an injection. Make you feel better."

He turns his head and mutters something. I hear it faintly.

"Get that white coat off! All of you get 'em off. Signal Walter Reed. No one's to be around him with a white coat. I'll kill the bastard who wears a white coat near him – tell 'em that."

He turns back to me and smiles. "We're gonna fly you Stateside, sir, to Washington; Walter Reed Army Hospital. You're gonna be fine. Just fine. But first you gotta have this little injection."

I nod and he moves away slightly; still holding on to my hands. Another figure is next to me. Dark clothes. Soft voice. "Won't take a second, sir." I feel something cool on my arm, then a slight prick. A moment later he's gone. Slocum smiles.

"It's gonna make you sleepy. Then we load you up and head for home."

"You're coming too?"

"I sure am. I'll be there all the way."

His face is becoming indistinct. I drift away.

The room is light and airy. Sunlight filters through mesh curtains. I have woken from a long sleep. How long? Days?

No. Years and years and years. I feel a wonderful clarity of mind; of purpose. My mind feels clean. I am looking at a very white ceiling. I turn my head and now I'm looking at the very black Slocum. I am not at all surprised. He is sitting on a big soft chair with his head back and mouth open, snoring gently. I roll my head to the other side. There's a tube snaking down to a bandage around my right wrist. I've hardly ever been sick in my life. I guess it's a saline drip or something. I'm hungry and thirsty. I swallow. My throat is still a little sore. I crane my neck looking both sides for water. There is none. Softly I call, "Slocum."

He jerks erect, his eyes widen and then his mouth splits in an enormous grin. He climbs to his feet and ambles over. "Jesus, sir. I thought you were gonna sleep for ever."

"How long has it been?"

"Six days since we left 'Nimitz'."

I'm not surprised. I feel like I've slept a lifetime.

"Could you find some water?"

"Sure, sir. But first I got to buzz for the Head Nurse."

He reaches for a bell beside the bed.

"Can't that wait awhile?"

He grins and shakes his head.

"No, sir. She told me to call her the instant you woke up. Now those doctors are one thing, but Nurse Clay's tougher than an angry buffalo."

He pushes the button. I say seriously, "You have the right to call me by my first name."

He smiles. "Okay, Jason. I'm Silas."

"Silas, if you were me how would you go about thanking a man for what you did?"

He shakes his head. "I wouldn't waste the breath. I'm a soldier. I was doing my job. I'd be real glad if you'd keep that in mind and not embarrass me. I mean it."

I'm trying to think of an answer to that when the door opens. A short, plump, middle-aged woman with blonde hair bustles in.

"Move yourself, Colonel."

He backs away down the bed. She leans over and gives me a critical once-over.

241

"How do you feel?"

"Very well. A little weak I guess. I'd like some water."

Her eyes dart to the metal bedside table and her mouth tightens in irritation. She picks up the bell and gives it two sharp presses.

"Major Calper will be here in a moment."

"Major Calper?"

"Your doctor."

I'd forgotten I was in a military hospital. She turns to Slocum and says tartly,

"You may leave now Colonel."

"Aw, maam . . ."

"Colonel Slocum. You gave me your solemn promise that you would leave as soon as the Ambassador was awake and feeling well. You heard him. He said: 'Very well.' Besides, you have things to do . . . important things."

Reluctantly he nods his head. "Okay, maam. Jason, I'll see you later this evenin'. Anything you need?"

I shake my head. What the hell can I say to this man? I mutter, "Thanks, Silas . . . for everything."

A pretty young nurse opens the door.

"Water," Nurse Clay says succinctly.

She's back in less than a minute with a flask and a glass. She gets a look that says: "I'll be talking to you later." I'm embarrassed by her expression as she looks at me. I've never been the object of hero-worship and I find it disconcerting. Slocum follows her out and as Nurse Clay fusses around straightening the bedsheets I ask, "He's been here all the time?"

She sighs. "Yes. Colonel Slocum arrived in the ambulance with you and simply refused to leave. In thirty years in the profession I've never seen anything like it . . ."

The severe lines of her face abruptly soften into a smile.

"He told the doctors that if you died he'd come through this hospital with a sub-machine-gun. I think some of them believed him. You were in a very bad way. Your condition was complicated by severe pneumonia. He even wanted to go into the intensive care unit with you and was only dissuaded by Major Calper explaining about the risks of him

242

passing on germs. When you were moved in here two days ago he slept on the couch over there or in the chair. General Mallory, C.O. of the hospital, just about went out of his mind. His position was impossible. Only force could have moved the Colonel. It's even rumoured that the General asked the President to intervene and he replied: 'I'm not about to order Colonel Slocum to do anything.' "

I'm not surprised. "I guess Colonel Slocum is a big hero now."

"You both are, Mr Ambassador."

I'm wondering how to handle the situation when the door opens and a fair-haired man with a cheerful face comes in. He's in army uniform. Nurse Clay says, "This is Major Calper."

He shakes my hand and says heartily, "So the sleeping Ambassador has woken. Were you kissed by a princess?"

"No, Major. Not even a frog."

"And how do you feel?"

"Really fine. A bit weak but I feel surprisingly well."

He nods. "You surprised all of us. You were four days in intensive care. For the first two you were in an extremely agitated mental state; your subconscious in turmoil. Then quite abruptly you passed into a very deep and serene sleep. The pneumonia cleared up and all vital signs became normal. It's astonishing but you slept for four more days. I was getting a little worried."

He's been examining me rapidly but thoroughly while talking. Now he stands back and says, "Mr Ambassador, I'm going to listen to your heart which means I'm going to have to take a stethoscope out of my pocket."

I smile at the memory of Slocum's fiercely whispered words back on the "Nimitz".

"It's okay, Major. And white coats are not going to bother me either."

He smiles back. "That's a relief. Yesterday one of our young interns walked in here wearing one. The Colonel literally ripped it off his back."

He listens to my heart and nods in satisfaction.

"Do you know how long the abuse went on, sir?"

"What time was I rescued?"

243

"Shortly after midnight."

"Then, continuously for about twelve hours."

His face turns sombre and he mutters, "Animals." Then it clears. "You've made a wonderful recovery, not easily understood within medical parameters. Nevertheless such treatment often affects the mind . . . sometimes it's a delayed reaction. I'm going to ask Colonel Elliot to pass by and visit you tomorrow. He's our senior psychiatrist."

I shake my head. "No thank you, Major. I could have used him a long time ago, but not now. Whatever effect that torture had on my mind, believe me, was beneficial." I smile at him. "Shock treatment is used in mental hospitals to try to bring insane people back to sanity. I guess something like that happened to me."

He's looking very puzzled. He shrugs.

"Well, okay, sir. If that's your decision. But if at some future time you experience any difficulties be sure to call us. Immediately."

"I will, thank you. Can I eat something, doctor?"

"Sure." To Nurse Clay he says, "That drip can come out. Put him on a light diet and he's to have no visitors until tomorrow afternoon at the earliest."

"Yes, doctor. But Colonel Slocum said he was coming back this evening."

He shrugs resignedly. "Well, you can classify the Colonel as a fixture rather than a visitor."

I ask him, "How long will I have to be here, Major?"

He purses his lips, thinks for a moment and says, "I want to keep you under observation for at least another week. Besides you need time to build up your strength, and it's better that you do it here where no one will bother you — especially the press. I'll see you this evening."

He leaves and Nurse Clay says, "I'm going to send you some fresh chicken soup and minced beef with vegetables. Is there anything else you'd like?"

My reply is prompted by the Major's mention of the press.

"Would you have any newspapers? I'd like to catch up on what's been happening."

"Yes. I've kept you the *Washington Post* for the last six days."

I read the papers in sequence while I eat. The first is full of the rescue; and outrage at my treatment. I feel a pang of guilt as I learn about the casualties suffered by the rescue team. I also learn that Slocum has been wounded. A bullet had taken a chunk of flesh out of his right side. My condition is reported as being critical. The editorial called for the immediate invasion of San Carlo.

I'm still critical on the second day. There's a clamour for Slocum to be interviewed but a bulletin from Walter Reed Hospital states that he is still recovering from his wound. Again the editorial calls for the invasion of San Carlo.

The headlines on the third day proclaim the invasion of San Carlo. After a brief but bloody battle the capital was taken and the Chamarristas had fled to the mountains. An interim Government was to be formed and a constitution drawn up leading to free and fair elections. My condition was stable. Slocum's wound was still being treated and in the meantime the President had announced that he was to be awarded the Congressional Medal of Honour, and all his men were to receive high decorations. Meanwhile the State Department had protested to Cuba in the strongest terms about my being abused and interrogated by a senior member of the Cuban Intelligence organisation. I was now stable and improving. I push aside the other papers. My eyelids are heavy, sleep has become such a warm companion.

I wake at the sound of the door. Slocum is standing there, his arms cradling packages. He manages to raise a finger to his lips, and winks. He deposits the packages on the couch, goes back to the open door and peers first one way down the corridor and then the other. Carefully he closes the door and gives me a conspiratorial grin.

"I came in through the service entrance, eluding Nurse Clay's spies."

From the packages he produces two Big Macs, french fries, packets of cookies, a bottle of Black Label Scotch, and an aerosol can of air freshener. I've never had a Big Mac; always considered fast food plebeian. I chomp into it like an errant schoolboy. He pours two slugs of whisky and adds a few drops of water. It's the first drink I've had for more than three weeks. It tastes like nectar. I remember something. I raise my glass and say solemnly, "Silas, let's drink to your Congressional Medal of Honour . . . richly deserved."

He's sitting on the end of the bed. He sips at his whisky and says, "I got it because I was in command. It's a pity that all my guys couldn't get it."

I'm suddenly conscious of the casualties. I've been feeling relaxed and happy. Now I feel guilty. I tell him that and he shakes his head vigorously.

"Jason, considering the conditions, we were damned lucky. We only had one man killed in the compound. Those wounded are recovering well with no permanent disability. They're right here in this hospital. I'd be glad if, when you're on your feet, you'd go visit them for a while. It would give them a real charge. Two men crashed on take-off right on the deck of the 'Nimitz'. One walked away and the other had a broken ankle. Eleven others went into the sea. Eight were rescued due to some brilliant work by the navy. Three drowned. In all we had four fatalities . . . a lot less than had been projected."

Quietly I remind him, "Four lives lost on my behalf. I hate to think about that."

He stands up and gives me a very straight look.

"I knew those guys well. Let me tell you this. They joined the army to fight. They were all veterans. They'd done a lot of fighting and they knew what it was all about and what the risks were. They all volunteered for that mission. Right now they might be warming their asses in hell or up in heaven ogling the angels. Wherever they are they sure as hell don't blame you. They'd rather have died that way than of senility . . . believe me."

I do. He said it simply and sincerely. He pours more whisky into our glasses. I ask, "When are you getting your medal?"

He grimaces. "Tomorrow morning at the White House.

My men are all gonna be there. Big ceremony, TV, Congressional leaders. The whole damn works."

There's no false modesty about him. He's genuinely not looking forward to it. Quietly I remark, "Well, Silas, it looks like you're going to end up the most senior black officer in the entire history of the United States Armed Forces."

He swallows some whisky and says grimly, "I don't know that I want to end up the highest black anything. I'm thinking of retiring."

"Retiring?"

"Sure. I've got a ranch in Wyoming . . . and Jason, if you ask where I'll find a horse big enough to carry me I'm gonna get mad . . ."

"A ranch?"

He grins. "Yeah. An' I'm not even gonna look for a horse. I'm gonna be the first cowboy in the West to round up his cattle from an Ultralight!"

"So tell me about it."

He does. But first he pours more Scotch, saying, "Doctors tell you not to drink alcohol while taking medication like antibiotics. I got a little secret for you. It's not dangerous. It just reduces the effect of the drug. The secret, ol' buddy, is not to forsake alcohol, but double the dose of the drug. Don't tell matron I told you that. The little lady is already calculating which way to castrate me. She just hasn't found a knife blunt enough yet."

He refills our glasses, tucks the whisky bottle out of sight behind my pillows, sprays the room and dumps the empty paper bags in a trash can in the bathroom. Then he perches on the end of the bed and tells me all about his plans. His enthusiasm comes through. And also his trepidation. It's like he's starting a new life, and it reminds me that I'm doing the same. I ask a few questions. They come easily . . . personal questions. An intimacy grows between us as he talks of his life. His early broken marriage, his dedication to his "tough ol' bull" image. I marvel that I, with all my latent prejudices, can feel so close to this man. I see parallels in his life and mine. Suddenly he leans forward and says earnestly, "Jason, why don't you come down and visit me in

Wyoming? Damn it, man, you're gonna need a good period of recuperating. The air out there is real fresh . . ." His enthusiasm suddenly fades. "But hell, it's not much of a place I got. I mean, just a pineboard cabin . . . with an outhouse an' all that . . . I guess it's not the kind of place you'd . . ."

Quickly, passionately, I cut in. "Silas, you invite me and I'll come. You just talked about changing directions in your life. I'm about to do the same. Some things were important to me before; now they're trivial. I don't mind roughing it a bit. I think I might enjoy it."

He grins. "I'll teach you to fly an Ultralight. We'll punch cows together."

"At my age?"

"Hell, why not? You're fit enough an' it's damned easy . . . but I promise you one thing. We ain't ever goin' up if the wind is more than ten knots."

My eyes are drowsy. There's a silence and I doze off.

I don't know how long I slept. A few minutes, maybe an hour. I open my eyes and he's still sitting there nursing his drink, at the end of the bed, gazing far beyond the enclosing walls.

"What are you thinking, Silas?"

His head snaps round in surprise, and then he relaxes.

"I was thinking about a little talk I had with a guy just a few days ago. About how sometimes it's possible to communicate without words . . . about exceptions that prove rules . . ."

The words don't make a lot of literal sense but in a strange way they're comforting.

I drift back into sleep.

Late morning and shit hitting the fan. Nurse Clay came in and sniffed the air: "Lemon scented air freshener, Mr Ambassador? Not regulation issue."

In seconds she located the empty paper bags in the waste bin; lowered her nose into one and pronounced ominously, "Onions . . . ketchup. You've been eating hamburgers!" She sniffed at the empty glass on the bedside table. How could I have been so stupid?

"Whisky!"

Now the tirade is washing over me. Silas, what have you got me into? I feel like a schoolboy caught with his hand in the cookie jar. Thankfully she shifts her attack.

"It's that damned Colonel Slocum! This is the best run hospital in the world and in one week he's turned it into a tavern!"

She stalks around the room, small, shapely and vibrant in her indignation. Her words are directed at me again.

"I'm surprised at you. A man of your position! Must I ask General Mallory to post a guard on your door?"

I notice the gold band on her finger and decide to go on to the attack. Sternly I ask, "Do you talk this way to your husband?"

"My husband died five years ago."

I mumble contritely, "Sorry."

"So was I. He was a wonderful man . . . but time passes and life goes on."

She draws a breath. Expecting another whiplashing I point at the television in the corner.

"He'll be at the White House now. I'd like to watch."

She snorts. "No doubt he's got a hip flask in his pocket!"

But she turns on the television and pulls up a chair.

It's a moving ceremony. The President's natural charm is entwined with obvious emotion. First he pins the medals on Slocum's men. God, they're a fearsome bunch! Then it's Slocum's turn. He ducks his head and the President carefully lowers the blue ribbon and adjusts it around his neck. The camera lights reflect sharply from the metal of the nation's highest award for valour. It nestles at the base of his neck clearly delineated against his ebony skin. The camera zooms in on it. His head and shoulders fill the screen and his face glistens with the sweat of discomfort. I have the definite impression that he would rather be in Wyoming. The President makes a short but emotional speech. He talks of democracy and sacrifices for freedom. Finally in husky tones he invokes my name and talks of my suffering. He urges the

nation to pray for my swift recovery. Nurse Clay gives me an
admiring look and I'm absurdly conscious of the half-full
bottle of whisky under my pillow. The broadcast is live and
at the end there's a little confusion. Obviously Slocum is
expected to say a few words and very firmly he does not. The
microphone, held in front of his face, looks forlorn. Cut to the
studio where a smooth, effete broadcaster gibbers on about
masculine modesty. Nurse Clay turns the TV off and says
positively, "He's a lonely man."

"Who?"

"Colonel Slocum."

"You think so?"

"Yes."

She's bustling again. Pulling and patting the sheets into
place. I keep my head firmly on the pillow.

"I've seen others like him in this hospital. Tough as
rawhide on the outside and desperately lonely underneath.
I can bully them because they want me to. They invite
it because sometimes they get sick of being tough. They
pretend to be scared of me because the pretence gives them
comfort in their loneliness. Colonel Slocum is like that."

She is standing at the end of the bed, her hands gripping
the footrail, her face infinitely sad and ethereal in its
introspection. I'm intrigued and trying to formulate a
question when she says, almost defiantly, "I'm glad he was
the one who rescued you and the others. It's right that it was
a man like him. Right that he didn't say anything just now.
Others would have had glory poured on their heads. It was
right."

It's late afternoon when General Mallory comes into my
room. He's short and stout with a plump, worried face. We
exchange pleasantries and then he tells me, "I had a call
from the White House. The President would like to visit you
at seven o'clock this evening."

Immediately I feel nervous. I know the confrontation has
to come and I've tried to rehearse it. The scenario scares me.
I say, "That's okay, General. But no media. I'd like it to be a
private visit."

250

He nods briskly. "So would the President. We'll serve you coffee."

I have an hour to think. I try to compose words and clarify thoughts, but when the tap comes on the door my mind is still in turmoil.

The start is melodramatic. General Mallory enters, stands to one side and says portentously, "Mr Ambassador . . . the President of the United States of America."

It makes me even more nervous but then the President strides in, grins and says, "Hi, Jason. How are you?"

I know what I'm going to say but I'm no longer nervous. I'm propped up against a pile of pillows. I take his outstretched hand and shake it firmly. The General is pushing a chair up to the bed but the President waves it and him away and perches on the foot of the bed. As the door closes he says, "They looking after you?"

It should be mundane but there's genuine concern in his eyes. I nod.

"Very well, Mr President, thank you."

He's carrying a paper bag. He reaches out and puts it on the bedside table.

"Grapes. I don't know why but hospital visitors always bring grapes. When I was in here I got enough to start a winery!"

We both smile. I cannot sustain the anger that has been smouldering inside me. But still I'm going to get it off my chest. I take a breath but I'm interrupted by a tap on the door. Nurse Clay bustles in with a tray holding coffee and cups. She is totally at ease. As she pours the coffee she casts a critical eye over my visitor and says sternly, "You're overdoing it. You look damned tired. You need at least a week at Camp David or on the ranch."

He smiles affably. "Mary, it won't be for much longer."

She puts two spoonfuls of sugar into his coffee, passes him the cup and says, "Half an hour and no more . . . and I don't want my patient agitated!"

He nods solemnly, a twinkle in his eye.

She goes out. We sip our coffee and he says,

"A fine woman."

"Yes, very."

The tension is mounting now. I wonder if he will broach the subject first. He does.

"Jason, you will know that our agents in San Carlo tried to kill you."

"Yes."

He is looking down into his cup as if trying to find an explanation in the black coffee. Harshly he says, "I don't apologise for it. I turned a blind eye. I've had to do that on several occasions over the past years. It was an immoral act but sometimes morality has to be tempered to reality. You were in a situation which affected the security of our nation."

He has, in that statement, made it easier. I was dreading either a denial or an apology. Before this moment I had respected the man. Now I admire him. The anger has left me, but quietly I state my belief.

"Mr President, I don't think that an agency of our Government has any business dealing in murder. Reality must never be the master of morality."

I feel disconcerted. The words sounded good in my head, but pompous as I uttered them. He is nodding solemnly.

"Jason, of course you're right. Your case has resulted in a general review of the Agency."

I can't help but say it.

"Because the operation failed?"

He smiles wanly.

"No. The shrinks said you would crack. We take too many decisions based on theory. You didn't crack. As a result we'll bring democracy to San Carlo . . . and maybe later to Cuba. Now I didn't come to apologise but to try and make restitution. I intend to ask Congress to strike a single and unique medal to mark your courage."

Slowly I shake my head. I look into his eyes and see the understanding. He murmurs, "You won't accept it. I guess I realise why. Then what can I do?"

"Allow me to take early retirement."

He sighs. He really does look tired. He puts down his cup,

stands up and stretches, then walks to a window and looks out over the city. There's a long silence. When he turns, his face is different; his expression determined. No hint of tiredness. He strides to the door, opens it and sternly calls out,

"Tell Colonel Slocum to report here at the double."

He walks back to the window and stands tall and straight. Without turning he says, "I know of the friendship that's grown between you and Slocum. During the past days you've both had an effect on me and on this country. You may as well hear what I've got to say together. The Colonel is waiting to escort me to visit his wounded men. He will be here directly."

Another long silence while I wonder what's coming. My visitor has an air of barely suppressed irritation. He turns at the tap on the door.

"Enter!"

Slocum enters in full dress uniform and snaps off a salute. The President points to a chair.

"Sit down, Colonel. Last month you paced up and down in my office while I sat and listened to a lecture. Now it's your turn."

Slocum glances at me, looking bemused, and then meekly sits down.

The President paces and talks.

"Colonel Slocum, this morning at the White House you asked me to allow you to take early retirement so you could go ranching in Wyoming. I told you that I would think on it. Well I have. The answer is no. By your lecture and your recent actions you have caused me to institute a major review of our armed forces. You will be involved. These are your orders: you will take one month's leave. On returning to duty you will be promoted General and put in command of our rapid deployment force, which as you well know is perhaps the most important unit in our armed forces. You will inculcate, by training and example, your military philosophy and methods. You will do so for four years after which you may retire to your ranch. By that time I too will be retired and will accept an invitation to come to Wyoming

253

and teach you something about cows . . . is that understood, Colonel?"

"Yessir!"

The President has stopped pacing. He directs a gaze at Slocum that would penetrate steel plate. Slocum is nodding his head energetically.

The gaze sweeps round to fix on me.

"Mr Ambassador, you are a Foreign Service Officer of vast experience. My experts told me that you would crack under mental torture. You did not. Neither did you crack under appalling physical torture. That makes you a very special person. You asked me for early retirement. Now these are your orders: you will take a month's leave for rest and recuperation. You will then report to Georgetown University as Ambassador in Residence. As you know, that appointment is recognised in the Foreign Service as a special Presidential citation for outstanding Ambassadorial service. You prefer not to accept a medal but you will accept that. At the same time you will serve as a special Presidential advisor on Latin American affairs until the end of my term of office. At that time you may retire. Those are your orders!"

The words jump out of my throat.

"Yes, Mr President!"

He nods in satisfaction and turns to Slocum.

"Right, Colonel. Let's go and see those men of yours."

At the door he turns, grins at me and says, "It seems that the only way to deal with heroes is to give them a good kick in the butt!"

I eat some grapes and decide that I like the prospect. The posting to Georgetown is a sinecure. I'll be able to pick my own subject on which to lecture. It will be good to be surrounded by young people. I realise something. We take pieces from all those who affect our lives. I took a piece from Amparo and a lot from Jorge, and finally from Slocum. I'm sixty-three years old and at last I feel complete. I'm going to be a teacher and I think I have something to teach. I like the idea. I also decide that when I get out of this hospital I'm going to invite matron out for dinner. It sure is time I had a date again. I drift into a contented sleep.

When I awake evening shadows slant across the room. The door opens and Slocum comes in like the brother I never had. He puts a thick envelope on the bedside table, sits on the foot of the bed and asks, "So what do you think of your orders?"

"I like them. How about you, General?"

He grins. "Me too. It's a real chance to do something positive. The cows can wait. Now I'm off to Bragg for a couple of days and then to Wyoming for the rest of my leave."

"Fine. What's in the envelope?"

He grins. "My address in Wyoming and telephone number . . . and a United Airlines timetable . . . and something for you . . . something I want you to have."

He gets up and holds out his hand and I grip it warmly. I don't know what to say. I can't find the words and here he is giving me presents. He says severely, "If I don't hear from you in ten days I'm gonna put a call in to Bragg and some of my old buddies are gonna come up here and do a little escort duty. Meanwhile I'll be fixin' up the spare room."

I smile. "You'll hear from me, Silas . . . bet on it."

As the door closes behind him I repeat the words in my mind. "Bet on it."

I doze again for a while and then a nurse brings me dinner followed by Nurse Clay who fusses about straightening the napkins and knives and forks. I remember the envelope and pick it up. It's surprisingly heavy.

I shake its contents on to the bed: a slip of paper, the airline timetable – and a flat velvet box. Nurse Clay watches curiously as I open it. I catch my breath as I see the blue ribbon and the round gleaming embossed metal.

She murmurs softly, "It's his Congressional Medal of Honour. My God . . . he gave you that?"

There's a little card with sloping handwriting. It reads, "I've got enough fruit salad. You deserve it a goddam sight more than I do, Silas."

For a moment I'm speechless. Then I mutter the only words possible.

"Of course I'll have to send it back."

She nods her head slowly.

"I guess you will . . . but what an honour he did you . . . a soldier like that . . ."

I close the box and smile at her.

"I'm not going to send it back."

"No?"

"Definitely not . . . I'm going to take it back . . . real soon."